A Wildflower in the Dark

Second Edition

Michael E. Kozak

Author's Note

While you are reading my story, you will soon realize that there are many dream sequences. Almost all the dreams within this story are actual dreams I've had throughout my life. Of course, many are altered to fit the narrative and flow of the story. I wanted to share that. Enjoy!

"Dreams are today's answers to tomorrow's questions."
- Edgar Cayce

To my family, friends, and Air Force family I've met in the last 19 years, this one is for you.

One shall see,
See will all.
Who to become,
Shall never fall.

Our lives are quite similar to a chess board—every move prolongs or ceases life as time bides. Never was I, a self-proclaimed master of chess, nor have I ever pondered acquiring a sharp hand. One move at a time. Or, as I call it, playing blindly is the hand that rules all possibilities. Opportunities are endless, revelations are abundant, and expectations are commonly absent. By utilizing this strategy, it allows one to live in the moment, not in the future. The future may not be considerate, for I believe it picks and chooses in a perplexing algorithm that disappoints many. In turn, the many who play for the future have the greatest tendency to accept their placement on the board, or, as I like to call it, mediocrity. Mediocrity has never associated itself with my class. However, my reality is most likely misconstrued within my own mind. Yes, I suppose I am not always forthwith when dealing with my true self—but who unequivocally is?

My advice is to use your pawns wisely. They are the first defense to what one will hold near and dear to them. Many will justify pawns as overrated or inconsequential pieces that are nothing but space fillers. I do not agree with that notion, for I have a stout belief that a well-structured defense is the foundation for any level of attainment. Maybe this is why I have survived many hardships, obstacles, and an abnormal journey into the unknown. Maybe not. Maybe I am a lucky one—floating through life unfazed and unfettered by drastic change. This world is a funny place. A place that I may never truly understand or comprehend, for that matter. Regardless, I am still standing on my own two feet with everything to prove.

If I win,
Maybe I'll lose.
Destiny is absent,
Free will I choose.

The Backstory
(2160–2192)

The year is 2192. The war no one thought would happen, not even in a hundred lifetimes, came and ravaged the world. Old allies were shattered, history was rattled, and new relationships were forged through misery, derelict, and meek hope. Normality was no longer a thing. My grandmother once told me, "Society that observes, learns, and adopts advanced technology will share the same fate as the dinosaurs did." Sure enough, I can't say she was wrong. Dinosaurs had their run as superior rulers, as do we to this day. The only difference between us is that we are dooming ourselves much faster than they ever did.

This war was like nothing we have ever seen in our lifetime. The introduction of cybernetics and the ruthless use of nuclear methods by the colony of Peninsula set out a dangerous precedent—achieving world supremacy amongst other colonies. It was called the War of the Century; conversely, most people would label it as the War of the Apocalypse. Many colonies were lost, and many deaths were accounted for. Luckily, I was a survivor.

My name is Gretan Hutchen. Most people call me Gret for short. I actually like it, considering the nickname has a gritty charm to it, so to speak. My grandmother would always tell me how much courage and true grit I possess, so I suppose the nickname fit me well. I was born in the year 2160, on what many say was the coldest first day of spring that anyone could recall. Fifteen degrees was the low that day, but some would say that it truly felt like sub-zero temperatures, considering the wind chill that was in effect. Maybe the cold weather was a sign of times to come, or maybe it was coincidental.

When I was born, I was discarded and left alone in a public park bathroom. Soon enough, a homeless woman found me and kept me for three days before taking me to the nearby hospital. Medical records show that I suffered from severe RSV, along with other illnesses. Within the first ten minutes of my arrival, my lifeline took a drastic turn. I legally passed away, revived, and passed away again. When the medical staff went to inform and question the mysterious lady who brought me in, she had vanished like dust in the wind. However, she did leave a little something behind. Set neatly on the chair she sat on, she placed a note that read, "No act of kindness, no matter how small, is ever wasted." Luckily, I was told that sometime in between my second death and the staff seeking out the lady who brought me in, the doctors had one more miracle up their sleeve, clearing my path to where I am now.

I guess cheating death twice gave me an undeniable appreciation for life. The doctors never shed hope on me. They said I was legally dead for three minutes and twelve seconds. Fortunately, the miracle work of the doctors on duty that night brought me back to life once more. I was deemed a *miracle baby*, as the doctors described in my birth records. Whether it was luck, chance, or divine intervention, from that day forward, I was a fighter.

I often think about the homeless lady who brought me in. I wonder about the simple things about her. What did she look like? What color of hair did she have? How did she become homeless? Did she know the exact minute to seek help from the hospital? I have had a few dreams about her—once while I was ten years old, another right before I turned nineteen years old, and once more—not too long ago. It's funny, though; all three dreams were both vividly unforgettable and indescribable in a sensible way. I normally don't like to talk about them, but I will say one thing only: they were warm, detailed dreams that I hold quite dearly. The strange thing is that I cannot, for the life of me, describe what she looks like in all three dreams. Her face always had that *blurry* appearance in which one cannot simply depict the little details. The only thing physically I can recall was her tattered, white coat and cream-colored sweatpants. Maybe it was because of my deep, unconscious dream state, or maybe something was holding her identity back. I suppose some things are meant to be indescribable.

Regardless, this is where my story begins. Kindness and inspiration can go a long way in this world, and I feel like I was born from the depths of those two words. I guess I am living proof of that theory, or maybe it's a coincidence. Nevertheless, life is an interesting commodity that bestows hope and second chances.

My life was just beginning, all thanks to the faceless, homeless lady who saved me.

Once I received my full bill of health, the hospital turned me over to the government, which in turn placed me in a group home until they could find a forever family. Apparently, it was not supposed to be easy for me. I was diagnosed with minor epilepsy, a neurological disorder, and possible autism. Even with my so-called disabilities, my proclivity and curious nature led me to be a smart young boy. By the age of six, I was already reading at a third-grade level. Indeed, I was a little sponge for knowledge.

Behind my disabilities and intelligence, something else was quite nerve-racking. I was given a probable life span of approximately fourteen years. Anyone who cared about me never told me that estimate. While I was at a routine checkup one day, a neurological specialist left my file behind on a table while he excused himself out of the room for a moment. Habitually, my curiosity drove me to snoop through it and find it. I never once told anyone about my self-discovery.

The doctors predicted that around fourteen years, my neurological disorder would only progress, causing severe brain hemorrhaging so severe that death would call upon my number once again. Now that I think about it as I am older, that prediction to me was only speculation. Sometimes, I feel certain people need to say things that sound intelligent to turn speculation into self-relevance. My grandmother once said it best. Speaking on a similar subject, she said, "As long as you pretend to know what you are talking about and speak in confidence, you can convince almost anyone of falsifications." All I needed was a chance. A chance to overcome my disabilities and possibly become a precocious young boy. I have a chance to show the world that my life has a purpose. Most importantly, a chance to be *me*.

Fortunately, a distraught husband and wife who had recently lost two sons (aged nineteen and twenty-one) in the War of 2158 swiftly adopted me. My story spread like wildfire among the colonies. Lucky for me, I even made the nightly news as the station featured my story. In turn, my somber birth story and their heartbreaking story from the war turned out to be a perfect match.

I was what they needed—a new start to share the joys of life with. My wheels of life were in motion, and I was ready to withstand and dodge all the roadblocks and potholes I might encounter. My life was about to change, and the thought of an early death was exactly what it was—a thought.

As intimidating as death may be, it's a funny thought, in my opinion. I used to think that everyone had an invisible hourglass filled with sand hovering above their heads. The grains of sand were the life force, slowly trickling to the bottom until the inevitable became reality. Discernibly, everybody would not inherit the same number of grains and texture. If you were weak, susceptible to sickness, and intolerable to the cruelties of life, your sand was smooth and delicate—so delicate that it resembled a free-flowing river into a deep sea. The weak were pawns, pawns of the kings and queens who ruled the game of life. On the other hand, if you were strong, resilient, and vibrant, your sand would be grainy and dense, causing your life force to clog and prolong a foreboding end. If my youthful beliefs were true, I should have been dead before I reached my ninth birthday. I never gave up. Every speculation that the doctor proclaimed I would encounter turned out to be a huge farce. I am Gret, the master and ruler of my own destiny. I am a fighter.

My new mother's name was Florence Hutchen. She was simply a marvelous lady. My mother was forty-two years old when she adopted me, but she never looked a day older than twenty-five. She had such compassion for human life; rightfully so, she was a registered nurse. RNs are an extremely special breed of extraordinary people who exemplify the true meaning of sacrifice, dedication, and devotion. My mother had all three of these traits and never once asked for credit or reassurance about what kind of person she was. No doubt, she was a rare breed who simply exemplified love.

Her two sons (Jacob and Jaret) were the focal point of her whole life. One can only imagine the grief and sorrow she felt after their passing in the war. *No parent should ever have to bury their own kin.* Being the strong-willed woman she was, she picked up the tattered pieces of tragic loss and vowed to dedicate her life's work to those who meant the most to her.

I wish I could have met Jacob and Jaret. I am sure that if I ever had the chance, they would have embraced me as one of their own. It is ironic, though, because in life, there is death. In death, there is life. In my mother's case, the deaths of her two sons brought life back into her soul through my adoption. Some say it is a fine line and balance between both, and one must count their blessings and take account of their bad fortunes to maintain a life of harmony.

My mother had harmony, raising them to be the best sons any mother could ask for. I know this because she would refer to their personalities and ethical traits whenever she deemed it necessary. By doing so, I can only imagine that some may have thought that her sorrow was a never-ending day of rainstorms. I never thought that was the case. I always thought it was her way of keeping their memory alive forever.

Jacob was the older brother, an exuberant man who would give the shirt off his back to any stranger. Meanwhile, two years younger than Jacob, Jaret was more of a carefree spirit who went along with any situation, whether it was good or bad. Even if it was watching brave characters in an action-packed movie, past and current patients of hers, or even the simple customer service she received while dining at her favorite restaurant, Jacob and Jaret always came to mind. She would often tell stories about them before I went to bed. They were the kind of stories to ease my mental state—going to bed with a smile and waking up wanting to conquer the world. Envious to a point in which I wish I had that lifestyle and upbringing from my birth mother. Instead, I was simply a disregarded boy, left in a park bathroom. Until I got older and wiser, I always felt in the back of my head that I was bereaved by not being born into a loving family like the one I have now. I always felt that if I did not live up to the stories told or expectations from my mother, I would always be that *adoptive son* who would never draw a single comparison to Jacob and Jaret. Indeed, those were some tough shoes to fill.

Fortunately, my mother never treated me any differently. In her mind, I was on an equal footing with her two sons when they were my age. Still, that feeling of being the adopted outcast (whose birth mother tossed aside) lingered throughout my childhood years. Like any other young child, I was merely naïve growing up. I guess it simply comes with the territory of being young and adopted. I never knew any better until a certain day that vanquished those feelings forever.

I remember it like it was yesterday—my first day of baseball practice. I was around seven years old, ready to show the world that I was on the verge of conquering all my supposed disabilities. Along with all my teammates parents, my mother patiently watched me in excitement and cheered every moment I was in action. She simply did what any mother should do— provide a strong support system. At the end of practice, our coach called the team into a huddle and invited the parents on the field so they could listen to the plans for our season. Like a punch to the gut, a somber feeling suddenly struck. My joyous attitude suddenly took a nosedive, and feelings of jealousy, sadness, and a slight hint of anger raged within my head. Always intuitive, my mother had great instincts for all my feelings. She would take one look at me and instantly know something was off. In this case, her instinct chimed in like church bells signaling the start of Sunday mass. As soon as the coach dismissed the team, my mother ran her fingers through my hair gently and said, "Let's go home, son." As soon as we got into the car, she looked at me and said, "Why the sad face on the field?"

I tried my hardest to maintain composure, but she could tell I was half-hearted. "I wasn't sad, mother," Thinking fast to change the subject, I asked, "How many home runs do you think I can hit this season?"

My mother looked at me and smiled. "Son, I know when you are sad or bothered about something. I have these magical powers that I can't control. So, you might as well tell me what is wrong so we can get ice cream before we go home."

I let go as tears started to fill my eyes. "Your adopted son. I'll never be your real son. It's not fair. I hate it!" I was crying in agony as I felt a million emotions let out.

My mother took one look at me, took another look forward, and returned a serious look in my direction. "Son, don't you ever think that I am not your mother and you are not my son. A true mother doesn't necessarily have to give birth to her children." She continued as she ran her hand a few times on the top of my head. "No, no. A true mother acts according to how a mother should act. You are my son, and I am your mother. Period. I love you no less and differently than I loved Jacob and Jaret. I promise you that from the very bottom of my heart."

"Pinky swear?"

She reached her pinky out to mine and interlocked with me. "Pinky swear. Alright, let's say we go get some ice cream. Now, please don't tell your father about our little pit stop at the ice cream place because he'll get mad that we didn't invite him, got it?"

I smiled as the tears started to dissipate. "Got it."

My mother was my world at that moment. Simply put, she was my heaven in our little world. She was my guiding light. Most importantly, she was my mother for the rest of my life.

I never imagined that this day would come. On a cold autumn night in 2170, my mother clocked out from her 3:00 p.m. to 3:00 a.m. shift and never came home. Video surveillance showed her walking to her car in the murky parking lot, almost as if she was in a sudden hurry. About twenty feet from her car, a figure emerged from the corner of the feed as the camera miraculously faded to black for about thirteen seconds, refocused, and her car was gone. No sign of foul play or a violent struggle was ever recorded or confirmed. The local sheriff's office never solved the mystery of the figure who appeared. From what my grandmother told me, the local authorities said the figure had the appearance of a young female.

I remember waking up that morning to a dream I had. In my dream, my mother was watching me in a crowd of spectators while I was playing baseball. I was at bat and ready to make her proud. I hit a line drive to right field on the first pitch. As I rounded first, the ball went directly through the right fielder's legs. As the right fielder turned around to retrieve the ball, he suddenly tripped and fell to the ground. While rounding the bases, all I could hear was the roar of the crowd in a blistering cheer. Distinctively, I could hear my mother screaming, "Go! Run! Don't stop!" Once the right fielder retrieved the ball, I was already rounding third base and on my way to an inside-the-park home run. Once I touched the home plate, I instantly looked at my mother, and from a distance, she mouthed something to me that I could not hear or decipher from the motion of her lips. From that point, the crowd, players, scenery, and I entered a peculiar world of slow motion. No matter how fast I tried to walk or turn my head, everything was at a lumbering pace. Once again, I looked at my mother, and she kept mouthing the same unintelligible words to me. Almost instantly after her last word, everything and everyone started to move in real time again. As I walked back to the dugout, I instinctively glanced at the right fielder who had committed that awful error. On a dime, I stopped right in my tracks. There was no right fielder occupying right field anymore, for there stood what appeared to be a middle-aged lady standing where the right fielder should have been. From where I was standing, her face seemed unrecognizably blurry, but I could tell she was staring at me with a purpose. While our eyes locked, I could feel a warm sensation pulse throughout my body and into my bones. I cannot explain it, but at that moment, I felt more alive than I have ever felt. The next thing I knew, I woke up in a cold sweat. Somehow, and I cannot explain how or why, I knew that lady I saw in my dream was the homeless lady who turned me over to the hospital. There was no mistaking it—I just knew.

A couple of minutes later, my father frantically darted into my room in a worried panic. "Did you see your mother at all this morning?"

I shook my head in confusion. Something was not right— I just knew it. "No, I woke up a couple of minutes ago. Is everything okay?"

"It's just that…" He paused for a quick moment. "She never came home after work."

I was speechless. My suspicions were confirmed, but I never wanted to believe it or come to terms with it at that moment. My mother was indubitably strict with her routines, always early and never late. I was only ten years old at the time, but emotionally, I felt at least double my age. Deep inside, I did not have that innocent side that a typical fourth-grade child had. From all that I had been through in a short life, I was built tough. It took a lot to test my emotions; however, this test would key my emotions to the brink of infinite sadness.

After my father did his due diligence by reporting this issue to authorities, he received a call a couple of hours later from the colony sheriff. After a few seconds of silence, he instantly dropped the phone and turned to me and said, "Your mother… she's dead." I took two steps back, and it felt like my heart had slipped down to my toes. I then ran into my room, slammed the door shut, and cried until I fell asleep. Not once did my father knock on my door to console me or to see if I was okay. *Yes, father, it would've been nice to care.*

Authorities located my mother's lifeless body in a desolate, war-torn area that the local population refers to as the *wastelands*. In the report I read a few years later, it was said that her body was discovered near an old drainage ditch. As she lay on her back, her arms and legs were perfectly sprawled out, as if she were ready to make a snow angel in the ground.

Later that day, the lead detective came to interview my father at our house. I was alone in my room with the door shut, as my father instructed. Curiously, I pressed my ear against the door and could barely make out some of the words that were spoken during the interview. For those words I did hear, I have always kept them to myself and never spoken about them to anyone.

It turned out that the authorities were completely clueless. Her purse, money, and jewelry were all still intact. Not a single trace of DNA evidence was ever found in her car or around the scene. Not to mention, rape was thought to be a fallacy due to her hospital attire still being worn. As a couple of days went by, the coroner called my father to inform him that the cause of death was ruled to be "death by asphyxiation." What a dreadful way to go. Every time I watch television or even hear that phrase, I cringe and think about how much my mother probably suffered and struggled. Along with the cringing come thoughts of rage and justice. Sadly, those thoughts turning into reality are basically obsolete considering this so-called *female figure* has never been identified.

Life would never be the same. Some may say that it was life's predetermined plan to see how others react to adversity, but I have never understood that notion. My mother had so much to offer this world and even more to give. As I got older, I questioned my faith numerous times. Over and over, I tried to use this pain and manifest it into strength. This strength was nonexistent in my case. Being ten years old and going through this tragedy was arduous. Not once in a million years had I thought this would ever happen to me. My new life was perfect, and now it is forever changed. It is hard not to argue that a young child's brain is not as comprehensive as that of an adult. The explanation for why this tragedy occurred easily overshadowed the knowledge of concepts I had at ten years old. Unfortunately, this tragedy was simply the beginning of my father's demise.

y father's name was Jarrick Hutchen. Like my mother, he was also forty-two years old when I became part of the family. Unlike my mother, age was no friend of his. It was widely whispered amongst our colony how people would confuse my mother as his daughter. Certainly, those claims were not at all amusing to him. He was a quiet, yet modest man. I am not sure if he was always self-effacing or if the deaths of his two sons turned him into a stoic statue, ninety percent of the time. Regardless, he was a good man—not great, for what it's worth.

My father was a laborer by trade. He did all sorts of work for independent contractors, such as bricklaying, drywall, painting, and even landscaping. He was not the smartest man alive, but his work ethic and attention to detail were impeccable. A perfectionist, he simply was. When it came to his jobs or work around the house, every little detail always mattered. He was a contractor's dream, yet a co-worker's nightmare. If his attitude was anything like his silent criticism and back-door complaining about chores around the house, I could only imagine the joy his co-workers would express working beside him.

Sadly, my father never had a big influence on me. I think he expected that role from my mother, considering his busy schedule and dull personality. Part of me thinks he only agreed to adopt me because it was what my mother wanted. Regardless, he stuck it out as best he could. I firmly believe that once Jacob and Jaret passed, he wanted to live out his life in a state of mediocrity until his final day. I could not blame him, though; tragedy can easily jumpstart a vague perspective on life. I guess some people were not meant to overcome adversity but rather crumble to the ashes of hopelessness.

There are always certain days you have in your life that hit you hard and are harder to forget. My mother's wake was certainly one of them. I remember my father's stoic state, almost like he was looking right through everybody, like he was the only one in the room. I have always wondered if it was simply his way of grieving or if it was a natural expression. For my father, he had too much pride to grieve in public, so it was easy to understand that notion. Lost and broken were the first two words I could think of to describe him.

After the funeral, reality settled in rather quickly. My father would drop me off at school, while my grandmother would pick me up every day at 2:30 p.m. and take me back to her place until my father got off work. Sometimes, he would pick me up early; most of the time, it was later in the evening. My grandmother knew his late evenings were sometimes spent at the bar, but nothing was ever said to him. She accepted it, so she gave him his space and kept it to herself. Now that I am older and understand more, I guess it was his way of grieving and falling deeper into a never-ending depression.

Supposedly, my father was a big drinker before he met my mother. As for my mother, she never touched the bad stuff, as far as I knew. Willing to change and abide by being sober, my father put his past in the vault and decided to change for the better. I guess old habits die hard for some.

Painfully, the worst had yet to come. I remember the night—a warm but rainy evening. On this kind of evening, you would take a stroll around the block and not shed a care about the rain. To me, those nights are pure joy. They always gave me a subtle sense of life—like it was a good time to feel alive. Unfortunately, there was no joy or feeling of life to be found on this pleasant evening. The colony sheriff called my grandmother sometime around 9:00 p.m. to let her know that the police had picked up my father on suspicion of DWI. He had crashed his car into a ditch about a mile down the road from my grandmother's house. Luckily, it was a single-car mishap, and he was not hurt at all. Lucky for me, I was not in the car with him going home. Little did I know, my life was about to change drastically yet again.

It was a Saturday morning. My grandmother had dropped us off at our residence after picking up my father at the colony jail. My father did not say much that morning, only telling me to eat if I was hungry before he fled to his bedroom to sulk in his shame.

I was not hungry, though; my confusion and emotions were too much for me. I decided the best thing for me to do was to sleep it off and wake up with a better understanding of the events that unfolded.

I remember it like it was yesterday, my nap. I fell into a deep sleep and had one of those nightmares that sticks with you for an eternity. I dreamt I was somewhere in the wretched wastelands, trapped in the middle of a small pit full of quicksand, slowly sinking. Every time I attempted to escape towards the edge, I was met with curled-up cobra snakes with eager, erect heads staring at me, waiting to strike. The more I panicked, the cobras would become more anxious, taking up the greatest pleasure of my inevitable sinking. I thought it was either dying in one way or another. At that moment, I decided on the more peaceful way, which was to sink down under the sand. Once the sand hit my neck, I immediately woke up in a panic.

I remained in bed and thought about it for a while. I could not think long, though; the panicked state I was in left my mouth dry as a piece of sandpaper. Nonetheless, I rose out of bed, fixed a glass of water, and sat down at the kitchen table. I could not explain it, but I guess I was worried about what was to come.

A couple of minutes later, my father opened his bedroom door and stood there for a moment, mimicking a cold statue. I tried to pretend that I did not hear or see him, which was a little intimidating. I could tell my father was slowly losing his mind to a deep depression. As I was about to take another drink, he walked over to the fridge, held his hand on the handle, and paused for a moment.

He slowly turned his head in a crooked manner. "I need you to pack a bag for a couple of days," he said while staring at the floor. "You are going to stay with your grandma for the rest of the weekend."

"Right now?" I responded.

My father shook his head. "Yes, Gret. Granny Kline will be here in thirty minutes to pick you up. I have some… some business to take care of, and I don't need the responsibility of watching over you while I'm busy."

A part of me did not know how to feel. I was worried and relieved all at once. I did love sleeping in my own bed and listening to trains making their nightly runs. On the other hand, I loved spending time with my grandmother. Oddly enough, never once have I ever heard my father refer to my grandmother as *Granny Kline.* Something was off, I thought. Kline was my mother's maiden name. My father's parents passed away well before I was adopted—innocent casualties of the war. Therefore, he never had a reason to incorporate Kline while referring to my grandmother.

Before I could finish packing my weekend bag, the doorbell rang. I stopped packing my bag for a second to hear if my father would answer the door. No footsteps, movements, or creaking were heard. Shortly, the doorbell rang again. Feeling a little annoyed, I rushed out of my room to answer the door. When I opened the door, I anticipated getting a big hug from my grandmother, but she wasn't there at all.

An elderly man stood at the entrance and greeted me with a smile. "Hello, son, is your father around?" The man was certainly a stranger—a scary one.

A little sense of fear overcame me from the inside. "Yes, sir, he is. He's not... um, feeling well, though. He is resting in his room right now."

His smile grew even larger. "May I come in? I need to speak with him. It's quite urgent and necessary that your father and I have a little chat."

"I'm sorry, sir. I am not allowed to invite strangers into our house. My mother taught me so." As intimidating as an older man may be to a ten-year-old boy, I held my ground in a collective manner.

"Oh, I see. You learn quickly, young man. Your mother must be very proud."

Sadness started to sink in once again. "My mother is dead." I was a little jittery, and rightfully so. He donned a pinstriped black suit that was evidently a size too small for his stature. His black flat cap was slightly tilted to the right, leaving him to taunt his maniacal stare. He was evidently a mild, well-mannered man, but I was terrified of him. The look of this elderly man could haunt my dreams for days.

The old man shook his head. "Yes, I know, son."

I looked down and became confused. "How... how do you know?"

His head rose slowly and flashed a quick smile, avoiding the question. "Son, would you do me a favor? Would you let your father know that I will be stopping by once more? It is imperative that I have a conversation with him. It's very vital, son."

"Okay, I will."

"Thank you, son." The old man started to turn away but briskly halted himself, like he forgot something of value. "One more thing, son—before I take my leave. Someone once told me that mistakes are one of the most fundamental lessons in life. It's not the mistake that defines us. It's how we overcome and adapt to them. Never forget that." He kept an eerie smile as he awaited my response.

"My mother used to tell me the same thing."

The old man smiled even more graciously. "Mine too." He then nodded his head in a bowing fashion. "Have a nice day, young man. I hope to see you and your father soon."

"Yes, sir, you have a nice day also."

As he started to walk away, I heard him humming a rhythmic melody, casually looking in all directions—like the setting was new to him. It sounded like a praise hymn, the kind you hear in church every Sunday. I know I have heard it before, but I could not connect my thoughts to memory at that moment.

Three houses down, I could see my grandmother's car about to pull up as the elderly man made his way onto the sidewalk. As soon as she pulled in, she immediately got out of her car and briskly walked up to the front porch. "Hey, Gret! Are you ready?"

I smiled and looked in the direction of the elderly man. "Almost. Did you see that man that came up to the door, asking for my father?"

My grandmother shook her head and looked down the sidewalk. "No, I didn't see a man. Are you sure?"

I took a few steps towards the sidewalk and looked in the direction he left. He was nowhere to be seen. "Yes, ma'am, I am positive. I just saw him leave a few seconds ago; he—"

My grandmother quickly interrupted. "Listen, Gret. Regardless, you should never talk to strangers like that. The next time you encounter a stranger like that, you immediately grab your father."

"Yes, ma'am."

My grandmother smiled and was happy I understood. "Now, let's get going. Where is your father?"

"He is in his room. Sleeping—I think."

My grandmother clapped her hands a couple of times. "Okay, well, go get your bag and say goodbye to your father. I will be waiting in the car."

I could not believe my grandmother did not see that old man. As crazy as it sounded, it was almost like the man disappeared into thin air. As my grandmother made her way to her car, I ran back into the house and grabbed my bags, thinking about how that old man simply vanished. I then knocked on my father's door to say goodbye, but there was no answer. I was sure he was sleeping, so I left him alone and made my way into my grandmother's car.

****

A couple of days passed by, for it was now Sunday. My grandmother and I were to meet my father at Sunday mass at 11:00 a.m., then go out to lunch. There was only one problem—my father never showed up. By the time mass had started, my grandmother had an utter look of concern on her face, mixed with anger and confusion. For my grandmother, I could tell it was an instant red flag—my father rarely ever missed mass.

By the time mass had ended, I was starving. Feeling concerned, my grandmother explained to me that we were going to check on my father first, then go out to lunch. Our house was a three-minute drive from church; not one word came out of my grandmother's mouth. The concern started to escalate after realizing that my father's truck was gone, but the garage door was wide open. I thought to myself: *Maybe he went to the corner store and forgot to close the garage door.*

As a kid, you tend to not think about the worst-case scenarios that are possible. I remember it like yesterday—that morning when my father questioned me about if my mother came home from work. I never thought or expected that tragedies would strike our family once more. The brutal realities of this world, I suppose, overshadowed my innocence. I learned as I got older that a child's innocence dies slowly with age. Innocence, so precious and cherished, is the saddest quality for any child to lose. Once more, I was about to take another severe blow that would change my life yet again.

After entering the house, everything was in its place from the Friday I was picked up. My father's bedroom door was wide open, and even his bed was neatly made and set. Somehow, I could see it in her face that she knew all too well. She then opened his closet door. Gone. All his clothes, shoes, and possessions were gone. My innocence once again kicked in.

"Grandma, where did father go?" I asked. I already knew.

"Gret, go watch the tube, and please sit quietly for a moment. I need to make some calls." She was calm, but you could see the concern on her face from a mile away.

"Maybe he had a last minute—"

My grandmother quickly stepped in before I could finish my sentence. "Gret, please do as I say. I will not ask again—now, please."

After a couple of hours of phone calls, a colony sheriff visit, and sitting quietly with thoughts of curiosity, it was determined that my father took off without any notice. It was never known what day he left, but that did not matter to us. My father had abandoned us for no good reason at all. I was too young to even comprehend the reasoning as to why. For all his faults, my grandmother never spoke any negative words or displeasure toward my father from that day on. In fact, I could not even remember if she ever mentioned his name again. He was simply gone, leaving behind his duties as a sworn adoptive father.

Now that I am older and wiser, I feel like he thought that maybe he needed a new stab at life. A new beginning, intrinsically. I was a little hurt, and rightfully so, for it was not the first time I had been abandoned. Although it did not bother me that much because I knew that my grandmother was up to bat for me, I knew she would do anything and everything to never let me go. Indeed, I knew everything was going to be okay. From that day until the present, I was never to see or hear from my father again.

When I was in the sixth grade, I remember writing a poem for possible submission in my school's 'young author' contest. I never submitted it, for the fear of losing weighed heavily on my conscious mind. It was entitled, *"Depression Loves No One."* It went something like this:

> *Long days will pass,*
> *Short days will arrive.*
> *Bad days will obliterate,*
> *Good days will strive.*
>
> *Some weeks will bring pain,*
> *Other weeks will carry pleasure.*
> *Lousy weeks will bring agony,*
> *Superior weeks will bring measure.*
>
> *Months then years, surely will come,*
> *None to be forgotten, we shall stand.*
> *To understand and conquer depression,*
> *United we become, hand in hand.*

This is the first time I have ever shared this poem, for I always kept it to myself. I was twelve years old when I wrote this, roughly two years removed from both of my parents. My grandmother and I had a special relationship, which has influenced this poem. We had an unbreakable, systemic approach to lifting each other up while we were down. When I was down, she would cheer me up in ways I could not explain. While she was down, I always tried my hardest to lift her spirits. At all times, we both knew that one had to remain strong, and it never seemed to fail. What we had was certainly a blessing beyond all measure.

Shortly after my father left, my grandmother filed for sole custody of me. It was a little difficult at first because my father's whereabouts were still unknown. In turn, colony officials were hesitant to decide on legally declaring my father missing or deceased, for that matter. Their argument was that he could return at any time and continue his duties as my legal guardian. This absolutely angered my grandmother. I would often hear her arguing on the phone, sometimes screaming at whoever was on the other end of the line. With enough push and the right amount of patience, colony officials expedited our case so I would not have to move into a foster home. She did it; she now had full custody, which made me ecstatic beyond all words.

For the first couple of weeks, we stayed at my grandmother's house until she made a final decision on where we would live. She put three options on the table: her house, my parents' house, or a new house that she would purchase. Her house was much older, worn, dilapidated, and much smaller. Not to mention, there was always something off about her house. Maybe it was just me, but I always felt like someone, or something, was always watching me. I suppose old houses kind of set off that vibe for a youngster like me. My parents' house was roughly eight years old when they bought it brand new after Jacob and Jaret had passed. Buying a new house would take work and time, so that idea was a long shot at best.

In the end, my grandmother sold her house, and we moved into my parents' house. I was happy—happy to say the least. I never wanted to move; I was content and happy here. With the money she earned from selling her house, we made a few minor changes and additions to the house. She taught me that memories have a bad side and a good side. It's always important to keep an even balance because the foundation is where it all began. Whether you let that memory tear you asunder or let that memory make you smile, you always hold the key to a perfect balance. With that lesson, we decided that a few changes and a few minor additions were necessary. We both wanted the house to preserve the foundation of memories that my parents built. No walls were knocked down; only fresh paint was added in most of the rooms. We did make one minor change to one of the rooms. My father's storage room became my video and playroom. My grandmother would not let me have a television in my bedroom, citing that a bedroom was made for sleeping, not watching the tube. Generally, that was the first item on her list of changes. I even got my wish. She added a huge swimming pool and a new deck in our backyard. The pieces of my young life were starting to mend once again. I was happy. Sure, I missed my mother, but my grandmother filled her role with utter surety.

****

Seasons changed, years came and went, and good times and bad times were plentiful. The world was slowly healing from the wars of the past. Life was pretty decent, to say the least. My grandmother and I had life in a firm grasp, for there was nothing too big or small that we were afraid to take on. She stuck with me through thick and thin. I graduated high school with honors and completed my community college degree in finance, and we started our own side business selling medical equipment for a distributor. She was a hospital administrator, but once she retired, she took on this business venture with my help. The money and experience were great, but once her health started to decline, she sold our side business to a young married couple.

It was around May of 2191. My grandmother had attended her monthly checkup and came home with the kind of news you never want to hear. She was diagnosed with stage three lung cancer and was given about six months to a year to live. I was sad, but content in a humanistic manner. I was content because she was ninety years old. Her life was the kind of life that was beyond admiration—living a full life and accomplishing so much. From that moment of the news, I made a conscious decision to not mourn but rather celebrate her life when she passes. She will always be my mentor, my hero, and my best friend.

****

January 3, 2192. I knew this day would come sooner than later. It was a matter of when, considering she was admitted to hospice three days ago. I had received a call from hospice

27

informing me that she was most likely to pass any hour now. I immediately dropped the phone, grabbed my keys, and left work. Tears rolled down my face as I sped down the unusual, desolate streets as quickly as I could. It was a funny feeling, though, because I kept telling myself that I was not going to mourn or cry my eyes out when it happened. I guess emotions are ever so unpredictable, for one can truly not control them until they face death head-on.

Lucky for me, she was awake but barely audible when I arrived. It took one smile from her to ease my sorrows almost instantly. I would never forget the way she looked. Even in her last moments, she looked like someone out of a fairy tale. An angel, to be exact. As I sat next to her bed, she grabbed my hand and held it firmly with both of hers. If I had known that this was our last three minutes together, I would have said something more meaningful and worthy rather than shaking my head with one-word answers.

She took a deep breath and looked me square in the eyes. "Gretan, look…"

A tear started to roll down my cheek. "Yes, grandma?"

Her voice was becoming a silent whisper. "My time is up. Yours is about to begin. You have a rare gift—I've always known. I had it too. From me to you, you will now see how enhanced you've become."

My eyes became wide. "What do you mean, grandma?"

"I love you, my child."

My insides started to shake. "I love you too."

"You must… must protect…"

"Protect? Protect who?"

"Yes, look f-f-for…"

Flat line at 2:13 p.m. She was gone and off to the afterlife. She was ridden out of all her pain and taken in peace by the angels from up above. I sat next to her for the next five minutes and held her hand. Even though she was gone, I said everything I wish I would have said to her in my head, hoping she would know what I wanted to say. After I cleared my conscious mind, I said a little prayer in the hope that she would find eternal peace and that my mother might meet her. Even though I was sure my mother was always watching down from above, I was sure my grandmother would tell her what a fine young man I had become. I gave her a little kiss on the forehead, tucked her body in the blankets, and left the room while the nurses patiently waited for my last goodbyes. I was on my own now.

The Present
2192–Beyond

1

Routines, Reveries, and Realization

In a world full of uncertainties, come strange and unpredictable times. One thing that I am certain of is death. Death was now a regularity in my life, parading and flaunting around my proclivities. In a way, it was like it masqueraded around my every step without a care in the world.

How many others were like me? For that, I did not have an answer. It had now been eight months since my grandmother had passed. Since then, I have acquired (enhanced, as my grandmother claimed) this uncanny ability deep within my soul. I wondered for how many years she had this exceptional capability. *Was she born with it? Did she inherit it somehow? Did my mother have it too?* Maybe these questions were better left unanswered, or maybe not.

I was now alone in this world, searching for answers that may come. Answers that may invoke limitless opportunities to make this life my best, or my worst, for that matter. "Everything in life comes full circle." I vaguely remember that phrase from that preacher on one of those late-night church infomercials that would play in the early hours of the morning. "Embrace the unknown, for the unknown is another obstacle to the known." I remember that one also.

For whom I am comes a deeper sense, a sense of what I must become. I was frightened by the thought of failure. Even more, how was I going to live with this rarity? "Protect," she said. *Protect who?* Full circle, I kept reminding myself. Everything will come full circle, even my death one day. Day by day, stride after stride, and night after night, this was my life—and the dead were all around me.

One by one, they would pass by me more than often. Routines and reveries were the norm, while others came and went, seeking whatever they might be looking for. The air felt different around them—an uncertain but warm feeling with a hint of a cold, brisk breeze. Numbness would overtake my senses. A loss of balance usually followed what seemed to be a second of shooting pain within my head. *Emotional sickness* is a proper phrase to relate to. If I had to guess, I would think that all these conditions were somehow related to my struggles when I was born.

I try my hardest not to stare, for they do not know that I can see them. Only once has anyone witnessed the truth I possess. I was at a toy store shopping for a gift for a co-worker's son. I shortly observed a little boy trying his hardest to reach for a toy on the top shelf. The poor kid must have been only eight years old or younger. His untimely demise made me feel weak and sorry, so I walked over to where he was and grabbed the toy. In an effort to try to comfort him and hand him the toy, he froze for a quick second and ran down the aisle and out of sight. I pillaged the whole store afterwards, hoping to see if I could find him. No luck. I instantly forgot why I came there in the first place and walked out immediately. Feeling low, I sat in my car for about fifteen minutes, contemplating if that move was the way to live with this. Since this day, I have never returned to that toy store again.

This curse, as many would call it, is now my everyday life. With this life, new challenges, trials, and tribulations took my emotions to heights that I had never felt before. Understanding these emotions could easily make or break the very foundations of who I was to become. Frankly, that was half the battle. The other half was simply living with them. This was my life, and I must embrace, fight, and conquer by any means necessary.

2

Soaring to Limitless Boundaries

Do not ponder or ask why.
Trust your instinct,
Set it free and soar high.

Clear is the beautiful sky.
Reach for the stars,
Do not ponder or ask why.

Your soul is a bird; it shall fly.
Overcome all obstacles,
Set it free and soar high.

Failure need not apply,
Never give up.
Do not ponder or ask why.

Never quit; always try.
Your spirit is within,
Set it free and soar high.

Limitless is the clear blue sky.
The future is yours,
Do not ponder or ask why.
Set it free and soar high.

I was strolling through an open field in Old Falls Park. My mother used to take me there on her days off when she claimed we needed some *fresh air.* Looking back on what I had learned, I believed it was her escape from the brutalities of her job, tragedies, and even marriage. She would sometimes sit on the bench and gaze into the vibrant blue sky, cracking a half-smile.

Occasionally, I would witness a tear or two rolling down her cheek, striking her collared shirt. I believe it was her method to cope with all the obstacles within her soul.

During my walk, I remembered stopping near the center of the field and soaking in the beautiful sounds of nature. The smell of freshly cut grass lingered all around me, enlightening my joyous mood. I remember buzzards flying in an ever-circling pattern in the far distance, possibly honing on a nearby animal carcass. Nature and all its entirety were all around me. I closed my eyes for a second, took a deep breath, and paused.

To my surprise, I was no longer standing stationary on the ground. My feet were carelessly dangling in the warm air, about three hundred feet off the ground. I was on top of the world, moving forward thanks to a slight wind gust. Out of the blue, a predatory hawk positioned itself about five feet below me, possibly scoping out its next prey.

Suddenly, as it dove toward the ground for the kill, my gravitational pull shifted simultaneously in correspondence with the hawk. Once it nabbed a small field mouse, my body instantly propelled me to a height much higher than any bird can sustain. As I started to climb higher, my body started to convulse. Oxygen intake became shallow and hard to manage. Once I was at a point of impossible breathing, I instantly woke up in a cold sweat. It was one of the best dreams I have ever had.

August 24th, 2192. Monday. Another summer had passed. Leaves were turning brown, a cold wind was blowing from the north, and what seemed to be a frigid autumn was in the making. The older I became, the less I seemed to care about the change of the seasons. Warm, hot, warm again, cold— it was all the same to me.

I remember this morning, for I was woken up around 6:00 a.m. from an intuitive vision I dreamed. Today was like any other normal start to the work week—get out of bed, shower, eat a quick snack, and head to work. For the last two years, I have maintained a Monday-to-Friday job as a loan specialist for 1st Wing Bank. It was far from exciting, but I loved the people I worked with, and it paid the bills. Positive work atmosphere, easy job, bills paid—it was all I needed.

Nevertheless, since my dream woke me up an hour early, I decided to leave my house a little early and go somewhere that I had never been to. The place was called *Claire's Coffeehouse* and Eatery. I guess I needed to venture out more and explore more businesses. The little place just so happened to be right across from my bank. Looking out my window from my office, I have always stared and wondered about this place. I would think to myself and wonder what Claire was like, or if Claire, if she even existed, worked there. When time at work seemed to drag, I always found myself lost in my thoughts about this place. I would glance, sometimes stare, out my window, wondering what this place was like. It seemed like it was one of those little coffeehouses that was run by hardworking, blue-collared people—the kind who would scrounge for a living. The kind who would have to save every penny to buy it one day. The kind who simply did not take life for granted. Genuine people, I imagine, are the kind who care about the human being—people easy to envy, easy to admire, and easy to love. Soon enough, I would find out if this place was everything I had imagined it to be.

It was unusually cold outside in late August. Once I arrived and stepped outside in the parking lot, I instantly thought of that crazy guy from that one conspiracy theory show. I remembered one episode in particular; global warming was the main topic. He adamantly insisted that global warming was a false reality, insisting that the world was heading towards a major ice age. Nevertheless, my car read fifty-three degrees that morning. Far from an ice age, but good gracious, it was damn cold outside for a late August day.

Breathe. Stay calm. Breathe. Remain calm. Just my luck. Once I opened the door, the unknown hit me like an eighteen-wheeler. It had been a couple of weeks since I last felt it, so this one caught me by surprise. Frozen, numbness, vertigo, numb tongue—here it comes again. An eerie presence was surely inside.

"Sir?" the hostess asked. "Are you okay?"

Snap out of it. I heard the welcoming greeting, but I couldn't react. "I-I-I-just…"

"Just?"

Regain control, quick. Luckily, I did it in the nick of time. "I think I left my wallet in my car, or at home, for that matter. You know, opening the door and thinking where my wallet was. I got a little confused, I guess." *That was awful.*

The hostess smiled and presented a look of relief. "Oh, good golly grief. You had me worried for a second there! You looked like you were having an episode or something. Was it PTSD from serving in the war that triggered it?"

"No, ma'am, not at all. I'm sorry; I sincerely am. I'm probably as confused as you are." *Boy, I felt insecure and stupid.*

I get this a lot. For some reason, I got asked questions all the time about whether or not I served. Usually, I quickly explain that I could not join if I wanted to due to my medical history, but this time, I left it alone.

The hostess still had a look of concern on her face. "Are you sure you are okay?"

I signaled a perfunctory nod. "Yes, I am fine. I'm going to grab my wallet. I think it's in my car, but I may have left it at home."

"Would you like us to prepare a table for you?"

"No, thanks. I would not want to keep any other customers waiting."

The hostess looked back at the dining area, looked back my way, and smirked. "Honey, have you looked around this morning? It is like a ghost town in here. I don't think you will keep anyone waiting."

I quickly smiled and obliged. "Okay, I cannot promise I'll be back, but if not, I'm terribly sorry. I-I… need to check on some stuff first."

"Suit yourself, honey. Thanks for stopping by, and feel free to visit anytime. I'm Gabby, by the way."

I had no choice but to offer my hand in a handshake. "I'm Gretan, but you can call me Gret."

She reached out her hand and obliged. "Okay, Gret, I like your name! Have a great day, and thanks again for stopping by."

"You too, Gabby. Nice to meet you also."

I instantly felt a connection between us. The grasp of her warm and comforting hand pioneered a blissful feeling within my body. Not to mention, she was one of the most exquisite girls I had seen in quite some time. I wanted to know more about her. Gabby—she seemed fantastic.

I walked out to my car and totally forgot about what initially caused that discomfort. I did not see one inside, nor was I looking. I was fixated on my composure—and Gabby. Embarrassment filled my consciousness, and it embellished my body for a few moments. In those moments, I felt a sudden feeling of certainty, a feeling like there was some kind of plan for that scene to happen the way it did. Gabby seemed genuine, caring, and certainly gorgeous. She had beautiful, wavy blonde hair that accentuated all the precious features on her face. A sarcastic but funny attitude was written all over her personality. You could put her in a room full of a hundred people, and yet everyone would gravitate towards her. She seemed to have it all, and here I probably did not make the best first impression. I knew that I had to go back soon. But what if? What if déjà vu happened again while I walked in? I guess the worst that could happen was a repeat of the same scene, and maybe she would think I was psychotic or something. I guess it wouldn't be the first time or the last. Anyway, I knew I had to take that chance. Not today, though, for tomorrow is a brand-new day for new beginnings.

4

Precursor to Transparency

Cryptic messages,
Ambiguous they are.
The tower shines bright,
Seemingly, still far.

The path may stray,
Strength from within.
I will never give in.
I will never give in.

I was walking in a crowd of people from all around the world. We were not anywhere recognizable or familiar, as our surroundings depicted like us as all entrapped in a structure shaped like a dome. Nonchalantly, I kept to myself and maintained the pace of the people in front of me. As time slowly went by, I noticed that a few people started flashing hostile and vicious glares my way. These were soon combined with subtle bumps and nudges. I started to feel uneasy. Fear was settling in as it started to overtake my body. I started to panic hard— uncontrollably hard. Trying not to make a scene, I began to dart in between the massive crowd of people. As I slouched down to catch my breath, I caught a truly disturbing and morbid scene. A group of about fifty people were standing in a circle, chanting a peculiar phrase. Over and over, it sounded like an ancient language that had been rendered obsolete for thousands of years. Inside the circle stood a figure donning a black cloak, staring up into the sky as if it were harnessing a power from above. The circle started a gentle shift, contorting to an entrance straight ahead of me. As the chanting became louder, I knew my presence was put on notice as the figure from within fancied a wicked smile my way. Instantly, my subconscious felt an electroshock, and I awoke in my bed, terrified.

To be precise, it was 3:12 a.m. Another bad dream, another cold sweat, and another instant panic. Some say your dreams and nightmares are depictions of your life or what your life may become. While others even believe that they depict a troubled past and warn people not to follow that path again, regardless, my nightmare left me with questions that may go unanswered for quite some time.

5

Within the Confines of Claire's

Tuesday. After my nightmare, 6:30 a.m. came quickly. Of course, 7:30 a.m. was my normal get-out-bed-time, but since I was up early again, I was going to attempt breakfast at Claire's again. Truth be told, I was extremely nervous. My mother always used to tell me, "Don't be such a nervous nelly!" I could not help it; I was normally a nervous wreck. It felt like the first time I gained enough courage to talk to a girl—actually *talk*, if you know what I mean. I asked my middle school crush, Beth, to dance at the winter social. She said yes, but my nerves and confidence still clung to me like a stench. I guess it was part of me that would never fade away.

On the way there, I thought about Gabby, the nightmare from last night, and the unknown presence I did not see yesterday. It was not all necessarily in that order, but Gabby was a close first. I legitimately liked her, and it had been a while since I had gotten close to someone. *Wishful thinking, I know.* I tended to keep myself 'well reserved' when it came to dating and meeting new people. I would rather have four close friends than one hundred so-called friends, if that makes sense.

Well, here goes nothing. I walked up to the door, stopping for a short minute to regain my composure and pretend I had gotten a text message on my phone. Once I pretended to text whoever the phony person was, I slowly opened the door to a nice surprise. The air was pleasantly clear. No presence meant no uncontrollable seizing.

On the other hand, it was dead as a door nail in there. From the looks of it, Gabby was nowhere to be seen as a short, older woman named Nancy (from her name tag) genuinely greeted me and escorted me to a table.

As I sat down, Nancy presented me with a smile. "Would you like to start off with some coffee? Maybe some juice or water?"

I must admit, I was still nervous. "Of course, what kind of beer do you have?" *Horrible joke.*

Confusion overtook Nancy's face for a second, then she realized it was a dumb joke. "Oh, good gracious." She let out a short burst of laughter. "You're too funny."

 "I apologize—corny joke." I quickly glanced at the menu. "May I… may I please have a black coffee—no cream or sugar. Black coffee, please. You know—a coffee cup and coffee." *Stupid, stupid.* My awful jokes are seemingly abundant when my nerves are in overdrive.

Nancy let out a quick bit of laughter and smiled. "Is everything all right? You seem nervous for some reason."

"Oh yeah, I'm fine. I'm a little groggy, I suppose. Plus, I have a long day ahead of me. So, you know… just a *wee* bit tired."

Nancy shook her head and smiled again. "That's me pretty much every morning. I'll be back with your coffee. In the meantime, I expect to hear more funny jokes from you."

My eyes grew wide. "I'll try my best."

After Nancy turned and headed towards the back, I quickly looked around to see if Gabby was anywhere in sight. From a quick look, it looked like I was out of luck. I guess I got my hopes up, but the day would go on. I briefly thought about asking where Gabby was but figured it may be too soon. I did not want to sound desperate, I guess, so I refrained from the thought in inquiring—at least now. A minute later, Nancy returned with a menu and coffee and graciously presented it to me while informing me about the specials.

"You know, I think I will stick with my coffee for now," I said while a strange lady walked in and casually strolled to the front counter. It was unexplainable; my eyes were glued to her the whole time I finished my sentence. "I'm honestly not that hungry right now. However, I may order something to go."

I could not stop staring. Admittedly, it was hard not to consider that she and I were currently the only patrons in the whole coffeehouse. Not to mention, her attire, her appearance, and her general presentation were *off* to me. She looked to be in her mid-to-upper thirties and had a hairstyle that probably died twenty years ago. Strange enough, I felt like I knew her from somewhere—a strangely familiar face that I could not pinpoint my finger on. As I casually sipped my coffee, I watched her converse with the cashier for about twenty seconds. When the conversation was over, the strange lady turned around, headed straight forward like a mannequin, and walked out of Claire's. Not once did she not look around or even care to notice my presence—not that I was expecting her to. Odd, to say the least.

Once I finished my coffee and wrapped up my short conversation with Nancy, I walked up to the counter to pay my bill. There stood the same middle-aged woman who was conversing with the strange lady. I thought to myself: *What the heck? I might as well ask.* Trying minds are dying to inquire—guilty as charged.

I noticed the cashier's name was Bree (on her nametag) as I handed her the bill. "Just the coffee today."

Bree took the receipt and began to type on the register. "Not hungry, today?"

I shook my head. "Nah, I needed some caffeine." *Here goes nothing.* "This may sound a little strange, but may I ask you a question?"

"Shoot."

"That woman who walked in and talked to you, what did she ask you?"

Bree stopped what she was doing and looked right at me. "Why? Do you know her or something?"

"No, no. She looked familiar. I don't know; I deal with a lot of customers at work. She just looked familiar; that is all."

"I see. She was wondering about the hours, that is all." Bree rolled her eyes, but not at me. "Even though they are posted on the door, she had to come in and ask. Anyhow, what kind of work do you do?"

"I'm a loan specialist across the street."

"Oh, that sounds quite interesting. Do you specialize in mortgage loans?"

"Mostly personal loans, but I refer those who want a mortgage loan to my counterparts." I playfully smiled at her. "Do you need a loan?"

Bree let out a sudden chuckle. "Oh no, not me. I can barely pay my bills, but I'm still afloat with my head barely over water—if you know what I mean. Unfortunately, there are many people here in our area who are indigent and suffering. Those rich bastards across the world don't give a crap about any of us."

It was outright obvious that Bree was casually bitter about modern-day affairs across the world. I truly could not blame her, though, for that was the feeling of many citizens I have encountered throughout the years here. For the past ten years, our colony has seemed to remain in a stagnant condition with no hope of overcoming tragedies from the past. Honestly, that thought never seemed to bother me. Coming from where I came from, I knew that things could be much worse than they are.

I shook my head in agreement to be cordial towards her. "I feel you on that notion. For what it's worth, though, I am thankful beyond measure that I am still six feet above the ground and continue to breathe."

Bree presented me with a quick smirk. "Well, that's good. People these days are always looking for a way—you know, a way—to survive and live day by day. You must keep your head up, as hard as that is these days. Always hope for the best and expect the worst. That's my motto."

I was not sure what she meant by 'a way', but I went about it like I understood. I have always tended to give people the benefit of the doubt. We who survived the wars and attacks had been through a lot, some more than others, and others had mostly lived vicariously for those who had suffered.

Bree was eccentric; her so-so attitude was something that probably would have to grow on people to be accepted. I suppose she was the type of person who had that 'never a dull moment' personality. I could tell she could talk anyone's ear off in the most curious situations, along with the awkward ones. She had spunk. You could tell that when she had something to say, people would always listen and take heed to her words.

"If you don't mind," I said while itching my nose. "I have a couple more questions for you before I leave."

"Well, I have two more answers for you."

"Number one: Is Gabby off today? Number two: Do you guys have a restroom here?"

Bree smiled from ear to ear. "You know Gabby?"

I suddenly became nervous again. "Well, I stopped in yesterday and briefly chatted with her, but I had to leave before I could get coffee because of sudden work business."

"I see. She actually left yesterday for college. She is a student at Hoborg University. She will be back, working weekends here and there. After all, her mother, Claire, owns the joint."

"Really?"

"Yes, they opened this place about eight years ago. I've been with them for about six years now. Man, how time flies. Oh, the bathroom is down the hall and to the left." Bree squinted her eyes for a moment and gave me a strange look. "You know … that lady who came in here… you and her have the same little beauty mark right under your left eye. I mean, everyone has freckles, beauty marks, and molls, but I swear… same place."

"I guess that's kind of odd. Anyways, thank you so much. By the way, my name is Gret."

"Nice to meet you, Gret!" Bree then pointed to her nametag. "My name is Bree, obviously."

"Well, thanks for the great hospitality and conversation. I will definitely be stopping here more often in the future. Have a blessed day."

"Thanks, and you also, Gret!"

Wow. Gabby was a student at Hoborg University. Hoborg was the only college within a radius of 150 miles. To be accepted there, you had to be a genius or have a lot of money. Her being away made me somewhat sad, but I was happy for her. Even though I did not know her well, it felt like I did.

Anyways, business at hand. I had to use the restroom quickly before I ventured into work. Caffeine does it to me all the time. I noticed as I walked to the restroom that there was a dilapidated seating area toward the back that sat behind the kitchen. It seemed like people were only seated there when the front was full, which, I can imagine, was not very often. There were three rows of tables, which included five tables in the first two rows and two tables in the last. There were a total of twelve tables, each seating two people. Nonetheless, I did my business and opened the door to exit. Instantly, it happened—numbness, freezing, shaking, a sense of helplessness, followed by a sharp pain in my head. *Snap out of it. Composure—maintain it at all costs.* With one hand holding the door open, I closed my eyes and looked down. Suddenly, my composure came back, and all the unpleasantries had dissipated. To my surprise, the relinquishment of all my symptoms was just the beginning. As I looked up, there was a mysterious woman sitting in the back corner by her lonesome. Undoubtedly, she was one of them—the dead.

6

The Hidden Past

---

*D*eep breath. Stay focused. Do. Not. Stare. Many thoughts ran through my mind at first glance. *Did I not notice her on the way to the restroom? Did she just appear during the time I was in the bathroom?* Regardless, it did not matter. From the short glance I stole, it felt as if everything was in slow motion, and all her details easily registered within my memory. She was utterly beautiful. Her hair looked to be shoulder-length and dirty blonde, the kind of hair that portrayed that natural, clean look. She wore a short jean jacket with one of those cream-colored collars that pop at first glance. Her eyes told a different story. Bitter sad they were, as her somber state was not well hidden behind what I gathered were baby-blue eyes. I could not get those sad eyes out of my head. I knew I had to see her again.

Unfortunately, boredom for the next eight hours was on the horizon, for I had to go to work. It was only Tuesday, but it felt like a Monday that began with the notion of a slow week. Normally, Tuesday was my slowest day due to Monday's rush of my department being closed on weekends. I was bracing for it to be an excruciatingly slow and dreary day in my building.

I could not get her off my mind. I thought Gabby would be re-running nonstop through my thoughts today, but that was not even close to the case. Becoming upset was easy at this point due to my work schedule being a possible impediment to my inquisitive nature. I simply needed to know more. My mind was running in circles. *How long would she be there for? Where did she come from? Would she be there every day?* Many questions festered inside my brain. Sitting here and staring out the window at Claire's was enough to almost drive me insane. Helpless, but never hopeless, is how I felt. A wise man once said, "Patience and diligence are for those who never give up and seek the answers to be sought out." Be patient, be persistent—I knew I needed to be both to satisfy my thoughts.

During my lunch, I thought about the *others* I had encountered. Not that I made it a habit to stalk or inquire about them, but I did recall seeing a few in the same places at the same times. I recalled the elderly lady at the grocery store. Vaguely sluggish and indigent, she was—her presence while searching the produce section for the best deals around 5:30 p.m. never failed. Clockwork, as I would call it, is as predictable as the sunset every day.

For the rest of the day, my mind was in a complete haze and somewhat in disarray. Until fifteen minutes before I was to clock out, it hit me. I thought about my grandmother's passing and her last words. 'Protect' and 'look for' were what she told me. Protect was a big mystery because I was not sure who or what she meant by that word. But the very fact she was trying to tell me to look for something triggered a thought in my head. After she passed, I found a few old boxes under her bed that were taped up and sealed firmly. Still grieving at the time, I did not want to re-awake any sorrows or sadness, so I kept them sealed. I felt the best course of action was to stick them in the garage attic until I felt the need to sift through them or forget about them. Anyway, I had figured it would be many years until I touched them from up above the garage—never eight months. Answers. I desperately needed them to appease my mind.

Every Tuesday and Friday, I would meet up with Brian after work for some grub and drinks. Brian is one of my friends—actually, probably my only friend. Usually, it was always at the same local pub, but at times, we would change it up. It was our little ritual—a time for us to chat, drink, and eat. Unfortunately, I knew I had to cancel today for obvious reasons. I told him I was coming down with a vile cold and needed to relax and shake it off at home. He was fine with it, claiming lethargy from his work schedule.

I hate my job some days. Just my luck, a customer came in at 4:52 p.m. and needed assistance with a qualifying loan promotion we had been advertising. A total of two customers came in in eight hours, and the third came in right before I was to leave. The story of my life. I had no choice but to stay and help this young man. I easily did not mind, though. Most likely, it was not like he came at this time on purpose. Maybe he got off his job a few minutes early, and this was the only time he could visit us. It did not matter, though, for the excitement of these boxes had me in an eager mood.

When it was all said and done, it was 5:20 p.m., and I was ready to check out. Once I gathered all my belongings and locked the doors, I was so eager to get home that I forgot my wallet on my desk. I did not need it though. I had leftovers in my fridge from last night—no drive-through fast-food purchase was necessary. Cautiously driving home without my identification and license, I could not help to think about my grandmother's last words again. It was finally time to transform those words into answers, or something close enough to understand.

Go to the bathroom, eat, and change clothes. Those were first on my agenda for the night. Considering my curiosity overthrew my appetite, I put my appetence for dinner on hold. It did not matter how hungry I was; I was about the task at hand.

The dreaded garage attic. To access these boxes, I once again had to climb up the garage ladder to the attic. I hated going up there, for good reasons. It was mainly because of my excruciating allergic reaction to insulation. When I was a child, I had to help my father take down items that we were to sell for our church's flea market. Unknowingly, I must have accidentally brushed up against some insulation while handing off boxes and items to my father while he carried them down the ladder. The next morning, my skin broke out in rashes and hives all over my hands and face. Mother once told me that it was also possible to breathe in the dust from it, so I was to stay out of the attic at all costs. I was not worried or perturbed, for I was to retrieve the two boxes as quickly as possible and comb through them in the house.

The attic string was a little high, so I had to reach on my tiptoes. As I pulled down the attic door, the old attic smell from eight months ago was the same as it is now. It had the smell of mildew, mixed with mothballs that were probably older than me. As I crept up the ladder, each step seemed a little more brittle than they were the last time. As I remembered, the first step had a big chuck missing from the left side, which rendered it completely useless. Gloves would have been smart, as I nearly gashed my index finger from a splintered piece of wood on the railing at the third step. The eighth step was the worst, for it has been missing since I could remember. I was sure my father must have broken it at some point but never got around to replacing it. Thirteen steps total there were—not the safest, but they did the job.

Damn dust. Once I recovered the boxes, I dusted them off outside thoroughly before bringing them in the house. Eight months of dust could have easily been eight years from the thick layer of grime. Unbeknownst to me, I never noticed that my name was on one of the boxes. I must have set the box with no name on the bottom when I settled them into the attic—hence missing my name. I wondered, *why did only one have my name on it?* I thought it was a bit odd, but it piqued my curiosity even higher. Regardless, it was time to disinter these and hopefully discover some answers.

I started with the box with no name first. It was the heavier of the two, weighing around 25 pounds, if I had to guess. As I opened it, a great, big smile from ear to ear spread across my face. Inside were my grandmother's favorite possessions. On top, her favorite knitted blanket was neatly folded on top, as if it were to provide extra padding for the breakables under. Directly below the blanket lay some antique figurines that I had never seen before. If I had to ponder, these figurines looked to be around eighty years old and probably worth a pretty penny. The value of each was quite evident by the neatness and meticulous care with which they were sealed in bubble wrap and neatly placed. The rest of the box was filled with old pictures placed securely in what looked to be turn-of-the-century photo frames. Some were older than others, while others were probably from when my grandmother was in her young adult life. As I browsed through each frame, one picture caught my attention instantly. The picture was dated 2126. It was a simple family picture that looked to have been taken during a picnic or a family gathering of some sort. My grandmother, who was visually young, was holding a newborn infant who could not be more than a few weeks old. To her right, a little girl was wearing a yellow spring dress. It was obvious that the child was my mother, probably around the same age I was when she passed. To her left, a man stood wearing a dark blue suit and brown loafers. It was quite evident that he was my late grandfather, who passed away in the '40s from an apparent suicide. My mother and grandmother rarely spoke of him, for I did not know much about him. This infant, however, sparked my interest. Could there possibly be more members on the Kline side of the family, from what I have known? Maybe it was a niece or nephew? I had no clue and decided not to dwell anymore on the photo. My attention started to curiously shift to the second box.

I stared at the box for a moment, still wondering why my name was on it. My stomach let out a hungry grumble. I thought about taking a quick break to eat, but ultimately decided to press on. Books and papers were what I was set to look through. I did not even know where to start. Most of the papers were old tax records, hospital papers, medical records, handwritten dinner recipes, and even an old newspaper about a car accident—I didn't care. Nothing particularly piqued my interest. However, the books painted a different picture. Many looked to be over a hundred years old and mostly dealt with spirituality and religion. I was a bit surprised; my grandmother never spoke of these topics with me. She kept these books private.

One book in particular struck my attention. It was entitled *The Glorification of Accepting Spiritualism and the Afterlife*. It was an old, leatherbound book. This gigantic book looked to be at least two hundred years old, with well over one thousand pages. The leather smell was all but gone, for it presented a smell of an old, decaying time. As I picked it up from the box, a pamphlet fell out from the inside and hit me in the foot. It was something I had never seen—my mother's obituary card. It read as follows:

Sadness overcame my thoughts as a tear gently flooded my right eye. I still remember that day like it happened yesterday. I remember what I was wearing; I remember my father standing there like a statue; and I remember my grandmother comforting me and giving me a few pieces of hard candy. I missed my mother and grandmother tremendously. I could not help but think about what my life would be like if my family were still around to this day. I would imagine the holidays would be blissful, birthdays would be joyous, and family picnics at Old Falls Park would be pleasant. I suppose everything happens for a reason, and to dwell on what could have been instead of what is now can drive anyone to the brink of a long, dark depression, which opens the floodgates to merciless insanity. Delightful memories will always linger with me, for they bring a glimmer of light to my most challenging and darkest days. Adversity and self-perseverance both taught me well.

I gave the book an inquisitive look while many thoughts started to roll inside my head. I started to flip through the beginning, briefly skimming through the paragraphs. Nothing in particular caught my eye. The pages were brittle, delicate, and somewhat hard to turn without tearing them asunder. However, once I reached page 48, near the end of the book, all the pages were hollowed out to form a perfect quadrate. Within the hollowed-out space lay a little red book with no title or any information to dictate what it exactly was. The tiny hairs on the back of my neck started to erect as I could feel the tingling sensation throughout my body. It felt like I had found a valuable treasure that maybe I was not supposed to find. As I turned the cover, I instantly knew what this was from the handwriting within. It was my grandmother's personal diary. *Why did she go to great lengths to keep her diary a well-hidden secret within this ancient book? Was I meant to find this?* As I started to quickly flip through the pages, another secret was to be revealed. One quarter into the diary, the stable and smooth rhythm of the pages being flipped took a sudden halt, for there was a page with both corners evenly folded as if were set that way for an easy find. The page reads as follows:

> *I will never forget last night. I am 14 years old, beyond young to even understand it all. My father is rapidly losing his battle with lung cancer, so maybe it was his time to clear his consciousness. He sat next to my bed, grasped my hand, and revealed the truth about this world and our family. Our world has been in a never-ending war. A war that was set in motion many hundreds of years ago. Very few will see it, and even fewer will act upon it. The Ancients are here, as they always have been. They will show no mercy toward the living and the Sleepless souls that still linger. What do they want? No one exactly knows, for I fear that total calamity is a grave possibility.*
>
> *He then informed me that I had the gift. The gift is to see, interact, and understand. He then confessed that his last living will was that he had accepted his demise, and it was the giver's responsibility to 'enhance' the gift. Some were automatically born with it enhanced, while others needed it finely tuned by*

an initiator. I was one who was not fully enhanced—dormant, to say the least. As it was his mother's responsibility many years ago and his now, his turn has now come.

This scares me to great depths to write this, for I do not know if I will become a walking target, as my father claimed. If I do not act, I may endure for a lifetime. To act, protect, and fight, my demise may come sooner than later, or I may live to endure to see the change for the good of this world. The choice is mine, he assured. If you accept it, your protection becomes an obligation, not a choice.

I do not know how to take this. I never asked for this, but he explained how it was like a hereditary disease, passed down from generation to generation. Considering I was born an only child, I guess it was an easy choice to be the chosen one.

In the meantime, I will choose to remain silent and neutral. Maybe when I am older, I will comprehend this to a level within my means and understanding. My father also explained how there are forces and people that will guide me, especially when I least expect it. When I asked him about forces, he explained that it was up to me to find out what and who they are. "The Ancients are always listening," he told me. If he informed me any further, he explained how he and I could be in near danger—for the Ancients know everything and everyone.

For now, I will pretend this conversation never happened. This is all too much for this age to take in, but according to my father, it was necessary due to his untimely demise. Regardless, I will pray for safety and kindness, and most importantly, I hope I will not disappoint my family.

Certainly, I was amazed by it all. It felt like I had found that proverbial needle in a haystack. Still, there were many questions that needed to be answered. I did not want to overthink this discovery, for I know it may drive me to the edge of madness. For now, I figured the best thing to do was to eat my leftovers, relax, and go to bed at a reasonable time.

7

The Missing Message

This young boy,
Shapeless and hollow.
Waves full of promise,
Seemingly to follow.

I see it, it's coming,
The inevitable end.
Cherry blossoms linger,
This beauty, it will bend.

Death, it's a thing,
I say it's living.
Many will disagree,
My spirit—will keep giving.

The first day of high school—a nerve-racking experience for almost any youngster out there. I was a young teenager—maybe fourteen years old, possibly fifteen. I was casually walking down the main hall by the northeast entrance. As I looked around, I noticed the faces were inexplicably unfamiliar. It felt like I was a brand-new student who had moved to a new colony. An outcast—I like to think in terms of how I felt.

The more I kept walking, the odder it became. I reached down to retrieve my schedule and locker information in my leather satchel. To my surprise, all the words on my schedule made no sense, like they were written in a different language from a land I knew nothing of. Suddenly, a lanky, male student bumped into me and fancied a hostile look into my eyes. Three seconds later, another shoulder bump hit me from the other side and almost knocked me off my feet. No apologies were rendered in my direction. *What was going on here?*

From a short distance, I could see my best friend, Brian, walking toward my direction. I turned my head and thought for a second—*he never went to my school.* Something was peculiarly off. As he approached my direction, I quickly forgot how he may be *misplaced* and expected a quick conversation to ensue. Of course, he kept a straight face and passed me by without any acknowledgement. As I turned my back in disbelief, another student violently bumped me and kept talking about their business. *Again, what in hell was going on?*

Panic mode started to kick in. I knew I was in the correct building, but in a way, it felt like I was not. Cautiously, I started to walk faster and faster as the occasional bump and countless glares raised a terrifying concern. Everyone was out for me. Scared and shaking frantically, I was trying to escape by entering any door I could. They were all locked, except for the last door on the left. It was room 213, used as a teacher's lounge for breaks and lunch.

Practically fumbling to get the door open, I entered in a mad panic. I was not surprised to see that the whole room was completely empty, considering it was before first period and teachers were probably setting up in their classrooms. I walked around the large break table with thoughts of hostile intentions from others if I were to exit. Suddenly, the lights flickered for a split second as I heard a noise from a large bookcase in the back corner. I took notice that a book (among the twenty or so) had fallen off the shelf. Instinctively, I walked over to the book with the intention of setting it back on the shelf. I was not ready for what was about to happen next.

When I bent down to pick up the book, every single book flew off the shelf simultaneously, as one in particular hit my knee. My nerves were shaking, but something was telling me that there had to be a reason for this phenomenon. I started to focus on the book that hit me in the knee; it was entitled *The Missing Message*.

Curiously, I picked it up and opened the front cover. There was a handwritten message inside the cover in red ink. It read:

> **Dear Julie,**
> **I will never forget you. I really hope this book helps in all your endeavors. Just remember, if you keep looking, you'll eventually find what you're looking for.**
>
> **Your friend,**
> **Max**

After I finished reading the inscription, the lights went completely black. All I could see were two faint red lights (smoke detectors) on the opposite side of the room from each corner. As I looked closer, my mind was starting to go haywire. Slowly, those two red lights started to descend to an eyesight level and formed as if they were red eyes, staring directly right through me. I took a step forward to try to find a quick exit. Something or someone grabbed me from behind in a hostile manner. Instantly, I woke up from yet another bad dream.

8

A Bag of Mess

Wednesday morning. *"If you keep looking, you'll eventually find what you are looking for."* That quote was on repeat, rattling through my head after I woke up. Along with the diary and family picture, it was certainly a lot to soak in at one time. The Ancients and the Sleepless. Since my grandmother passed, I have had no knowledge of these Ancients. *Who were they? Would I ever encounter them? Are they some kind of demonic force that has infiltrated this world?* I still had many questions that were unanswered, but hopefully, a little research and time could turn the unknown into certainty.

As for the Sleepless, I do believe my grandmother referred to them as the sublunary entities I see walking amongst the living. Questions about the *gift* still lingered in my mind. In her journal, she described it as a hereditary disease that was passed down from generation to generation within the family. Considering my mother was an only child, did she have it? My whole life, spotting odd details has always been easy for me. I found it quite interesting how my grandmother claimed she inherited it from her father and her father from his mother. The pattern was obvious: Female to male, male to female, and so forth. Since my grandmother never had a son, did it skip my mother's generation? I was at a loss, but I knew I needed more answers somehow.

Clearly, the only surefire answer I had currently was to take a sick day from work. A splitting headache, emotion sickness, and a lack of quality sleep took their toll. Mentally and physically, I was a bag of mess, overflowing with more mess. It was times like these that I wished my mother was here for me. I would do anything if she was a phone call away. Her warmth was what I needed the most. I wanted her reassurance that everything was going to be all right.

Calling off work was easier than I'd imagined. I thought about having breakfast at Claire's. She was still on my mind, especially those eyes. On second thought, it probably would not be the brightest idea considering my work was right across the street from Claire's. I guess I am paranoid like that.

Back to bed was in order, for I was exhausted. After last night, a little clarity shone down within my mind. Little by little, more clarity will come if I am adamant enough to seek the answers I find. Clarity, such as understanding who the young lady in the back booth at Claire's was. Of course, she was one of Sleepless. As the journal read, it was our duty (if we accepted it) to protect them from the Ancients. I still had no idea who these Ancients were or if I would ever encounter them. Deep down, I knew I had to somehow reach out and connect with this young lady. The question of the day was how. After much pondering, I laid down on my couch, turned on the television, and tried to let my mind go blank until I fell asleep.

9

Transparency
Stage 1 – Opaqueness

Patience lies,
Within her fold.
She awaits,
A moniker to uphold.

Magnificence diffuses,
Lengths of beauty.
Always ready,
To appease her duty.

Ambition pulses,
Striking at will.
Absent failure,
A destiny to fulfill.

Certainty prevails,
Rich in favor.
Never rigid,
Sharp as an engraver.

It must have been ten years ago. I was about twenty-two years old and working at my job—working a swing shift as a stocker at a large warehouse for a furniture company. Everything around me seemed hazy. Hazy to the point that it felt as if I was working, but not working in a different sense. I was on a mental trip. A trip through a hallucinogenic state where everything made no sense at all. I started to become nauseous, so I decided to take a quick ten-minute break. Unbeknownst to me, before I could open the door to the break room, an immensely tall, pale lady wearing a red business outfit with a black sash was waiting by the door—almost like she was expecting my presence.

She smiled to me and nodded her head. "Hello, young man. Blessings to you as we finally meet. I often wondered when we would meet. Today is that day. You are probably wondering why I am here."

I gave her an odd look. "Who are you?"

"That is a simple question with a complex answer. I am here with your subconscious in your unconscious realm for one reason. That reason is simple. Transparency."

"Transparency? What is that supposed to mean?"

"It's quite elementary, if I must say. There are three levels to transparency: opaqueness, translucency, and clarity. Right now, this is opaqueness. Are you familiar with that term?"

I shook my head in disbelief, trying to calm my state of confusion. "Vaguely, I suppose. It means something about a light shining through a surface. Or, not shining through… something to that nature."

"Somewhat… yes. You are on the right path. It means it is *difficult to see through or hard to understand.* Think of a car window that is tinted jet black. The sun will not shine through. Now compare that sunlight to a thought that hasn't reached full circle. Your grasp of why I am here makes no sense in your mind—at least not yet. We shall meet two more times for each step. Until then, you must walk through that door to understand the simple gratitude of my nature."

"You won't tell me who you are?"

The strange lady offered a presumptuous smile. "I promise you that when the time presents itself, your life—as you imagined it—will be so. I will see you soon."

I did not know what to say or how to react, for that matter. Everything was still a little hazy. I looked toward the door, thought for a quick second, and turned my attention back to the pale lady. She was gone. *Maybe I was imagining it?* I did not know what else to think; other than that, my mind must have been playing tricks on me, and I was to enter the break room. Behind that door, I certainly was not prepared for the scene that unraveled before my eyes.

Slowly opening the door, I realized this was no break room. This was a scene from my mother's funeral at our church. I started to walk down the aisle in reluctance. Attentively, my attention started to drift to the left side. My grandmother was front and center, next to my father, sobbing while he hung his head low. My best friend, Brian, was there, holding the hand of his beautiful wife. My mother's friends and co-workers were all flocked together, whispering to one another and expressing their sorrows. Most certainly, I recognized everyone seated to the left.

Something was disparate and queer on the right side of the aisle. Something odd was at play. I did not recognize a single person who had taken their seat in the pews. Their clothing was rather dismal—even depressing for an already dejected church crowd. Astonishingly, not one of them looked to be under the age of fifty. I could barely hear them muttering amongst themselves, probably talking about nothing worthwhile. I approached the alter, one elderly man stopped his conversation to the man in front of him and presented a semi-hostile glare in my direction. At that moment, I felt brittle and somewhat unwelcome.

Right before I approached the altar, I carefully dropped down to my knees, closed my eyes, and said a quick prayer. As I rose, my eyes opened, and the next thing I knew, my mother's casket was gone. In a reactive state, I quickly turned to the left side of the pews for answers and noticed that everyone I knew had vanished as if they were never even there in the first place. Scared and perplexed, I turned my focus to the right side of the pews. At that moment, my mind was in a state of total terror beyond my grasp. All the older strangers had halted their chatter and gazed at me with hostile intentions. I knew at that moment that not only was I not welcome, but I was in the wrong place. This was not my mother's funeral after all. Feeling aghast, they all simultaneously stood up while their eyes slowly turned to shimmering, red dots—fixated on the only unwelcome guest, myself. Feeling as if my heart had violently dropped to my toes, I abruptly woke up to yet another nightmare.

If I had one duty,
One duty to say.
I say to endure,
Endure another day.

The Curious Nature of Claire

Saturday morning, 5:12 a.m. I did not intend to wake up this early on a day off, but sometimes it happens without an explanation. It had been two days since I called off last Wednesday. During that time, I felt it was a healthy choice to focus on my sleep, work, and clearing my head. I had blocked out everything that had come to light for me, even my thoughts and emotions. Eat, work, sleep, and repeat. Even for the second time this week, I cancelled my plans with Brian last night. Nonetheless, Thursday and Friday were a couple of days of simple repetition for my meddlesome mind.

But today was a new day. My consciousness felt clear, and my mind felt like it was fully operational after a mandatory reset. The only thing I was lacking was a good cup of coffee, and I was fresh out of coffee filters. On the bright side, I thought it was a great excuse to go have a nice breakfast at Claire's.

By the time I showered and got ready, it was only 6:00 a.m. I was not even sure what time Claire's opened on the weekends, but I was optimistic that I would have no problem eating early. Speaking of optimism, my grandmother always used to preach to me about pessimism and optimism, explaining how people are a lot like batteries. Every battery has a negative terminal (pessimism) and a positive terminal (optimism). As for people, everyone has a choice to think and act like both terminals. By inserting a battery in the correct manner, both terminals equal the correct polarity, thus creating the proper path to success and optimism—hence everything will fall into place. When someone is flustered and naturally pessimistic, that person may not be in the right sense of mind and insert the battery incorrectly, thus reversing the polarity and creating an unfavorable outcome. I never understood her logic until I got older—always creating a bad habit of blaming my shortcomings on luck. I still fall into that habit occasionally, but my grandmother always made great points.

Of course, this was one of those mornings caught in between luck and optimism. My car battery was dead as a door nail. Apparently, I forgot to shut my lights off last night after I went to the convenience store. Luckily, I had a jump-start kit that I bought less than a year ago. From the time I started my car and let it idle for fifteen minutes, it was already 6:24 a.m. I was hoping to be out of the door and driving by 6:00 a.m., but twenty-four minutes would not ruin my morning.

Once I was on the road, I started to think about everything I had blocked out for the last forty-eight hours. The Sleepless woman, my grandmother's possessions, nightmares, and even Gabby. Not all necessarily in that order, but I felt the strongest stimulation was from my grandmother. I perceived that my grandmother had more hidden riddles for me to solve. Quite possibly, she could not tell me face-to-face because of the danger her father specified in her diary.

Once I pulled into the parking lot at Claire's, I sat in my car and braced myself for who could be inside. I became nervous once again, for the uncertainty of losing my composure was ostensibly possible. Not to mention, Gabby may be working since it was the weekend—if she decides to come home this weekend. Expecting to see her was a eustress feeling—the kind that would give you butterflies in your stomach. If she was working, I thought about the possibility of asking her to dinner and a movie tonight. Nothing special—a casual hangout between two friends.

As I stood outside the door for a moment, I felt no loss of composure, just a little nerve. As I was about to open the door, Nancy (from the inside) beat me to it and opened the door.

"Oh, I remember you… your name… Gret, right?" she said, greeting me with a cheesy smile.

I smiled back with subtle laughter. "The one and only."

"How are you on this lovely morning?"

"I am doing pretty well… besides having a dead car battery this morning," I nonchalantly pointed to my car. "But I jumped her, and she made it here in one piece."

"I can see that." She could not help but smile and laugh. "Are you here for some breakfast today?"

"Nah, I figured I would use your restroom if that's okay. It looked like a good place to go." *I really don't know where that joke came from.*

Nancy suddenly looked confused. "Oh, well—"

"I'm joking," I said while interrupting her in mid-sentence. "Remember? I'm the guy with the corny jokes."

Nancy quickly changed tunes and began to laugh hysterically. "You are too darn funny! Here, let me seat you and get you a menu."

"Sounds good to me."

Note to self, do not make stupid jokes ever again. I honestly did not know where that came from or how it came about. Maybe it was a way to clear my nerves without thinking; I did not know. It was an awkward, yet funny, moment.

While sitting down in front of the kitchen, I could not help but look around and observe in a non-conspicuous manner. There were a few customers already seated, all sipping their coffee and digging into their breakfast entrees. Bree was behind the cash register as she presented a colossal smile my way and flapped her hand in the air to wave at me. Thus far, Gabby has been nowhere to be found. Nancy swung around the corner and was approaching me.

Nancy stood right by my side. "Here is your menu. Did you need some time, or do you know what you already want to order? Maybe a beer?" She started to laugh again.

"I'll start with a plain, old cup of coffee. Black, please. No beer today." I can see she was playing along with my jokes. "And you know what? I think I'm in the mood for some eggs and pancakes. I'll have the three eggs and pancake platter that you guys have been advertising. Scrambled on the eggs, please."

Nancy nodded her head and smiled. "Sure thing, Mr. Gret. How have things been going for you?"

"I suppose it's the same old, same old. The everyday grind of work and living." I shrugged my shoulders. "You know, it is what it is—living I guess."

"I hear you loud and clear. I'll be right back with your coffee and—"

I abruptly interrupted. "By chance, is Gabby working this weekend?" *I saw it in her eyes. My intentions were kind of obvious.*

"Actually," Nancy looked back toward the kitchen, "she should be here any minute now. She called earlier and said she was running a few minutes late. Wait … I think I heard her in the back. I'll go get her for you and your coffee, of course."

Before I could even reply, she ran off quickly toward the kitchen. The temperature suddenly became balmy inside, but I knew it was just my nerves. My heart felt like it was going to burst through my chest, pounding a mile a minute. Any second now, Gabby would probably walk out that kitchen door and see me. As corny as it sounded, I nonchalantly pretended to be on my phone to present a calm and collective appearance.

Her voice was loud and clear from the cash register area. "Gret! Hi!" She walked up to my table and put her hand on my shoulder. "How have you been?"

"Hey, pretty lady," I replied. "How have you been?" *Pretty lady? Good grief. Where did that come from again?*

"I'm good. I started school again at Hoborg. So, you know, it's a lot of studying with a grueling schedule. What about you?"

"Same old, same old. Work, sleep, and save the world one day at a time." *Another bad joke.*

Gabby started to chuckle as she playfully punched my shoulder. "Must be tough. I kind of took you as some kind of undercover superhero from the first day I met you."

She was good—very good. "Let me tell you, it's not easy work. You never know; I may have to save you one day." *Again. I need to stop right now.*

Gabby continued laughing and began to twirl her hair. "I'll keep my eye open for trouble around, so maybe you won't have to. Anyway, I need to start my shift. My mother is supposed to be here today at some point. She already thinks I'm lazy, so I better get to it."

"Your mother, as in Claire?"

Gabby quickly smirked. "That would be her, the one and only. She's a real joy, let me tell you."

Gabby—she is wonderful. Behind my corny jokes and her subtle mentions, I sensed a spark between us. My nerves were totally off the table now. I was feeling comfortable and at ease, although I started to feel a tiny, sharp pain in the back of my head. I was sure it was nothing.

Nancy hollered across the way. "Gret, your food will be out in a minute."

I hollered back. "Thanks, Nancy. I'm going to use the restroom quickly."

A slight nod from Nancy, and I was up. On my way to the bathroom, I took notice of the dining area in the back. It looked the same as it did the last time I saw it—neglected, dilapidated, and empty as a broken icebox. No Sleepless lady, not yet.

Easy restroom objective: Do my business, wash my hands, and return to my seat to eat. Unfortunately, it was easier said than done. A strange man entered, and then a cool breeze followed him to the sink right next to me. I did not recognize this man in the dining area, for it would have been hard not to. A slight shiver and an uneasy feeling embodied my insides, rattling my bones instantly. This man looked to be in his early fifties or even his late forties. He donned a long, black trench coat that appeared to be from the '70s. His hair was greased back and pulled into a little two-inch ponytail that began at his neck and hairline. He was fixing his hair as I was, almost in unison, like his intentions were to mock myself. A second later, he decided he wanted to speak.

"Nice day out today. What do you say?"

I kept with fixing my hair—not looking his way. "Yes, it's not too bad."

Immediately after I finished my sentence, I started to feel it. It started with head pain—brief and miniscule this time. My balance and composure were slightly off, along with the absence of feeling numb. I closed my eyes for a second or two and reopened them, and it was like it never happened. As I looked to my right, the odd man had vanished. Maybe I lost my composure longer than I thought, or maybe there was more to his sudden absence. Regardless, I was starting to feel like myself again once he left.

As I made my way out of the bathroom, she was not seated in the dilapidated dining area, for she was walking in through the main entrance straight towards the back dining area. The air suddenly got cold again, although I could feel her warmth run throughout my body. I started with a slow pace back to my seat, ensuring that I would not be a blockade for her. Her pace was exceptionally casual, as her field of vision was strewn straight across. With each step closer to one another, an unexplainable feeling started to overcrowd my body. Sadness, curiosity, anxiety, frustration, and happiness. It was all five of those words rolled into one giant ball and pieced together with scotch tape.

Once we crossed paths, it felt like that giant ball burst inside of me. I did not know how to articulate my thoughts, but sublimating my feelings and trying to act like nothing happened was my only choice. She continued to make her way to the aft seating area. I turned my head around and stared for a few seconds. Little did I know, I was being watched. As I turned my head forward, I could see Gabby and an older lady staring at me from about twenty-five feet away.

"What's the matter?" The older lady curiously asked. "Did you see a ghost or something?"

Gabby threw her hands on her hips and turned her head. "Mother, stop! Gret, this is my mother, Claire. You know… the owner. I apologize; my mother is crazy and thinks this place is haunted."

Claire lightly smacked Gabby on the shoulder. "Well, Ms. Gabriella, you do not know what I know or have heard what I've heard."

Gabby jokingly shook her head. "Give me a break, mother. I have customers to take care of."

I flashed a huge smile. "It's certainly a pleasure to finally meet you, Claire. My name is Gret, and I must say, I absolutely love your place."

"Are you my daughter's new boyfriend or something?" She was unnecessarily brazen.

Good grief. "No, not at all. I barely know her, to be honest. We are just—"

"Friends?"

"Yes, friends. Like I said, I met her earlier this week."

Claire nodded her head. "I see. It's a pleasure to meet you also. So, what were you looking at behind you when you walked out of the bathroom?"

"I-I… nothing. I was looking at the back dining area. It's nice." I had to think of something. "Look, I'm sorry. You caught me off guard, that is all."

Claire's demeanor suddenly became a bit hostile and serious. "Oh, come on. I wasn't born yesterday. Unless you like to stare off at random spaces in a worn-down dining area, you must've seen something."

"Oh… well, there was also a gentleman who was in the restroom with me. I thought I heard him come up from behind me." I knew after I said that, it didn't make much sense.

Her look became marred with doubt. I could tell she was on to me like a moth to the flame. Considering I had just met her, I could not tell if she was serious or joking around with me. "Right. That gentleman in the restroom. He walked out right before you did and had already left."

Think quick, smart, and hard. Be vague if I must. "I did not even notice, to be honest. I tend to do that a lot. You know, not pay attention to my surroundings."

Claire looked directly into my eyes, like I was transparent. "I see. You may think I'm some kind of nut or a whacko, but I promise you, I'm not. So, is my place haunted?"

"I hope not for your sake." The tension could be cut with a knife. "I don't really believe in that stuff anyway." *This was getting bad fast.*

She nodded her head in doubt. "Right. You don't believe."

Intimidating, condescending to liars (like myself), and a no-nonsense lady—Claire was all that. She was certainly someone who seemed to have no trouble calling anyone out for their falsities and lies. I could not help respecting someone with all those qualities, and it was easy to see that she commanded respect right off the bat. I envied her; I surely did.

After my brief encounter with Claire, I returned to my seat to have my breakfast waiting for me at my table. My appetite was somewhat suppressed. My mind felt as if it were warping through time dimensions while noticing something intriguing during every stop. Gabby, Claire, the mystery man in the bathroom, and most importantly, the Sleepless woman. Without a doubt, the Sleepless woman was number one on the list. I knew I needed to see her again, but how was that possible without making it too obvious that I was up to something? *Next to impossible,* I thought. Claire was already watching me like a hawk, so walking to the bathroom again was out of the question. Her occasional smug looks she flashed towards me throughout my breakfast made it seem like I was stuck between a rock and a hard place. Just like me, it felt like she had her own puzzle to solve, and she considered me a vital piece. Maybe she was like me, but on a different level, to a lesser extent. I felt like a square peg trying to fit into a circular hole. In a lesser sense, I would be no help to her, at least not yet. I had my own puzzle to solve first.

I was sparsely eating the rest of my breakfast when a quick thought ran through my mind. For my next visit, I could bring my laptop and pretend to do figures and reports for my job, teleworking away from my office. I could ask to be seated in the back section, where it was quiet and desolate, hence the minimum distractions. Therefore, I would have a clear view of what I was seeking. It all sounded too perfect, and I knew I had to try. The biggest question I faced was exactly when. I thought about tomorrow, but considering the Sunday church crowds and family get-togethers, I decided it was a no-go. It was too risky. My soonest option was Monday, but I was scheduled to work that day. Then another idea sprung in my brain. I currently have eighty hours of vacation time and sixteen hours of personal time off. I was in good faith with my boss, so a simple phone call would easily suffice on my end. Footsteps were coming closer to my table—it was none other than Gabby.

"Hey Gret, is everything all right?"

"Couldn't be better." The eggs were a little runny, but I like them like that. "Except, my eyes are obviously bigger than my stomach."

She smiled and patted me on the back. "Would you like a box?"

"Nah, that's okay. Something about re-heated breakfast food doesn't sit well with me—if that makes sense."

"I totally know what you mean. Pizza is about the only food I will eat reheated. To be honest, half of the time, I eat it cold."

Her speech and body language were obviously insinuating, as she seemed nervous while twirling her hair with her right index finger. I felt she had something to ask me. *Of course, she did.* "What do you do around here for fun?"

I shrugged my shoulders. "Not much, really. To be truthful, I have no family, and I can only count the number of friends I have on one hand. So, as you can imagine, my options are limited."

"Aw, that's a sad thought. No lucky lady at all?"

I knew it. "Nope. No lady at all. It's hard to meet someone around here. It seems like everyone these days is either married with kids or stays at home."

She playfully tapped me on the shoulder twice in jubilation. "I know what you mean! All my friends are also married or away with their boyfriends." Gabby paused for a moment. "Well, here's the thing. I'm home for the weekend with not much to do. I must say, I do not want to spend tonight with my mother. I was thinking if you're not busy tonight, maybe we can meet someplace for coffee, a drink, or whatever."

Indeed, I was deeply flattered, the most I have ever been. I had never been asked out like this before, so it was a new feeling for me. Nonetheless, I had no choice but to graciously accept. "Yeah, most definitely. I would love to. Do you have anywhere in mind? What should we do? I'm good for wherever and whenever."

"Well, obviously not here—we are closed. Sorry, corny joke. Have you ever been to the Meeting House?"

I slowly nodded my head a little. "That's the little high-end cocktail spot that is a few minutes away from here, correct?"

Gabby nodded in return. "That's the one."

"Yes, I've been there once with my friend Brian. It's a nice joint. Would you like to meet there?"

"If you don't mind. Let's say… 7:00 p.m.?"

"Sounds like a plan. We shall meet for a meeting at the Meeting House." *I needed to stop with these awful lines.*

"You are too cute. By the way, I want to apologize for my mother. She's a little rough on the edges, if you know what I mean. I'm sure you'll get used to her one day. I like to tell people she's an 'acquired taste'."

I shook my head in disagreement. "That's not necessary. I think she is a nice lady, and I look forward to more conversations with her."

"If you say so," Gabby said, expressing a burst of laughter. "Well, I will see you at seven. Until then, I got to get back to work before my mother yells at me for something I didn't do or something I did wrong." Gabby smiled once more. "See you tonight."

Well, it was all set. I had plans to meet Gabby at the Meeting House at 7:00 p.m. I was excited, but I was trying my hardest to not get my hopes up in case she were to cancel. I could not remember the last time I felt so *giddy*. I felt like a young man again, full of promise for the makings of a good Saturday night.

I was finished at Claire's. The next step was walking up to the register to pay my bill. Just my luck, after waiting a few seconds behind the register for someone to show up, Claire walked up from the kitchen and snatched the bill out of my hand. As she began to ring me up, she looked up once and presented a witty smirk.

"Was everything good? Did it meet your standards?" She arrogantly asked.

I smiled back in her direction. "Of course, no complaints here."

"Good. Are you still not going to tell me what you saw earlier?"

Good grief. Here we go again. Relentless, this lady was. Her determination was on point, and I had to respect that. I was completely perplexed, to the point where I wondered why she thought I had responses to her claims that free spirits were roaming around her establishment. *Was I advertising my ability in public?* I did not think I made it too obvious, but then again, I always felt one could not decipher oneself by speech and movements; only others could.

"I honestly thought I heard the man in the bathroom behind me."

"Right, that man again." She said as she modestly shook her head up and down, "Well, please do come back and see us again."

"Thanks, ma'am. I definitely will."

After the bill was paid, I was walking out and subtly waved goodbye to Gabby and the rest of the staff, who were assisting customers. Her immense smile back was a reassurance that tonight should be interesting and fun. My mind completely shifted from the Sleepless lady to tonight. It was not that I did not think of her; I was overjoyed at all the possibilities of a great night.

Speaking of tonight, it was supposed to be the warmest night we could have in the months to come. It was already warm outside, until that same cool breeze that I felt in the bathroom hit me once again. As I was about five feet out the door, I glanced to my right, only to see that same peculiar man leaning against the pillar with dark sunglasses and smoking a cigarette, glaring my way with a slight smile. The ever-so-idiosyncratic look he possessed was almost too difficult not to take notice of. I pretended not to notice him, for it was a daunting task to imagine with every puff of his cigarette. He puzzled my mind, but I did not bother to make anything out of it. I had to head home, clean the house, and relax until tonight.

11

A Descending Truth

Impetuous, he becomes,
A past full of haste.
Shrouded by reality,
Bitter in taste.

His compass teeters,
Morality equals depravity.
A walk amongst clouds,
Defying his own gravity.

Elevators. I have always had a fear of them. I could not recall what age it started or even when I first rode in one; I did not like them. I was on the top floor of an extremely tall building, not sure exactly what floor or what I was doing there. As I approached the elevator, I pressed the call button, and the door instantly opened as if it were waiting for me. As I started going down, I could sense that something was amiss—maybe I should have taken the stairs. The lights flickered a couple of times and then slowly stopped at the twenty-sixth floor. As the doors opened, an elderly lady paused as one foot crossed the entrance. For as old as I perceived her to be, her face was truly a menacing act. She glared at me in terror, then suddenly started yelling at me in a hovering voice in her native language. Confusion started to set in as I did not know how to respond. As she entered and settled in, her eyes were locked on me, and she continually lashed out her vulgarities in my direction. I just stood there, shrugging in confusion, as we continued our descent to the ground floor. The farther down we went, the louder and more dramatic her voice became. My confusion violently turned into panic and terror, for I felt I was not welcome on this elevator.

The elevator cart apparently had one more stop—the twelfth floor. Much to my surprise, my father proceeded with his entry. As he entered, he turned around and stared at the door, acting as if he were the only passenger aboard and without a care in the world. He took no notice of the screaming lady or me, for he was purely about his own business.

The cart continued to descend while the old lady kept screaming her indifferences as my father ignored it all—it felt like the longest descent ever. Meanwhile, I took notice that the floor notifications had completely stopped above the door, and it felt as if the elevator was picking up speed. Seconds started to feel like minutes, and minutes began adding up fast. I was in utter terror—terror I could never imagine in my wildest dreams.

As the mayhem continued, my panic suddenly turned into confusion again—the emergency phone began to ring. The amplified ring was abnormally earsplitting, as if it were the most important phone call known to mankind. Looking down and to my right, I noticed the phone was an arm's reach away—painted the brightest red I have ever seen. With the rapid descent continuing, constant yelling from the lady, my father still looking straight ahead, and the blaring phone, I decided to answer it at the end of the fourth ring.

"Hello?" I calmly answered.

All I could hear was heavy breathing and what sounded like a faint squelch operating on a two-way radio. Someone, or something, was on the other end.

"Hello?" I eagerly repeated.

Once again, same result. I began to become a little frustrated, as it felt like someone was toying with my emotions.

"Hello?" I said, demandingly awaiting a response.

The squelch finally seized. *"Loooooook. Agaaaaain."*

Just like that, I woke up in a deep sweat on my couch. *Will they ever stop? I think not.*

12

An Unexpected Night Out

It was 5:00 p.m., but it felt like 3:00 p.m. A four-hour nap seemingly felt like a two-hour nap. I have come to understand that the fast and intense dreams seem to constrain myself into a deep and long slumber; meanwhile, the slow and meaningless ones pull me out of slumber at the snap of a finger. I call it a *slumber anomaly*. Sometimes, minutes in a dream turn into hours of real-time, while others feel like endless hours but turn into an hour or two of restless sleep.

At times, one's body does not take heed to or comprehend the need for a long nap, thus seemingly propelling those fast dreams forward. This dream portrayed that fast, anomalous mirage in slumber. Four minutes on that elevator ride mirrored four hours of sleep. I felt refreshed, but if confusion was a marathon runner champion, that champion was running miles on end in my head. I remembered every little detail of that elevator ride, especially the mysterious phone call. *"Look again". What did that mean?* I was lost in the dark—seemingly without a flashlight—because I had no idea what that meant. That message was now stuck in my head, only to think of the vagaries falling behind it. It piqued my interest to the point in which I had to turn it off inside my head and focus on the night at hand.

It had been a while since I had been out with a lady— almost two years, to be exact. I guess you can say I was shy to a fault, but the term modest would be more accurate. My grandmother would always inquire about how a date went or if I was seeing anyone. She was highly intuitive in that aspect of my life. It did not bother me, though, for I knew she only wanted what was best for me. I remember she once told me, "If you believe you don't deserve the best, you will never achieve the best."

****

The time had now come. It was 6:35 p.m., and I was dressed, prepped, and ready to go. The Meeting House was only a five-minute drive from my house, but arriving early was always my moniker. Surprisingly, I was not as nervous as I thought I would be. The inside of me was glimmering with confidence. Tonight, I just felt right. Although I have learned from the past that hopes could be easily dashed at the drop of a pin, regardless, I wanted to make the most of this Saturday night.

By the time I arrived and parked, it was 6:45 p.m. I stepped inside, and I made a quick look around to see if Gabby was already seated—she was not. It was rather slow inside; there were maybe about fifteen patrons, with half of them seated at the bar. It was a *seat-yourself* place, so I decided to select a table with an easy view of the entrance to see her walk in. As soon as I sat down, a hugely tall and attractive woman server came over to my table.

"Hello, sir, my name is Kristina, and I will be your server today," she said as she quickly pulled her hair back. "Can I start you out with a drink? Margarita? Cocktail? Beer?" She then gave me a funny smile. "Wait… I apologize. I can tell you're waiting for someone, aren't you?"

I smiled in a gracious manner. "Yes, indeed, I am. If you wouldn't mind, may you please bring over a couple of waters, and once my guest arrives, we shall order some drinks."

She nodded her head and smiled again. "Sure thing, sir. I'll go grab those waters. Meanwhile, the menus are on the table, and if you have any questions, feel free to ask, okay?"

"Will do and thank you very much."

Wow, she was tall. If I had to guess, I would guess she was 6'3". For some odd reason, I was infatuated with her height. Of course, she was also pretty, but how often do you see a lady that tall? As I was watching her chat with the other bartender across the bar, Gabby was standing by the door from the inside, curiously looking around. I stood up and frolicked my hand in the air so she could take notice. She immediately saw me and started walking towards our table.

"Hi, Gret!" she said as she struck a playful smile as we embraced each other with a quick hug. "It's nice to see you again… especially out of my work element."

"Likewise. The server is bringing us two waters and is going to take our order. I didn't want to be rude and order a drink without you."

Her face started to blush a little. "Aren't we such a gentleman? Have you been waiting long at all for me?"

"Oh, no. I literally arrived about five minutes ago. It's all good, no worries." *Just a tad nervous, but cool and collective.*

Gabby simply looked amazing. Beautiful, stunning, and clean—she had it all. I almost did not recognize her with no work apron and uniform. She was wearing a long-sleeved black shirt with two neat buttons and a pair of casual gray jeans. Her sandy blond hair was gently curled, which complimented her outfit and dollish face. She was a natural beauty. She looked like someone I had seen before, but I could not put my finger on it. She had my undivided attention.

"So, how was work?" I casually asked.

She shrugged her shoulders. "The usual. Slow… putting up with my mother, for which I want to apologize to you again for her rampant behavior."

"No, it's fine. There is no need to apologize. I honestly didn't mind at all."

"Still, I'm embarrassed for what she was saying to you. It's what I like to call her '*kooky talk*'. I swear, she's going to lose her mind completely one day."

"Gabby, listen… It's okay. For real. I don't mind."

From the first time we made eye contact tonight, our smiles were continuously complimenting each other. A little giggle here and there, and we were both deep in the moment. I always found that happiness connected to small talk was quite normal on first dates, but this felt different—I did not want it to end. From a couple of tables away, I could see Kristina making her way over with our waters.

"Here is your … Gabby, hi!" Kristina said while joyfully smiling. "I didn't know you were back in town."

Gabby immediately stood up and embraced Kristina in a hug. "It's great to see you again! Yeah, I'm leaving tomorrow. I'm here for the weekend to help my mother out with her business and what not."

"Oh, that's very nice of you. Lucky for you two, I will be taking care of you tonight." She suddenly turned in my direction. "And ugh… I'm not sure if I got your name yet."

"Gret, that's my name." I smiled and stood up to shake her hand. "It's nice to meet you, and I must say, you are one of the tallest women I have ever seen… no harm meant; you're a rare breed in my opinion."

Kristina placed her hand on Gabby's shoulder and began to laugh. "Yeah, I get that a lot. Anyways, what may I get the both of you to drink?"

Without hesitation, Gabby pointed up with her index finger. "Malbec for me, please."

"I will have a gin and tonic," I responded. "With a lime and lemon, please."

"Okay, let me go put those in for you." Kristina acknowledged. "Anything else I may get you?"

"I'm good." I replied. "What about you, Gabby?"

"No, thank you." Gabby responded. "Maybe, just maybe, some shots later."

Kristina smiled and walked to the bar to put in our drinks. So far, the whole night has been clicking without any loss of beat or rhythm. Quite frankly, I was still somewhat shocked that I was out tonight with her. Watching movies while home alone—that was always my weekend plan. I knew I had to keep things interesting. I had to keep this conversation going.

I took a quick sip of my water. "So, how do you know Kristina?"

"I used to come up here a lot, almost too much." Gabby paused for a moment. "This used to be my bar, I guess. Well, more like a place to sulk in my depression, as bad as it sounds."

"Depression? If you don't mind me asking, how so?"

"It's a long story. I wouldn't want to bore you easily. Especially on my first night out with you. I promise you, I'm not a depressing person or someone who falls into that category."

I shook my head. "No, I wouldn't think that. You seem happy-go-lucky with a great outlook on life." I took another sip of my water. "Bore me? Never. How about you enlighten me, and I promise not to judge. After all, we are all on the outside, looking into everyone's life. The human mind is a very meticulous wonder. No one should ever judge another one because everyone's mind is composed of different aspects and interpretations of what and who they are. If we were all the same, the world would be a boring place."

Gabby quickly flaunted a natural smile. "Are you sure you're not like... a college professor or a psychologist? You sounded highly intelligent explaining that to me."

I smiled back instantly. "No, I'm speaking real to you. In me, what you see is what you get. No substitutes."

Gabby's claims of depression piqued my interest levels. She didn't seem like the kind of person who would experience severe depression that was alcohol-fueled. From what I knew about her, she seemed to have a great grasp on life and what it had to offer. Maybe I was wrong, or maybe it was nothing too serious. Regardless, my intuitive nature wanted to know more without pushing for answers and explanations. Meanwhile, Kristina was right around the corner with our drinks.

"Here we go. I have your malbec and your gin and tonic with lime and lemon." Kristina placed the drinks on our table. "Please, if you need anything else, let me know. As you can see, it's not too busy yet, so I'll be easy to locate."

Gabby took a quick sip. "Thanks, Kris. We most certainly will."

Getting to know Gabby was what tonight was all about. The topic of depression seemed to fade away once the drinks arrived, and I was fine with that. I was not going to press that topic any further unless she wanted to. We spent the next fifteen or so minutes chatting about our jobs, ambitions, and dreams for the future. Everything in her life sounded intriguing, until I dared to ask her a simple question.

"So, what about your family?" I curiously asked. "Are you close with them?" *I can tell I may have changed her tone by the look on her face.*

"That's a rather difficult question to answer."

"Okay. You don't have—"

She quickly interrupted. "No, it's okay. I don't mind. It's just that…" Gabby paused for a couple of seconds. "My family used to be super close with each other. Then, one day, we weren't close at all. Of course, you already met my mother, and she's the extent of my immediate family now."

"It's you and your mother right now?"

"Yep. Last year was detrimental to us. My oldest sister, Daniella, drowned in the lake down the road. You know, Hugo Lake. You may have heard about the story on the news. I don't know; maybe you hadn't. I hate that place."

"I'm sorry to hear that. You know, I think I do remember hearing about that story on the evening news." I could see her emotions starting to show. "Look, we don't have to talk about this. I had no clue. I'm sorry."

"No, no… it's okay."

"So, she drowned?"

"Yes, she did. She went missing one day, thought to have unexpectedly moved away for a few days after she and my mother got into a huge argument. Long story short, her body was found washed up on the shore by the park and swimming area. Have you been there before?"

"Yes, a couple of times. Maybe a few more. It's not really a place that sits in my mind as a vivid memory. To me, it's a lake and picnic area—nothing special."

"To top off that story, my father passed away two weeks later from cancer. When he was first diagnosed, the doctors said it was 100% curable. He was on the right track and all, then, when Daniella passed, it was like the cancer accelerated and took him quick. I personally think he was so grief-stricken by her death that the cancer became incurable, like it took advantage of a broken heart. As you can see, last year ravaged us. Since then, my mother has always been in a bad mood and seems to have more and more resentment towards me as the days go by. It's awful."

My eyes became wide as this poor girl poured her heart out. "Wow, I have no words I can express other than I'm sorry. It takes a brave person to pour their heart out to me like you did. I have a lot of respect for you."

"I appreciate that. The sad thing is that my sister had minor epilepsy. My mother believes she took her own life due to her manic-depressive outbursts. I don't believe that, though. No one knew Dani the way I knew her. I know she would never take her own life, no matter how hard she had it. She was always a happy person, despite her problems and issues. I believe differently. There had to be something other than suicide. I know it."

"Maybe one day you'll find out the truth. You never know."

"Yeah, maybe. Until then, I'll be here waiting, I guess." She took another couple sips of her drink. "Anyways, tell me your story. What makes Gret do the things he does?"

Here we go. "Well, for starters, when I was about 3 days old, I was left in a park bathroom by my drug addict mother and was found and brought to a hospital by a homeless lady. I was gravely ill and about to die, according to what I was told. I persevered and was fortunate to find adoption from a grieving couple who had lost two sons in the war. Not to mention, I was given a supposed death sentence when I was found to be about twelve to fourteen years old. The doctors said I would have autism, seizures, and other ailments that would probably end my life prematurely. I guess I proved them wrong.

"Many years later, my mother was abducted from her work at the hospital and found murdered in the wastelands up north. My father was a suspect for a broadly short time, but that was ruled out rather quickly. They never found the killer. The only lead that ever came about was the figure caught on tape for a split second, which had the body composition of a female. I know, it's kind of strange, but it happened.

"Also, about a week afterwards, my father packed all his belongings and flew the coup. I never heard from him again. Is he dead? I don't know, nor do I really care. My grandmother then adopted me, which was probably my saving grace for who I am now. She unquestionably gave me a great life. Unfortunately, she passed about six months ago, so here I am, with no family whatsoever, and living in this lovely place we call the world. One day at a time, I always say."

Gabby reached her hand out and placed it on top of mine. "Oh my, that's horrible. I think we've both had our share of misgivings and unfortunate circumstances come our way. I suppose we have a lot in common."

"Indeed. It seems adversity has been no stranger to you and me."

She held her glass up high. "Cheers to that." I connected my glass with hers. "It only makes us stronger."

"Strong enough to conquer this world one day."

Just by that little comment, a little humor slowly lightened the mood. I did feel sorry for her as her story hit home. I could not imagine losing a sister and a father in the same month. But then again, I did lose a mother and a missing father in the same month. We both had been dealt bad hands at one point in our lives, so it was easy to relate to one another.

I was having a great time. As for her, I felt as if she needed this night out, as did I. A night to relax, unwind, and forget all our cares in the world. I could sense she was feeling it. Behind the sad stories, I was happy, and that happiness was contagious. After our third round of drinks, she presented me with an unusual proposition.

"I have an idea if you're down to do so." She quickly took her last sip. "It's a nice, decent, and clear night. I know I told you how I hate the place, but let's go stargazing at Hugo Lake. That's If... you want to go."

I offered the biggest smile. "Don't tempt me with a good time. Yeah, let's do it. Let's go."

"Perfect. I really don't like that place, but I can't take away from its natural beauty. Something about seeing the stars reflect on the lake certainly put me in a calm and happy place."

"It sounds all perfect to me."

"Alright, let me pay my tab, and we'll get going."

I shook my head and let out a quick chuckle. "Wait a second. What kind of gentleman would I be if I didn't pay for your drinks?"

"No, I can't have you pay! I'm not—"

I interrupted quickly. "Ms. Gabriella, it's my treat. I won't take no for an answer, and if you even try to pay, I'm going straight home." *I was obviously joking.*

"Ms. Gabriella? Geez, you sound like my mother. Okay, fine. You can pay. Only under one condition."

"That may be…"

"You must drive. My mother dropped me off, and before you make fun of me, she only did it because she didn't want me to drink and drive. I know, it's pathetic in its own way."

"It's not pathetic at all. Your mother is looking out for you. You need to cherish that, because one day you're going to end up like her. I mean that as a compliment, not an insult. And don't worry, I will drive, and I'm not even close to being tipsy."

"No, I understand. It's a little weird thinking that someday I may be just like her."

"I know the feeling."

"Anyway, I guess once you're done milking your drink, we can get going." She made it a point that she had already finished her wine. "Do you need one of those kiddie cups with the twirl straw to help you finish?"

That was a funny one. "Oh, I see. You have jokes. Don't you worry; I'll get you back. Just wait."

Three malbecs, three gin and tonics, six drinks total— $44.74. Considering Kristina was a great waitress and extremely personable, I left her a twenty-dollar tip. For some odd reason, I still could not believe how tall she was. Admittedly, I had a strange fascination with her height that I simply could not explain.

8:30 p.m. After the bill was paid and I finished my drink, we were set to embark on a trip to Hugo Lake. I was happy and a little concerned. Happy in the sense that I would be able to spend a little more time with Gabby, but concerned that bad memories may flood her mind once more. From what I gathered, she was the emotional type. Regardless, it was her idea, so maybe there was a logical reason she wanted to go.

Hugo Lake was a short drive—five to ten minutes. It was a little awkward at first, possibly factoring in what she told me about her sister, Daniella. For the short ride there, I could tell that her sister may have been on her mind due to her quiet state. It felt as if she wanted to vent to me, but I dared not ask. Maybe I was wrong, for assumptions are not always what they seem to be.

Once we arrived, the lake was nothing but a ghost town. The beauty, the warm but somewhat chilly temperatures, and the clear night were a subtle reminder of a getaway from the harsh realities of life. It was a little slice of paradise for me. Once we found a nice bench near the lake, the conversation began.

"You know, Dani and I would come here at night frequently," she said. "I miss those nights."

"Oh yeah?"

"Yeah, we used to come here and talk endlessly for hours, especially when we wanted to get away from our parents."

"It sounds like you miss her a lot."

"Yes, I really do. Some days are hard, while others are easier than others, if that makes any sense at all."

"It makes perfect sense. But you know what? Time heals all wounds. That's a life lesson I learned growing up. Even at thirty-two years old, I'm still learning that lesson in different facets."

"Geez, you're old," she said as she jokingly punched my arm. "I honestly don't think time will heal this one. Maybe, but maybe not. Until I get some ironclad answers on how and why she drowned, I'll chalk it up as ever-long pain and sadness. I can't help it."

Oh, no. I feel it a little. "Gabby, listen. The thing is you… you… you… yoooou…" *Not now, please. Maintain composure.*

Instantly, I felt that feeling inside. Slurred speech, shooting head pain, and sadness within my soul. This time, it was a little different. I felt a presence near, but in a way, I did not. I could not explain it—almost as if it were a false reading. Regardless, something, or someone, was pinging me hard.

A look of concern overcame Gabby. "Gret, are you okay?"

"Yes, just… please, give me a minute," I said as I closed my eyes. "I'm sorry. It's just a thing with me—a medical condition that has never left my side since I was born. It's hard to explain. It happens out of the blue at times. My apologies."

"No, no, Gret. You don't have to be sorry at all. I feel bad that I'm pouring my whole life story on you in one night."

"It's okay. My episode had absolutely nothing to do with you, I swear."

"Promise me you're telling the truth?"

"I promise."

"I'm sorry, Gret. I miss my sister beyond belief. I should've known better that this place would stir up bad memories."

I knew it. "I understand. I wholeheartedly do. I miss my grandmother and mother every single day. But you must take it day by day and keep living. If you live too much in the past, you will never see what is in front of you—the present. I'm not one to dwell or act like I know everyone's purpose in this life, but I do know it's not to live in the past. I'm sure if your sister could speak to you for one minute, she would tell you to not worry about her and to seek what this funny old life has to offer."

"You know what? You are absolutely right. Day by day, that's the route I need to take. It's so hard at times. Deep down,

I want to keep thinking that full closure will come one day. Until then, I must remain patient, or I will lose what is in front of me."

"Look at it this way. Today is the first day of the rest of your life. Live it good, and most importantly, live it for her."

Gabby immediately hugged me and planted a kiss on my cheek. From what I saw and heard from her tonight, I believe she needed to hear what I had to say. I never considered myself one to give life advice, but I could see she was grateful for what I had to say. At that point in my advice and lectures, I thought she was done talking about sadness. I was wrong.

"Can I tell you one more thing? I feel like I still need to vent to clear my conscious."

"Yeah, for sure."

"When Dani went missing, something inside of me told me to go out and look for her. I never thought she was in mortal danger. I never wanted to believe that. My mother and the sheriff didn't seem stressed or worried. They thought she would show up one day unexpectedly, like it never even happened. It wasn't out of the norm for Dani to do that either. But something—and I cannot put my finger on it—just didn't feel right. So, the day she went missing, I got into my car and drove endlessly around town looking for her. I stopped at restaurants, bars, hotels, and even places that one normally doesn't go. I kept looking and looking, hoping to find the answer. Because, you know, sometimes answers don't present themselves on a silver platter. You need to look and find them yourself. Anyways, I did this for the next couple days, and the whole time, my mother didn't care or worry one bit."

"Really? I would like to think she may have been a little concerned."

"No, not one bit. Great mother, huh? Finally, we got the call from the sheriff. They had found her lifeless body washed up on Hugo Lake. Once my mother told me, I lost it. Not only was she eternally absent, but I also searched every location besides this damn lake. Despite the fact that it was an abhorrent two minutes' drive from my residence, I never bothered to look. All the time she and I spent here, it never occurred to me to come here and look. That's what bothers me the most. Who knows, if I'd come here first, I may have saved her. It weighs on my conscious every single day. I never told anyone this, so please keep it between us."

Fighting back tears, and by the tremble of her voice, she became even more emotional than she was five minutes ago. I felt for her, for I could not imagine the grief and uncertainty she felt for those couple of days. At that point, I made up my mind that I wanted to help her in any way I could. I now saw her in a different light; unfortunately, I knew I only had my friendship to offer her.

"Look, as a friend, I want to help you get through this any way I can. In your darkest nights and brightest days, I will always be there for you. I know we practically recently met, and it sounds kind of crazy, but I feel a strong connection of solidarity between us. When you're away and in need, call me. When you're near, we can hang out. Days, nights, or weekends, I'm here. Never forget that."

I could see in her eyes that she understood my indirect mention of *friendship*. No vocal clarity was necessary, for the feeling was perpetually mutual. I was exhausted from all the emotion, and I could feel that she was too.

"Well, if you don't mind," she said. "May we call it a night? I must get up early tomorrow to make my way back to Hoborg."

"Yeah, not a problem. I'm kind of getting sleepy myself."

This was an interesting night. My expectations were split in half, but the only way to give someone a chance was to take a shot in the dark and hope for the best. Bittersweet, I guess I would call it. She was not what I expected or hoped for, but in the end, it was a win because I made a new friend.

Luckily, her residence was only a couple of minutes down the road. During that time, we did not say much to one another— we mostly listened to the music that was playing. Once I parked in her driveway, the night was officially over—at least I thought it was.

"Well, I want to thank you immensely for taking me out," she said. "I really needed this night, and it was perfect in my book."

"It was my pleasure, Ms. Gabby. Safe travels tomorrow, and don't forget to keep in touch."

"Certainly. You know, it's a funny thing sitting here in your car in my driveway. I only say that because I remember when Dani would go on dates. I used to wait by the window to try to catch a glimpse. Most of the time, she and whoever she was with would sit in the car for minutes on end, like we are doing right now."

I cracked a bit of laughter. "Spying, huh?"

"Nah, just curious, I guess. You know, it dawned on me. I have a picture of her and me in my purse. Would you like to see it?"

"Yeah, I would love to."

"A lot of people used to say that we look alike, but I never thought so."

She pulled out the picture and presented it to me. I had to turn on the interior lights to take a closer look. *Commence the slow-motion theater.* A sudden jolt shocked me, like 100,000 volts running through my body. It had felt like my heart had exploded into a million pieces. I could only count on one hand how many memories were imprinted in my brain. The kind of memories that you wish a simple button could be pressed and it would vanquish into a black hole, never to be remembered. This was one of those memories. The picture she bestowed upon me was of her and the Sleepless woman at Claire's.

13

ETP-2612

Desolate forest
Flourished greenery decay
Secrets in the deep

Right before dusk on a cool autumn night, I was walking through a senescent forest dominated by vast pine trees. The majority were dead, weathered down by the brutality of time. The air was thick with mold and mildew, which would make a sensitive person wince in disgust. Sadness also lingered throughout, for this forest was once prosperous and thrived with life.

As I continued to walk, I could see an old, abandoned four-door sedan rusted and rotted beyond worth in the short distance. An abnormal location, I thought to myself. As I got a closer look, it was strikingly similar to my mother's car before her life ended prematurely. Same model, color, and box-shaped taillights, from what I could remember. The license plate reads ETP-2612. I was not sure if those were my mother's plates, for I was too young to remember. On the front windshield, a rather menacing message was written on the thick layer of dust. It read, "We all self-destruct in this life or the next." For what that was insinuating, I did not know.

The wind had started to pick up, carrying that wretched stench forward and intensifying it to a level of unbearable self-containment. Darkness started to fade in, assuring its certainty of misfortunes to come. As I turned my attention forward, I could see a peculiar red object propped against what used to be a brilliant pine tree. It looked as if it were perfectly placed, only to be lost in time but never forgotten. Instinctively, I knew it was meant for me to find.

Reaching out for the object, it turned out to be a tiny book of some sort. As I held it in my hands and observed the vagueness around it, I realized that this was no ordinary book, for it was my grandmother's journal. Coincidentally, it was the same one cleverly hidden within that spirituality book within my grandmother's boxes. Immediately after I opened it, every single page fell out and dispersed amongst the ground. A violent gust of wind suddenly appeared, blustering every single page away in the distance. Panic-stricken, I tried to salvage any page I could muster—the wind was too callously ruthless.

Frustration and confusion started to overcome my senses, for it was only the tip of the iceberg. What sounded like an old rotary phone chime was heard in the faint distance. Three-second ring, two-second pause, repeat. The ring sounded all too familiar, but I could not remember where I heard it from. I eagerly moved about in every direction to pinpoint the source of the mysterious chime.

After about thirty seconds of discontent and hopelessness, I tracked down the chime back to the abandoned car. To my surprise, the car was not the same when I first saw it. The harrowing message on the windshield was wiped clean, as the car looked as if it had been parked a few minutes ago. The chime was coming from the inside as a cell phone lay perfectly on the dashboard. I opened the door, grabbed the phone, and paused as it continually rang. I was nervous to answer, for I did not know what to expect. Phone in hand, I took a few steps back, tripped over a stump, and suddenly woke up from another intense dream.

14

The Back Dining Area

7:52 a.m., Sunday morning. I awoke from another vague dream describing an unfamiliar scene, possibly meaning something. I wonder if these dreams will ever cease or if they will keep continuing without an end in sight. Regardless, that thought was not weighing heavily on me at that moment. My mind was strictly reserved for one thing and one thing only—that photo.

That photo was what I called a curveball—a perplexed pitch with the intention to sway the recipient into bewilderment. The way I saw it, one either strikes out from the pitch or smashes that ball out of the park. I knew I was on deck, and it was soon to be my turn in the batter's box. I had to calculate my next move carefully, or this whole thing could go south quickly.

I continued to lay in bed for a few moments after I awoke, thinking, wondering, and soaking everything in for the past twelve hours. A part of me wanted to forget the whole thing. Forgetting that Gabby, Claire, and Dani even existed. Of course, that would be a rash decision bent on sudden emotion. That was not my game at all. I knew I had to be and was already invested in this narrative, considering the promise I had made to Gabby last night. I was perfectly fine with that, but I knew I needed time to myself to ponder the answers I wanted and sought. Every good story holds an even greater ending.

Today was to be a day with no set plans. I thought about going for a long drive—maybe someplace along the countryside would be refreshing. Another possibility was to go to Claire's for breakfast or lunch. To be truthful, I was curious to see if Dani would be there today. Another part of me thought: *Maybe it was too soon.* Lastly, maybe relaxing at home and watching a good movie was in order. My options were plentiful, but for now, it was time to get out of bed and start the day.

I got up to go to the kitchen to get a glass of water. On my way, I glanced at my grandmother's boxes on the ground in the dining room. I knew I had to sift through them again for more information, although it seemed like a good idea to do that around nighttime. My mind was simply not ready for more curious finds, for it was too early in the day.

Once I settled with my glass of water and planted myself at my kitchen table, I turned on the news to see what was happening around the colony. A story came on about how three people were stuck on an elevator for almost twelve hours. Unfortunately, the building had lost all power and the generators had seized, thus creating the inevitable delay. I thought this story was a stretch to be on the morning news. After all, no one died, and it seemed like the news center had to stretch the news out of a boring day.

However, this story triggered a wonderment inside of me. Seeing that photo of Dani threw me off track this morning due to the menacing dreams occurring as of late. The phone call in the elevator ride, the walk in the forest, and even the funeral scene with the pale lady who talked about *transparency*. It's an unsettling feeling that each of these dreams felt real. It was hard to discern between what was real and what was not. I felt that this was going to be my new normal. As my great-grandfather told my grandmother, "There will be forces and people that will help guide you, especially when you least expect it." *Maybe this is what he was talking about, or maybe not.*

For the next few hours, I sat around and did pretty much nothing. Thoughts circled around my head about everything that had entered my life, but they were exactly what they were: thoughts. It was approximately 11:00 a.m. when I decided that I would try my luck with some lunch at Claire's. I could have decided to pick something up quickly, but I knew I wanted more from this story. As soon as I showered and got ready, I was on my way.

It was rather warm outside like last night. The birds were chirping, and the smell of warm autumn air was all around me. As

I pulled into Claire's, I was lucky to get one of the front parking spots while the parking lot was unexpectedly full. To my surprise, Gabby and Claire were conversing outside by the door as I made my way to the entrance. I figured she had already left for school, but I guess I was wrong.

"Gret!" Gabby yelled out. "I didn't expect to see you today. How is everything? Sleep well?"

I presented her with a quick one-armed hug. "Hey, Gabby," I said as I looked over to Claire. "Hi, Claire. I'm doing well… slept like a log, I guess. I came up here for some lunch considering I haven't tried the lunch menu yet."

Gabby looked over to her mother. "Mother, please. May I talk with Gret for a minute before I leave?"

"Yes, Gabriella, you may." Claire nodded her head toward me. "Give me a kiss, and please drive safe. Call me when you get back. Please, not one of those, 'I'm sorry I waited right before I went to bed to call you.' Call me the minute you get back to campus, okay?"

Gabby rolled her eyes towards my direction. "Yes, mother. I promise."

"Good. Drive safe and keep your eyes on the road." Claire looked in my direction and flashed a half-smile. "Gret, I will see you inside."

I did not expect to see Gabby here today, nor did I expect her mother to be here either. I honestly did not know how to react around her. There was a little awkwardness mixed with a dash of sorrow when I saw her. I was hoping that last night would not be brought up, for I did not rehearse or even think about what I would say. Wishful thinking—I thought too soon.

"Gret, about last night. I'm really sorry. I hope I didn't ruin your night with my sorry story. I didn't mean to do that at all."

I had to speak from the heart. "Gabby, look. Please trust me when I say this. You're fine. We are fine. What was said was simply said. I had a nice time, and I hope you did too."

Gabby reached out and put her hand on my right shoulder and looked me in the eye. "I had a great time. I think you are the most wonderful person. I truly do. For what it's worth, I really hope we stay in touch and can hang out more when I come home on the weekends."

"No doubt. I would like that. You have my number, so don't be a stranger. I don't know what your schedule is like, so whenever you're free, reach out to me. I would never want to bother you in the middle of your studies."

"I like that. I definitely will."

After exchanging pleasantries, we embraced with a warm hug and voiced our goodbyes. I did not know when I would see her again or if she would even call, as she willingly agreed. From my past, I have become accustomed to empty promises. Ordinarily, I am not surprised by any outcome these days.

As Gabby drove away, I started to head inside, and instantly, I felt the pinging. This time, the feeling was calm, comfortable, and controlling. She was here, along with a vast lunch crowd. I had never seen it this busy, but then again, I started coming here. I wasn't surprised that I was greeted by a familiar yet somewhat challenging face: Claire. *Just my luck.*

"Mr. Gret, did you have fun with my daughter last night?"

I nodded and smiled. "Yes, ma'am. I had a good time. Your daughter is quite the conversationalist." *I guess that was the best I had.*

"Oh, really? It never struck me as Gabby to be what you said—a conversationalist?"

"There was never a dull moment."

"Well, that's good. I'm glad she was able to go out and have fun. Are you here to dine in or takeout?"

"A table would be nice, if it's not too much trouble."

"Of course not. Unfortunately, the only tables we have available are in the back section." Claire then looked at the crowded tables. "The two open tables you see there are reserved."

Claire. What a piece of work. It was an obvious lie about the tables, as she was up to something, and I had a pretty good idea as to what. Let alone, the tone of her voice insinuated a clever scheme within. Like a lot of people, I do not like being lied to. Well, I can't complain about this lie. What she did not know is that I wanted to sit in the back for obvious reasons.

"Yeah, I'm perfectly okay with that. Any lunch specials today?"

"Everything here is special, Gret. It's a matter of what you want or what you need."

Claire's dry hostility was wavering full-flag this afternoon. Meanwhile, while escorting me to the back section, she was there—sitting pretty and seemingly lost in her emotions, as the last time I saw her. I made certain to sit facing her so observations could be made less obvious as to turning around. Her blank and somber face, mixed with the occasional glance downward, made me wonder what she was thinking. My goodness, she did look a lot like Gabby. Even more gorgeous, I must admit. Now that I knew the truth, I found it ironic that I could not put two and two together to realize how strikingly similar their physicalities resembled each other.

It's a strange sensation that I can't put into words. I was at complete ease. Just as I entered, there was no confusion, no headache, and no episode that would warrant a public scene. All I felt from the start was a little sadness and the subtle pinging from when I walked in—like absolute radar. That sadness was quickly replaced by the feeling of warmth. Maybe I was mistaken, but it almost felt like she was sending the warmth as a non-threatening sign of acceptance because she knew I posed no threat or danger. Speaking of threats, Claire suddenly made her way back to my table.

"So, what will it be?" she asked.

"I take it you'll be taking care of me today?"

"Yeah. If you hadn't noticed, we are kind of slammed. Nancy and Bree are busy with everyone up front, so I figured that I would lend a helping hand. May I start you off with something to drink so you can browse over the menu some more?"

I quickly glanced at the menu with the intention of ordering suddenly. "You know… I think I'll take a raspberry tea to drink, and that club sandwich looks pretty good. Yes, that's what it'll be."

"Fries okay with that?"

"Of course."

"Good deal, I'll go ahead and put that in for you." Claire started to walk away, but then suddenly ceased and turned back my way. "One more thing. Out of curiosity, did my daughter happen to mention anything about me last night?"

I shook my head in confusion. "I'm… confused. What are you referring to?"

"About our family and growing up. Did she mention anything about her sister?"

At the drop of a dime, Dani's head looked up towards us after that very sentence. This time, I knew better not to look, as I could see her in my peripheral vision.

I shook my head side to side slowly. "No, not a thing. She didn't mention it at all. Is there something she should've mentioned?"

Claire gave me a somewhat non-believable smile. "No, not a thing. Your order will be up shortly."

My mood abruptly turned bittersweet. On one hand, I got to observe Dani, something I had been wanting to do since I first laid eyes on her. On the other hand, I had to deal with the ticking time bomb known as Claire. It was what it was. Not even two minutes later, Claire walked back to my table again.

"I put your order in. My cooks are a little backed up, so it may be a few minutes more than expected. Would you mind if I sat with you for a little bit? I need to get something off my conscious, if I may say so."

"Yeah, sure. Take a seat and let's chat."

Of course, she pulled out a seat at the table to the left, facing me, which put a minor visual blockade on Dani. I slid my chair roughly a few inches to the right, hoping Claire would not notice so I could keep my peripheral vision of Dani. It was an interesting scene—the kind you would only see in a movie. As my peripherals were locked on her daughter, I took notice that she took a quick glare toward her mother, followed by a stoic stare into nothing. I could only imagine what she was thinking.

Claire put her hands together and began to speak. "First, I want to apologize for my behavior toward you. The way I have spoken to you, my attitude, and my total presentation… unacceptable. I had no right to do so. I feel as of late that I have lost everything near and dear to me. Honestly, I don't know who I am anymore or why I'm telling you this. I know it's no excuse to act rambunctious toward good customers, especially ones who take my daughter out."

I noticed that Dani glanced at her mother after that last statement. "Look, it's water under the bridge. Please don't get down on yourself. I never took offense to anything you have ever said or done. The times are tough these days. Everyone has different ways to cope with adversity. I understand it all. So how about we start over?"

Claire gave me a funny look. "What makes you think I'm coping with adversity? Did Gabby tell you anything? She must've said something."

Here we go again. "No, you said you haven't felt like yourself. That's all I was implying."

Claire scoffed and glanced to her right. "Well, whatever. Look, I'm going to be unapologetically blunt with you. Gabby and I don't see eye-to-eye. We never have. The sad thing is, I'm sure it's all my fault. I wish I could go back in time and take things back that I've said and done. I was anything but an ideal mother to my daughters."

Dani's head suddenly perked up again, almost as if she were awaiting her mother's admission of guilt for a long time. While her eyes were fixated on her mother, I could not help sneaking a quick glance toward her. Bad timing. Like a child being caught stealing candy from the candy dish, Dani turned her attention my way. I was caught. Our eyes met only for a split second, but that second felt like an eternity. As soon as I turned my eyes back to Claire, Dani sat up and started to walk away toward the exit. She was gone. Where she went, I had no clue. I feared she would never return, and it was all my fault.

I started to panic within. "Pardon me, Claire; may you please hold that thought? I desperately need to use the restroom quickly."

"Yeah, sure. I'll go check on your food."

While entering the restroom, I felt as if I had lost my appetite. Emotional sickness, I suppose. I walked in, made my way over to the sink, and stared in the mirror. The reflection I saw, I could not fathom. Disappointment, sadness, anger, doubt, and regret are beyond measure. I knew a simple glance was only humanistic, but I knew I could not help myself as I let this drag me down. I now feared that all the answers I sought were now impossible and unattainable. I had to go home; I had no choice.

Of course, my lunch and Claire were waiting for me as I made my way back to the table. I felt my heart sink yet again. This time, it felt like my heart weighed as much as a fourteen-pound bowling ball. Reality had set in as I had to pay my bill and leave as quickly as possible.

"Excuse me, Claire? I hate to do this, but I must go. I feel nauseous suddenly. Here's twenty-five dollars. This should cover my lunch and tip. I'm sorry, I truly am."

"Wait, just like that? Do you at least want a to-go box?"

"No, it's fine. I must leave now. I... I must go."

Claire's look suddenly became stern. "Gret, what did you see?"

"What? What did I see? I'm ... I'm not sure what you mean."

"Don't play dumb with me. If you think I didn't notice your glance behind me a couple of times, then you have another thing coming."

"Look, I got to go. I'm sorry again."

As I started to walk out, she persistently followed me. "What did you see!?"

"Nothing, I have to go."

"You're lying! What did you see!?"

An intense scene for an intense moment—even the patrons took notice. I figured Claire would follow me out the door considering the outburst she exuded inside, but she opted not to. I can only imagine what her customers were thinking. I felt horrible—just horrible. There was no other way to put it. It was all my fault. I wondered if I would ever be welcome there again, and it tore me up inside. I had no choice but to drive home and sulk in my regret.

15

The Kulning

Visions of beauty,
Rest upon the weary eye.
Soothing to the soul.

It was the most delicate voice I had ever heard. Fields of green surrounded my every step. The reeds were tall and full of life that the slightest touch from my right hand made me feel as if I were somewhere warm. So peaceful and calm, I imagined I was venturing into a different world. A world of ecstasy and happiness where fears are never recognized or shunned. Where I was, I did not know. It did not matter, though. At that moment, I was where I was supposed to be.

Every step further, I heard that voice. The high-pitched tone followed by a glass-shattering echo was so pure, it had to be a song of prominent significance. Undoubtedly, my heedful ears started to lure me closer and closer.

As I walked to the edge of the downhill horizon, my eyes were met with a breathtaking spectacle. There stood a blonde, long-haired woman wearing a long white dress—kulning to the free-range cattle in the near distance. Her back was facing me as the cattle started to draw near. It was like a page out of a fantasy book—a scene so dazzling and surreal that my soul felt as if it were instantly healing.

Curiously, I descended the jagged terrain, watching my every footstep and being careful not to trip. As I grew closer, the ever-so-alluring kulning became more powerful. I could hear the clanking of the cowbells slowly sailing in the gentle breeze. The closer I approached, the more hypnagogic it became.

It was when I was about ten feet behind her that the kulning ceased. The cattle all around her seemed to watch in curiosity as the mysterious blonde-haired woman slowly turned around. Our eyes had met, and it felt as if I was in a trance of some sort. She was gorgeous. Her soft facial features were highlighted by her piercing red lipstick. She looked like an angel from up above. Without hesitation, she began to speak. "Do not be troubled, young man. Our fear and sadness are only obstacles to the journey to what is to be. You shall overcome it all. We are always watching you."

Instantly, I awoke gasping for air. For a second, I felt confused as to where I was, for it was still dark and in the early hours of the morning. An intuitive dream during a rather difficult time.

16

Good Boy

6:00 a.m., Wednesday morning. Two days had passed. On Sunday night, I called my boss and explained that I had a family emergency and desperately needed a week of vacation. Lucky for me, my boss knew nothing of my non-existent family and willfully obliged. I felt horrible for lying, but my mental state was far above that of telling a little lie. During the confrontation with Claire, I felt slightly perturbed. No calls from Gabby or even Brian, whom I have not heard from or seen in some time. All I could do for the last forty-eight hours was sulk, rest, and keep a somewhat clear mind to regenerate my sanity.

This dream, however, made me see things in a different light. Reassurance was what I desperately needed to remind me that life goes on. Not all was lost, for I have had good and bad days. I simply needed to pick myself up out of the despair and start over.

That episode at Claire's was none other than another curveball. I struck out awfully—there was nothing more to it. It had shifted the tide of my mission toward answers. I had to remind myself that not all tides remain strong and rough, for smooth and sunny days will be abundant. I had to think positively, for positive thoughts were only justified through positive actions.

Claire was weighing heavy on my conscious. I knew I had to go back and try to rectify what I had done. Also, I had to see if Dani were to ever return. It was obligatory to me—both matters, to be exact. For Claire, I was not sure how awkward it would be between us. My lies spoken with her did not disappoint me, for it had to be done. I pondered if the truth was my best choice. The truth about how I can see her deceased daughter every time I visit and the story that Gabby shared with me. Certainly, that would be a tough task at hand. It was something I had to contemplate a little more.

Beyond that contemplation, I decided that I would try my luck at Claire's this morning. By the time I showered and got ready, it was a little past 7:00 a.m. With all the thinking from the past two days, I felt a little rejuvenated. I suppose I was back to my old self once again.

Stepping out and locking the front door, I noticed something that immediately caught my attention. Across the street, old Mr. Perkins' house had been vacant for the last six months. After his passing, neither a person nor a car had been seen at his residence for the last five months. Until now. There, in the middle of his driveway, was a two-door coupe with distinctive square taillights. The license plate read, GEK-8873. Maybe it was a city worker or a relative checking on the house; I did not know. While walking toward my car, my eyes continued to fixate on the mysterious vehicle. What looked to be a silhouette of the top portion of a head was quite evident on the driver side. It could have been my imagination, but I could swear that someone was occupying that vehicle. *Was someone watching me? Was it coincidence?* I could not ponder the initial thought, for my mind was set on two things and two things only—Dani and Claire.

I arrived at Claire's right before 7:30 a.m. A few cars filled the parking lot; obviously, it was not too busy or crowded. It was expected, considering it was a Wednesday and not a busy weekend morning. A friendly and familiar face greeted me as I entered.

"Hi, Gret!" Nancy said, smiling. "How are you this morning?"

"Hey, Nancy. I'm all right. How are you?"

"Oh, you know, another day, another dollar. Same old, I suppose."

"I hear you loud and clear. We both woke up today, so I suppose it's always a great day to be six feet above."

Nancy's eyes grew wide and nodded. "Ain't that the truth? Here, let me seat you, and, if I remember correctly, coffee? Black?"

"Bingo. Coffee for now will do just fine."

"Coming right up, my young friend."

I sat down and cautiously looked around to see if Claire was in sight or if there were any signs of Dani. So far, it looks as if Claire may have taken the day off, and Dani was not present. I took Claire's absence as a good sign, for I was not ready to face her yet. The thought of her name still made me a little uneasy and nervous inside. I was not certain if she would even welcome me back. I did not matter, though; I was here, and she was not—at least not yet. Nancy was on her way back with my coffee.

"Coffee for Mr. Gret. Would you like any breakfast this morning?"

"Maybe in a little bit, but I'm good for now." I took a quick sip. "No Claire today?"

"No, she had to go see her daughter today at school. It was a last-minute trip. She'll most likely be out tomorrow also."

My mind started to wonder. "Oh. Is everything okay?"

"You know, I really don't know to be honest. She said it was personal. That's all I know. Not that it's any of my business, but Claire is notorious for keeping those who are close to her out of the dark in her family affairs. I suppose I would do the same if I had a family."

"I see. Well, if you see them soon, please give my best to both. I would appreciate that."

"Sure thing. Let me know whenever you're ready to order breakfast."

Once Nancy started to walk away, I quickly took notice of the three customers entering. They were two large men that could have been linebackers for a football team. The female—I could not put my finger on it— looked awfully familiar, like I had seen her from somewhere. It was like I seen her before with a different look—a much more unpleasant look than she looked today. I could not explain it or remember it, as confusion was getting the better of me. They were certainly *outsiders*. All three were dressed in black from head to toe. The two males wore matching black coats with black jeans, while the female donned a faded, black hooded sweatshirt and jeans with holes right over the kneecaps. I figured them out as bikers, but oddly enough, I did not hear any bikes pull up, nor did it look like they traveled by car. My view of the parking lot from where I was sitting confirmed this.

They sat in three rows in the front of me and one to the right of my table. The woman sat facing me, while the two others had their backs toward me. I positioned my hand somewhat over my face to make it look like I was not staring. My curiosity compelled me to get a closer look at this woman; it was killing me. I started to raise my hands behind my head, pretending to act out a big yawn, and stole a quick look. Unfortunately, while I stole a glance, she took notice as our eyes met for a split second. It was then that I knew where I saw her. From one of the first times I was in here, Bree's voice started to echo inside my head to the tune of, "You and her have the same little beauty mark right under your left eye." It was her—that strange lady—who entered and asked Bree questions while she was at the cash register. No big deal, I thought. Although a bigger deal was about to enter the front door.

That warm feeling was felt within, and there she was. Dani was back. Unquestionably, feelings of warmth and happiness have replaced that perplexing feeling now. I could not explain how or even why, but I knew this warmth brought me total ease. However, the ease would suddenly turn into leeriness and trepidation.

While she made her way to her normal spot in the aft dining area, I observed all three outsiders glaring at her like a trio of hungry lions stalking their prey. *Who were these people? Were they like me?* I suddenly grew concerned and even more apprehensive as the woman caught me observing their undeniable stare toward Dani. From that point on, things started to become very peculiar. This woman would not keep her eyes off me. It was one of those stares with her mouth half-open, as if she were salivating over a piece of meat. Her phlegmatic stare simply chilled me to my bones. I continued to monitor her the best I could through my peripherals, noticing she turned her attention towards the two men, so I stole another glance. She said one sentence to both, and I am no expert lip-reader. Surely, from the interpretation I took from the movement of her lips, I could almost swear she said, "I know him."

For the next twenty minutes (give or take a few), I sat there sipping my coffee and pretended to not notice the outsiders. Of course, the woman's non-stop stare continued for minutes on end. Occasionally, her attention would turn to the men, say a few words, and then slowly turn in my direction and continue with her cold stare. I had lost my appetite as my nerves were starting to dominate my body and mind. The coffee was starting to hit me, thus creating a mandatory visit to the restroom.

I stood up and a cold feeling rushed throughout my body. I admit, I was a little petrified as the woman continued her stare toward me. Walking cautiously toward the back to the restroom, Dani was walking her way towards me—seemingly eager to bolt. Our paths would cross again, and I knew I had to try my hardest to avoid eye contact and go about my business. However, it did not happen that way at all.

Within two steps in front of me, I heard her voice inside my head. **Excuse me.**

Unbelievable. Simply breathtaking. I could not explain how I felt as all the emotions I could possibly gather rushed within my bloodstream, creating a warm place within my body. Once she passed, I stopped in my tracks, took a deep sigh, and turned around. Instantly, those emotions went from warm to bitter cold.

As she was halfway to the door, I took notice that the three outsiders all turned their heads, simultaneously glared in my direction, and then locked their sights on Dani. Time was in slow motion—at least it felt like it. Once Dani opened the door to exit, all three stood up and proceeded to follow her out the door. I knew right then and there that this scene did not happen out of coincidence or by some shear chance, for whatever reason was to be explained. I knew that these people had to be the Ancients whom my grandmother mentioned in her journal. After the initial shock, my fight or flight instinct kicked in so hard that I almost fell over. It was an easy decision to make, as I felt the rage and primal instinct to protect her any way I could.

I suddenly raced out the door, hoping no one inside would take notice, which might cause a scene. I looked to my right first. There she was, walking westward on the parking lot sidewalk, almost fifty yards away. However, the three outsiders were nowhere to be seen. Strangely, it was as if they vanished into thin air. I stood there a few seconds, staring and wondering why Dani had left Claire's so soon. *Was it me or even the outsiders who prompted her decision?* I did not know, as disappointment struck again.

Once she was out of my view, I turned my attention to my surroundings. The outsiders, or Ancients, were still out of sight. I started to look in all directions in hopes I would spot something to offer any clues. Nothing. Dani was gone, as were the others. I wondered how those three disappeared so quickly when I was literally five seconds behind them out the door. An anomaly that would forever go unexplained was what I thought. Strange times indeed, and this day was about to get a little stranger.

On the other side of the parking lot, close to the street, sat that two-door coupe with those distinctive square taillights. Maybe it was coincidental; maybe it was not. To avoid the obvious, I reached for my phone and started to walk closer down the sidewalk to catch a closer glimpse. A few steps forward, a sudden halt with a pretend phone call, and I was able to sneak a quick glance at the license plate—GEK-8873. Indeed, it was the same car that was in Mr. Perkins' driveway. This vehicle, whoever owned it, was tracking my movement. A part of me wanted to go over it and see if anyone was occupying it, but in this day of uncertainty, it did not seem safe. I had no choice but to step back into Claire's.

I sat down and took a second to collect my thoughts. From what transpired, I could not think all that straight. It felt like this was the beginning of something more to come—something that maybe I was not ready for. I was a player in this story, and the bell tolled to start. I needed more answers, and my motivation to go home and rummage through my grandmother's boxes was there again.

It was that time—time to wrap up my visit and head back home. As soon as I finished my coffee, paid my bill, and said goodbye to Nancy, I was on my way out. As I exited, I took a quick glance down the parking lot to see if that maroon car was still parked. It was gone. I was not certain if that was a good thing or not. Regardless, my car was on the opposite side as I continued to walk toward it. I opened my door, sat down, and started the engine. It must have rained for a second while I was inside, for there was a little precipitation on my windshield. I turned my windshield wipers on, and something caught my eye instantly. What looked to be a little folded note was stuck between my wiper and windshield. My insides quivered a bit as this day became even more bizarre. I stepped out and reached to grab the note. I quickly opened and read in utter confusion. The note simply read: *"Good boy"*. *What was going on?* I stepped back into my car and started to drive home. Good boy. *Who leaves a note like that?*

17

Notes of Confession and Concern

———————————

1:00 p.m., Wednesday afternoon. Once I got home from Claire's, I was more lethargic than I realized; hence, I decided to take a long nap. Woken and feeling refreshed, I walked over to the refrigerator and grabbed a couple slices of leftover pizza.

With my plate of pizza in hand, I sat down at my kitchen table, staring at my grandmother's boxes that had been untouched since that night. Roughly a week had passed by, although it felt like a couple of days since my grandmother's secret was revealed. I have always found it troubling how many believe that time accelerates as you get older. I do not believe that at all. I believe time tends to speed up as one becomes wiser. Old age does not grant wisdom. It is solely learned and inherited through experience and lessons. It is a simple explanation: the more wisdom one acquires, the more one tends to analyze every aspect they encounter. This simply creates a ripple effect—a movement that affects one's thinking, keeping them busy to the extent that they do not even think about time as it flies right over their heads. Many would agree, as many would not. After all, possessing wisdom opens the thought process of realizing that opinions vary from every person you encounter in life.

My life, however, was all about finding answers. Answers to riddles that hit me like a shock wave as of late. As I was finishing my lunch, my eyes were still locked on her boxes. I knew. I knew that maybe my grandmother was trying to tell me more in her last words. Considering the hidden journal, family photograph, bent page, and even her admission, something else was hidden within those boxes. Today was the day, and there was no better time to investigate than right now.

If I were to find answers, I figured that the box with all the papers and books would be my best bet. The other box with all her personal belongings was exactly what it was—personal belongings. Hence, I fixated myself on the box filled with letters and books.

At first glance, nothing immediately caught my eye. A whole bunch of letters from her late husband, financial statements, and various documents flooded her box. However, underneath all the papers were addressed envelopes with documents or letters still intact inside. There were about twelve envelopes, all open except for one dull yellow one. There was no return address on it or a receiver address like the others. I started feeling a little skeptical and slightly guilt-stricken about opening it. It could be nothing, or maybe it was something I was not meant to see. Even so, I had nothing to lose from opening it.

With envelope in hand, I placed my nose right above it and took a whiff. It smelled like an old library book that was lost in a mildew-infested cellar. Admittedly, I have the worst habit of smelling everything I encounter. I may forget what a certain inanimate object may look like, but a smell has a way to latch onto the brain and hold permanent residence. Whatever it was inside, it certainly had to have some age attached to it.

As I tore open the envelope, immediately a little card fell to the ground. Once again, it was the exact same obituary card for my mother that I found a week ago. Also, a note was neatly folded inside, made from a standard piece of notebook paper. As I unfolded the note, it read as follows:

Dear Mrs. Kline,

We have received your request for the revision of your daughter's obituary. We are glad to inform you that your request is being processed and should be available within the next twenty-four hours. Please, if you have any questions or concerns, feel free to reach out to our management team, and we will be happy to assist you during this difficult time.

Revisions. I wondered; this obituary was clear as day to me, so what revisions were possibly made? Spelling errors? Maybe. Grammatical errors? Possibly. The way it was written? Even more likely. I was at a loss about this letter, and why was it resealed? I could not comprehend the true facet of this revision. I suppose I was a little perturbed over the letter, but I had more digging to do.

I took a quick break from the box and grabbed my grandmother's diary. Starting from the beginning, I was to read the first few sentences of each entry to see if it was information I could use. It was a little troublesome because none of the entries were dated from when they were written. Also, I could not tell that every day was not logged. It seemed like my grandmother only wrote when times were tough and adversity was at its peak. Here and there, entries were mostly flooded with the tribulations of growing up and marital issues. However, after about ten minutes of browsing, one story caught my eye. It read as follows:

> *I don't know why I'm writing about this, but I feel that writing to myself is the simplest way to express my emotions and feelings on this matter. I am and will always be leery when it comes to my predicament, not to mention scared to a fault. Anyway, here it goes.*
>
> *It's been many years, but it still feels like yesterday, for the memory is forever locked in my vault without a key to set it free. When I was twenty-five years old and attending community college classes, I always went to the library on Mondays, Tuesdays, and Thursdays to study. Three times a week is simple enough. I would*

121

see her sitting at the same table, alone, helpless, and lost in this cruel world.

Her habits were predictable: holding her head low and focusing on folding the same piece of paper repeatedly. Maybe she was bored, or maybe she was nervous—I did not know. It was obvious what and who she was, but I kept about my business in a mild manner. Maybe, just maybe, if I had known that the last Thursday before finals was the last time I would see her, maybe I would've done something different.

On that Thursday, a mysterious man walked in and took a seat three tables behind her, one row to the right, and the second seat facing her. It's funny how I remember the exact location. I will never forget his look—the kind of look that would trigger every alarm within one's head. His hair was the most distinct feature—greasy, slicked-back hair with a little ponytail. He looked out of sorts, like he had no business visiting the library. Little did I know, his intentions were not remotely close to the kind intended for visiting a library.

Moments later, the woman got up from her seat and walked out in a hurry. The look on her face is something I will never forget. It was the look of death; there was no other way to put it. I believe she knew something was off as the strange man followed her out the door.

I remained in my seat, with no action taken. I never saw that Sleepless lady and that mysterious man again, who I presumed was what my father told me was an Ancient. For real, what could I've done? During that time, I

A son is on the way. It looks like a piece of the puzzle has been solved. Never once has my mother, father, or even grandmother mentioned this *'son on the way.'* I was kind of shocked, but more curious in the sense that this *son* left me wondering if he was still alive. *Why would they hide this from me?*

I was somewhat at a loss. Lots of thoughts were racing through my head. I thought maybe he passed young; hence, my grandmother and mother believed it was better to forget for whatever reason. The more I thought about it, the less logical it became in my thoughts. I believe they were hiding a dirty little secret within our family.

I stared at that entry and the funeral parlor note and read them over and over for the next ten minutes. *Was I missing something?* It all seemed cut and dry, with no hidden message about her son. I could not fathom that I may have or had a possible uncle whom I never knew existed.

I then started to browse through other entries past this one, hoping to find any useful information. There is absolutely nothing about her non-existent son. Frustration, driven by desperation, was starting to set in. This entry cracked the door open slightly, but I felt like it would lead to another dead end. I kept the journal out, closed the boxes, and sat at my kitchen table to think of all the possibilities. At that moment, an intriguing thought struck me like lightening.

In the other box, I recalled the family photo of my grandparents, my mother, and the mysterious child whom my grandmother was holding. Without hesitation, I walked over to the first box and seized that framed photo. As I sat next to the box to study the photo, there was an unexpected knock at my door. I placed the frame at the edge of the kitchen table and ran to answer the door. It was my next-door neighbor, eighty-eight-year-old Mrs. Freeland.

"Hello, Gretan," she said as she smiled at me. "How are you doing today?"

I was not in the mood for visitors. "Hi, Mrs. Freeland. I'm fine. I'm sorry to do this, but I'm kind of busy right now with something important. Did you need something by chance?"

"Oh, my dear, I'm terribly sorry. I wanted to stop by to tell you something. It's probably nothing, but earlier today, there was a man and a younger woman standing at the edge of your driveway, conversing back and forth for a couple of minutes. They—"

"Wait, a man and a woman? It wasn't two men and one woman?"

Mrs. Freeland started to look puzzled. "No, it was a man and a woman. Then they—"

"What did they look like?"

"Oh, well… the woman had a hood on. She looked to be very fair-skinned. The man looked to have a lot of… what do you call it—grease or gel in his hair. He was also smoking a cigarette."

Grease. Gel. Smoking. Instantaneously, it hit me. That description reminded me of the man I witnessed in the restroom and outside at Claire's. I'll never forget what he said: *"Nice day out today? What do you say?"*

"Did you see where they went?"

Mrs. Freeland looked puzzled. "Well, as I was watching them, my phone started to ring. I went to grab it, but by the time I answered, they had already hung up. So, I went back to the window to watch again, and poof, they were gone."

I scratched my head. "So, you have no clue where they went?"

"No, not a clue. I got the overall impression that they were scoping out your house or something. Please make sure to set your alarm and arm your cameras, if you have them. The last thing this neighborhood needs is criminals breaking into houses. I will do my best to keep an eye out for you. I'm sorry once again to bother you; I thought you would like to know."

"Don't be sorry at all; you did the right thing. Thank you, Mrs. Freeland. I must go now, and I hope you enjoy the rest of your day."

"You too, my dear. Chat with you later."

Instantly after I shut the door, a sound carried from the kitchen that made me flinch for a split second. Accidentally, it was the sound of glass shattering against the floor. I rushed over to the kitchen to find that the family photo had fallen off the table. Shards of glass were spewed across the floor, along with the right corner frame, which split from its origin. It was odd; I could have sworn I placed it in a position to not fall, but I was in a rush to answer the door. However, there was no spontaneous breeze or source of wind—no explanation there. No other person was in the house—easy elimination. Frankly, the only physical explanation I could think of was that maybe the vibration from the door shutting forced it to move a little, sending it off the table. Regardless, it did not matter; I had a hazard that I needed to clean up.

I picked up the frame and walked it over to the garbage can. As I was shaking the remaining shards off the photo, the right-hand corner of the photo from where the frame separated started to bend over. Carefully, I started to take the photo out, separating it from its tensile strength border. Suddenly, my heartbeat started to race. Nestled in between the photo and border was a standard piece of paper, folded into a perfect square. Wasting no time, I immediately opened the paper as my eyes began to light up. It was a note, and it read as follows:

Dear Beverly,

> *First things first, I am utterly disappointed with the obituary for Florence. I am not sure if this is your doing, nor am I accusing you. This obituary needs his name omitted ASAP. Between you and Florence, the two of you made a conscious decision to banish any involvement with him, period. For my sake, it sickens me to even write this note, let alone mention his name. The funeral is in two days, so please contact the funeral home to make the proper corrections. I will not allow some drugged-out loser ex-con of a brother on her obituary. Florence doesn't deserve this because her brother created his own grave. He did the digging; now he must live in the hole he created.*

> *Regards,*
> *Jarrick*

This note was huge. It was a simple affirmation that my grandmother had a son, who was at least still alive by the time my mother passed. I had an uncle whom I never knew existed. I was optimistic, even though this letter was written well over twenty years ago. I had a peculiar feeling within my heart that this uncle was still alive, but finding him seemed like a distant long-shot.

The question remained: What did my uncle do to be discarded and banished from the family? Was he habitually a drug junkie, like my father claimed in the note? I had ideas and thoughts, but none were too sure. Maybe it was all my father's doing, considering the demeanor of his condescending letter. Or maybe it was a huge fallout of some sort that prompted his absence. For whatever reason, my curious nature needed to know the reasoning behind it all.

Behind the discoveries, the lurking question remained on the site that Mrs. Freeland witnessed outside my house. These two people, the three at Claire's, and even the mysterious maroon coupe—were they all connected? Pieces of the puzzle were still scattered about, but the feeling of them coming together was a certain, slow burn. Time will tell, and I fear the uncertainty of it all will be a haunting spectacle once it all pieces together.

18

Dainty, Red Eyes

I swear, the picture was alive.
I swear, they do exist.
I swear, I would not lie.
I swear, I do insist.

It was around 8:00 p.m. The day grew dark, and I was feeling drained but restless as I slumped on my couch watching a movie. It so happened that one of my favorite movies was on—*Riders Amongst Men.* It was about a triage of three young men in the desert who were seeking a murderer in exchange for a lucrative bounty. During their expedition, they encounter many trials and tribulations that symbolize their journey into manhood. I think I love this movie because I sometimes envision myself in their boots. The way they act, the way they talk, even the way they move—I had it all to a staggering fault. It was a compelling and inspirational flick.

About an hour into the movie, I started to drift off a little. It was one of those incongruent dream states in which one was not certain if they were sleeping and dreaming or half-awake, falling into the phase of a daydream. It was about that time in the movie in which the three men evaded an attack from small time crooks and hid out in a cave for the night. When night fell, the thieves drew down into the cave to find the three men at a dead end. It turned out that they spared their lives on the promise that the men would turn over half the bounty they were seeking. Well, in my unknown dream state, that scene did not go as planned.

As I lay on my couch, the thieves were venturing through paths in the cave. With my eyes fixated on the scene, one of the men stopped in his movement, turned his head towards me, and presented a hostile stare in my direction. My heart sank, and I was lacking the ability to move or scream. Paralysis set in as the man suddenly began to step out of the television and make his way in front of my couch. He took a few steps toward me and stopped about three feet in front of my panic-ridden state. With his torch in his left hand, he pulled out a knife and wielded it as if he were going for the kill. Gasping for air in a mad panic, he walked over to my side and raised his knife above my body. This was it, I thought. Suddenly, I woke up from the unexplainable dream state to be completely terror-stricken.

After I somewhat regained my composure, I walked to my kitchen for a glass of water. Maybe it was the effects from the nightmare, but something felt a little off. Standing beside my kitchen counter and sipping my water, I suddenly flinched as my home phone began to ring. After a couple of rings, I hesitantly answered—the terror inside me was still present.

"Hello?" I answered confusedly.

"Inaudible noise."

"Hello?"

"Inaudible noise."

I had no choice but to hang up the phone. A few seconds later, the phone rang again.

"Hello?"

"Inaudible noise with excessive static."

I started to tremble inside. "Who is this?"

"Gret?" Good grief, it was Mrs. Freeland. "Can you hear me?"

"Yes, I hear you. Did you just try calling me a few seconds ago?"

Mrs. Freeland's voice was also trembling. "Yes, I'm sorry. It must be a bad connection, but hear me out. Those two people… they are in your backyard right now!"

"Wait… wh-what?"

"Yes, Gret… they are. I walked over to my back window to water my plants on the windowsill, and there they were, scoping out your house again!"

"Are they still there!?"

"Hold on, let me check."

I felt like a little boy who saw or experienced something beyond his innocence. As I continued to hold for a response, my whole body was shaking violently. Nothing would ever compare to this experience; I could recall being afraid of the dark, roller coasters, or even ghost stories.

"Gret, you still there?"

My breathing was becoming shallow as my pulse was rapidly increasing. "Yes, I am here."

"I don't see them anymore. Hold on, let me check the front."

I remained frozen by my kitchen counter like a solitary statue. I pondered calling the sheriff's office with my cell phone, but I could not even think straight now. Come to think about it, I had no clue as to where my cell phone even was, eliminating that option.

"Gret, I don't see anyone in your front yard. They were definitely in your backyard, though."

"Okay, I'm going to go upstairs to look out the front window. Mrs. Freeland, would you mind staying on the line with me while I check?"

"Most certainly, Gret. I'll stay on."

Immediately, I ran as fast as I could up the stairs to the master bedroom, which had a clear view of the front. Still trembling, I took a quick glance out the window—no one in sight.

"Mrs. Freeland? I'm not seeing anyone from my view."

"Yeah, me neither. I'll check the back and front again, and whoever they are, they seem to be gone. Strange. It's like they vanished without a trace."

"Well, I'm going to keep my eyes on the front for a few minutes."

"Good idea. Do you want me to call the sheriff's office for you?"

"No, it's okay. I'll probably call them in a few minutes. I want to see if I spot them first."

"Well, you should call them regardless and do it quickly. Just make sure your doors are locked, and you should leave your lights on tonight. I'll continue to keep my eyes open for you."

"Thanks, Mrs. Freeland. I owe you one."

"No problem. Oh, and Gret? One more thing."

"Yes?"

"I'm not trying to frighten you even more, but when I saw them, I could've sworn that they had the faintest yet dainty red fixtures where their eyes would be. As insane as it sounds, I know what I saw. It was like something out of those… whatchu call it… horror flicks."

"Okay, I don't honestly know how to take that, but thanks for the information."

"You let me know if you need anything. I still have Ted's crossbow if it comes down to that."

I smiled at that last statement. "Will do, and thanks again."

Dainty red eyes in my backyard; I did not know how to take that. Maybe she was right; maybe this was the beginning of some horror movie, with me portraying the victim. Mrs. Freeland was nearing her nineties, so maybe she was imagining things or losing her mind. I did not know what to believe. Regardless, I had to proceed with caution regarding this matter.

I remained steadfast on the lookout. Still, no one is in sight. It was about as calm and peaceful as a cemetery in my front yard. If I called the sheriff's office, it would be pointless. They would come out, find nothing, and tell me to keep my doors locked and to stay alert. However, maybe I should have called based on what I was about to see.

In the distance, two headlights were approaching my house from down the street. I was four houses away from the dead-end point, and the vehicle was rapidly approaching my house. It was moving at a steady pace—not too fast, not too slow. However, it slowed down rapidly right before it hit Mrs. Freeland's house. At that moment, this night took another dramatic turn.

The vehicle had pulled into the end of Mr. Perkins' abandoned house. It sat there for a moment, backed out, and then drove away. Sure enough, it was that maroon two-door coupe that I had seen two previous times. GEK-8837.

I swiftly ran downstairs to verify that all my locks were locked, turned off the tube, turned on my main lights (outside and inside), set the alarm, and returned to my bedroom. Locking my bedroom door, I grabbed my baseball bat from my closet, set it next to the nightstand, and crawled into bed, hoping to fall asleep as soon as I could. This was not going to be an easy night.

19

An Intricate Plan

6:00 a.m., Thursday morning. That thing called sleep—I was not sure it even happened last night. Tossing, turning, paranoia, anxiety, repeat. All night long. My body and mind felt as if they were sleeping awake—comparable to an insomniac, I can imagine.

Once I got out of bed, I walked downstairs to the kitchen to make some coffee. Waiting for it to brew, I walked all around the house to affirm that there was no evidence of a potential break-in. Call me paranoid, or even delirious; I was still a little on edge. In a way, I was a little ashamed of myself. The way I acted and how terrified I was made it kind of hard for me to walk in my shoes, let alone look at myself in the mirror. A grown man should not act like a child when adversity and threats come tumbling down. As I sat down, sipping my coffee, I knew that I could not let my fear dictate my actions. I must be better. I must endure the terror and protect myself and what is precious to me. I must change, and that change must come immediately.

Yesterday was one of the oddest, surrealest, yet most defining days of my life. To get a better grasp on it, I thought the way to understand the events that took place was to make a timeline of events and decipher each of the five *W's: who, what, when, where, and why.*

The timeline was an easy task; however, the only burning questions from the *W's* were *who* and *why.* In column A, I had the mysterious maroon coupe that seemed to have quite an interest in me. From column B, I had the supposed *Ancients,* or outsiders, for they have not been fully identified yet. *Were both somehow related? Were they the same people? Were they after Dani and me?* Despite everything, I needed courage to make my next move.

All my life, I was never one for confrontation. Until now. I now know that I must stand up for what is right in this world. Admittedly, I was not entirely sure what was right, but acting off my gut instinct was a start. My instincts were telling me that Dani and I may be in grave trouble. I knew if what I thought was true, I had to protect her and myself from whatever lurks in the darkness. If what my great-grandfather said was correct, protection was not a choice but an obligation if I chose to accept it. Nevertheless, I had to keep both eyes on Dani as much as humanly possible and be ready to fight if necessary.

****

A few hours have now passed since it was 10:00 a.m. I must have dozed off on my couch for a few hours watching the news. I felt refreshed and brand new from a logical perspective. My enervation had vanquished, my vision was unclouded, and my mind was now lucid. This thing, or *game,* as I like to call it, began yesterday at Claire's. The board was set, and the pieces were in motion. My opponent made their first major move, and now it was time to make mine.

After I finished getting ready, it was time to make my way over to Claire's. My plan was simple—stop in, immediately use the restroom (eyes on Dani), sit down, have lunch, and stay until close at 2:00 p.m. To make the time go by inconspicuously, I would bring my laptop to keep myself busy and give the impression that I was working on business from my job. From what Nancy told me, I was not worried about Claire being there, but I was preparing for the worst.

Right before 2:00 p.m. hits, I will use the restroom again to affirm that she is still there and then exit the establishment. From there, I will maneuver my car into a strategic spot where I will not be noticed and wait for her to exit. I had seen her enter around the same time every morning, so I was certain she would exit and not stay inside the whole night. I only had two burning questions about her exit: What time would she leave, and where does she go? As for the time, I was prepared to sit in my car and wait for however long I needed to. Once I would spot her leaving, I would follow her wherever she went. I was prepared to do whatever was necessary, hoping nothing went south.

136

As I stepped out of my front door, I paused for a second and stared at Mr. Perkins' house across the street. No maroon car was in sight. Also, I figured it would not hurt to take a quick look in my backyard to see if anything was tampered with. Nothing. That certainly boosted my confidence, and a piece of my mind was satisfied.

It was 10:40 a.m. when I pulled into the parking lot of Claire's. Only two cars were parked in the whole vicinity of her entrance, while the others were scattered amongst the other businesses down the plaza. Once again, there was no maroon car in sight. That thought alone simply put me at ease.

As I walked into Claire's, there was not a single customer inside; only Nancy and Bree were sitting down, conversing with each other.

Nancy stood up as she noticed me walk in. "Gret! So nice to see you again."

"Hey, Nancy. Hi, Bree. Nice to see you two also. You two look pretty busy, I must say."

Bree started to chuckle. "I can hardly contain myself with all this excitement here. Hell, you're our first visitor in the last hour."

"That slow, huh?"

Nancy nodded as Bree went to the back. "Yeah, it's been brutal. As you can see, the table choice is quite abundant. Take your pick, and I'll start you off with some water."

"I'm going to use the restroom first. You know, I was kind of in a hurry and figured I would use it here, I guess."

"Do what you need to do, young man. I'll see you when you come back."

As I made my way to the back, I did not even need to glance to see if Dani was there, for I could feel her warmth inside my body. Now, I was accustomed to it. All the shakes, headaches, and anxiety are gone. It was now a three-second feeling, for that was all I needed.

Same table, same seat—she was there. I did not need to make direct eye contact, as I could see her silhouette in my peripheral vision. Maybe I was mistaken, but as I was about to enter the restroom, her head tilted up a bit, which signified a quick glimpse of me. I was not worried, though. Deep down inside, I knew that she knew I was not a threat.

Exiting the restroom, I followed the same plan as entering head low, no eye contact, back to the main dining room. The plan was progressing accordingly, but it was still early. Once I returned to the seating area, I noticed that Nancy had set up a table for me, fully intact, with a menu and water.

"I know I said I would bring you water, but did you want anything else to drink?"

"Water is fine, for now."

"Okay. I'll give you a few minutes to mull over the menu, and I'll be back to—"

I quickly interrupted. "Say, did you hear anything from Claire or Gabby?"

Nancy tucked in her lips and nodded her head. "As a matter of fact, I did. You didn't hear this from me, though, but it turns out that Gabby is dropping out this semester and returning home."

I did not see this coming. "Really?"

"Yeah, it's unfortunate for that young lady. She relished being away. Well, at least from what I gathered."

"Do you know what happened? I mean, was it something she couldn't control or something out of the blue?"

Nancy took a quick seat across from me. "Well, between you and I, I don't know the full details, nor do I want to speculate. But if you keep this between us, I will speculate. I think her mind wasn't right to start school again. She and Claire have a somewhat *callous* relationship. Please, you didn't hear all this from me. I love Gabby like she's my own daughter, so I wouldn't want to say anything about her that is inaccurate. I know it sounds like I am, but it's what I have noticed from the outside looking in. That Gabby… she's such a sweet, innocent soul."

"Oh no, I would never say anything to anyone about what you told me. I'm far from that kind of person who is all about gossip and junk. I'm sure once she returns, she'll tell me everything."

"I greatly appreciate that. Both should be back on Saturday. Her mother is down there helping her pack up and whatnot." Nancy began to shake her head from side to side. "I can only imagine how many fights and disagreements they have gotten into down there. It kind of reminds me of ten years ago, but that's another story. Claire demands a lot from her—almost too much, if you ask me. But once again, I'm merely a viewer looking from the outside."

"I totally understand everything you just said. Please know this: I would never say a word of what you had said about Gabby and Claire." I thought about what I was about to ask her next with caution. "May I ask you something?"

"Sure, anything Gret."

"This is just me… and, like you said, from the outside looking in. You seem quite invested in their relationship. I like to think I'm a decent judge of character. No doubt, I think highly of you. But it seems like you are holding something back within— holding back regret of some sort. Is that the case?"

Nancy froze up for a second and was overcome with a look of sadness. "It's… I shouldn't get into this."

"No, I understand… speak no more. I apologize for mentioning it."

"No… I need to unburden myself. I suppose. My oldest daughter and I had a similar relationship. We could never see eye-to-eye on anything. *'Oil and water'*, she would always call us. She was a manic depressant. I can't say I'm not either. So, you may see how the disagreements would come about. Anyway, long story short, we got into a big argument about her childhood. Words were said, mostly regrettable ones. When it was said and done, we didn't speak to one another for eighteen months. Then, one day, I got a call. My daughter was found hanging in her closet with an extension cord. I couldn't believe it. I didn't want to believe it. For eighteen months, I never spoke to her. I kept asking myself, '*What kind of mother am I?*' So, you can see how I'm invested in both."

I shook my head in grief. "I'm sorry to hear all that. For what it's worth, I don't think you're to blame, and you shouldn't blame yourself. This life… it's funny. Nobody is perfect. We all make mistakes and have far more regrets than we can all count. I think everything happens for a reason, whether we like it or not."

"A reason?"

"Yes. A reason to live. A reason to learn. A reason to keep going. Don't get me wrong, I don't think that reason was to punish you for whatever reason you believe, but a reason to keep living."

"Do you think we ever get to come back from our mistakes?"

I took a deep sigh. "I do. I definitely do. Whether it be in this life or the next, I believe we all get to come back and fix the mistakes from the past."

Nancy looked at me with a sincere smile and almost shed a tear. "You're the best, Gret. I do believe you are now my favorite customer."

I shook my head and laughed in joy. "I appreciate that, I really do. And don't tell Gabby this, but I think you're my favorite server here now."

Nancy got up from her seat, put her hand on my shoulder, and smiled. "I'll be back in a few minutes to take your order. You're the best!"

I did not know how to take Gabby back into town this semester. I guess I deciphered her return as bittersweet. On one hand, I saw her as a nuisance, someone who maybe would pin a wedge between what was taking place. On the other hand, I did enjoy her company, to an extent. The emotional aspect could be quite tiresome, and I did not need that to occupy my life. Either way, I was quite positive I would be seeing her more often than I would like to admit.

About Nancy—she was great. I genuinely felt for her. At first meeting, her infectious, happy-go-lucky attitude was off the chain. In hindsight, I got to see a side of her I never expected. I loved conversing with her, as she was someone I could see chatting endlessly with without a moment of boredom. During our conversations, I often wondered if our voices carried over to Dani. Even during our little jokes, I hoped Dani would take notice, and they would put a smile on her face. A smile to remind her of the good times that once were.

Time flew by, whether it was countless chats with Nancy, eating my turkey club, surfing on my laptop, or watching the occasional customers drop in and out. It was almost closing time. Not to mention, the drama here from yesterday seemed to have found a black hole—absent without a trace to be seen. Compared to yesterday, it was a complete 180.

****

It was about 1:45 p.m. Before they were to close, I was to complete another simple task at hand. I got up and walked to the restroom and back—same result. Everything was going according to plan. Next, the bill was paid, and I left Nancy a little extra for the excellent service I received. I hugged Nancy, said my goodbyes, and walked out to my car. Once again, there were no outsiders, and no maroon coupe was in sight. A perfect plan was seemingly in place.

Inconspicuously, I drove to the other end of the parking lot, parked beside a company vehicle belonging to a hardware store, and turned my ignition off. I felt like I was on the other side of the law, initiating a long, drawn-out stakeout—a private investigator awaiting to find out the truth about a strange case. I must admit, I felt very different in an indescribable way. I guess the whole hiding aspect triggered a sense of guilt, like I was doing something immoral. I suppose I was out of my norm, and thinking about it endlessly added to the pressure of my task. Regardless, the waiting game has officially begun.

****

Several hours had now passed; the time was approximately 7:45 p.m. The day was fading fast as dark clouds began to surface. In the distance, a faint thundering sound was heard, as possible wet weather may be in the forecast. Night was fast approaching, signifying the ominous terror that is associated with darkness. It was smoothly quiet as the businesses around were soon to close shop. I was a little worried about that notion, hoping I would not be noticed as a suspicious person. Luckily, that was not going to happen, as the moment had finally come.

There she was. Dani was about five feet away from the door, walking westward in the same direction to her mother's house. I must have looked down for a moment, as I did not even see her exit. My heartbeat started to pick up a little, and my palms started to become enthralled in sweat. I thought for a moment: *Should I do this? What if I mess this up and things won't be the same?* Those thoughts alone put a curdling feeling in my stomach. I had no choice. She needed to remain safe under my watch. However, following her was going to be a daunting task.

As I saw her starting to walk westward on Route 13, I started my car and slowly started to exit the parking lot. Given the numerous sharp turns and sizable forest area along that route, following her was going to be a little challenging. It was a straight shot to her house, which was also about two minutes before Hugo Lake.

At the edge of the road, I could see her walking, as her pace was starting to pick up significantly. Traffic was miniscule, so taking my time to pull out was not going to be an issue. About two hundred feet away, she was now approaching the bend in the road. That was my cue to pull out and start tracking. I started off slow, trying to time everything perfectly to remain unobtrusive. As I turned at the bend, panic mode suddenly struck without warning. She was gone, out of sight as far as I could see. Shocked, I took my foot off the gas, and my mind started to go blank. I felt my plan had backfired—all for nothing. It was over. I had no choice but to keep driving and head home.

Normally, this was not the route I would take to go home, but I figured I had nothing to lose by driving the extra five minutes out of my way. *How did I lose her so fast?* It was a strange anomaly—one I did not even want to think about.

Disappointment, anger, anxiety—I had it all. Driving forward and maintaining a slow pace, little hope lingered as my eyes were focused on the hope that I could still spot her somewhere. Unexpectedly, my phone began to ring—it was Gabby. At first, I was going to let my voicemail answer her but ultimately decided to pull off the road to answer.

"Hey, Gabby. What's up?

"Hey, Gret! Sorry if I'm bothering you, but I figured I would give you a ring to see how you are."

"No, it's okay. You're not bothering me. So, what's new?"

"Well, I'm not sure if you heard or not, but I just got home from school. I had to drop out for a lot of reasons. I'll explain it all later in person."

With the phone pressed against my ear as I glanced in the rearview mirror, there she was. Dani was rounding a turn in the road and was roughly two hundred feet behind me. *How did I pass her the first time?* It was odd, almost like she purposely lost me. Every word Gabby was speaking literally flew right past my ear. I knew I had to end this conversation immediately.

"Gabby, I apologize. I need to let you go right now. Can I call you back in a few minutes?"

Her tone changed for the worse. "Um, sure."

"I'm sorry, I'll explain later."

I hung up the phone and kept my eyes glued to the rearview mirror. As she kept her pace forward, I had to think of something fast. Unfortunately, it was too late. From about one hundred feet away, she lifted her head up and spotted my car on the side of the road. She stood still, frozen to the point of unbearable fright. Her fright suddenly triggered a jolt of cold and sadness, and I could feel it in my bones. From the feeling I felt, I could only imagine the terror she felt as she ran into the dense forest to disappear again.

Shortly after that moment, something happened to me. Disappointment and regret were not a thing anymore to me. I felt something unusual, comparable to a perplexed feeling of hope.

The phone call from Gabby was a blessing in disguise. It prompted something within me—a week-old memory that seemed to have been forgotten in my mind. I now knew where Dani's destination was tonight. The date with Gabby, the pinging I felt that night, her story, the feeling I felt—I knew. She was going to Hugo Lake.

Immediately, I sped fast, for I had roughly a three-minute drive to the lake. My adrenaline was pure, and my buoyancy was high. The whole day had now come down to this moment. Make or break, I had to remain strong.

It was right before 8:00 p.m. when I pulled into Hugo Lake. Only two other cars were present in the parking lot, most likely visitors on a nightly walk. I had to remain invisible in the sense of not being noticed; therefore, parking next to the two cars was the obvious choice. Once I parked, I remained steadfast and low beside my car, my eyes fixated on the lake. Where she would go exactly, I had no clue. Therefore, my attention was maintained in every possible direction.

After two minutes had passed, there she was. In between the dense pines on the east side of the lake, Dani was making her way to the opening. This time, I felt the warmth combined with the cold deep inside my body for the first time. For what that meant, I assumed it was a mixture of feelings from within. I stood up and watched in amazement as she kept her pace without hesitation.

Fifty feet away from the lake, she froze and turned her head up to the dark clouds from up above. I did not have the best view to depict her face, but I believe she was starting to cry. The warmth was overridden by sadness, as the cold within could only be felt. Instantly, I knew her next move as she started to walk directly toward the lake. It felt like I was in a movie—surreal to the point where it felt like a dream. She was returning to where she met her untimely demise.

Cautiously, I started to inch toward the lake as I kept a close watch as she began to submerge herself in the water. The closer I got, the further she moved forward until her body disappeared from under the surface. Just like her death, the lake swallowed her under.

As my eyes remained glued to the spot where she went under, I could see a faint reflection of light hovering above the water. As the light got brighter, it finally became a realization of what it was. As I turned around, I could see two headlights approaching the lake from the entrance down the road. Immediately, I knew that was my cue for a quick exit. I hurried back to my car in a panic, realizing my car door was locked, and dropped my keys. As I bent over to pick them up, I noticed the car a couple spots over from me. Maroon coupe. *How did I not notice this when I pulled up?* I started to inch up to the back of the car. GEK-8837. My heart started to race as I took a few steps back.

BLACKOUT

20

An Unlikely Visitor

I saw a stranger the other day,
Who she was, I know not.
Lurking from the shadow,
She watches me, only at night.
Not too subtle, nor too cunning,
I wish she would go away.

My grandmother's old house always gave me an unsettling feeling of trepidation. As much as I loved visiting her when I was a child, her house used to frighten me beyond measure. During the day, it was like any other house—pleasant and cozy. However, night portrayed a different story. Creaking floorboards, an old grandfather clock, and odd sounds that resonated within the walls set an ominous tone in the darkness. Her house, even in my dreams, told the same old story countless times.

If I had to guess, the time was between 11:00 p.m. and 3:00 a.m. I was lying down on a stiff bed in my grandmother's dining room. On a normal day, a bed would not be placed in the dining room. I did not think about it, though, for I suppose my subconscious had other thoughts and worries.

From the living room, the faint sound of what sounded like a jubilant infomercial actor could be heard on the television in the living room. I could not see the television directly; only the bright lights were reflecting all around me. Confused as to why it was on in the first place, I stood up from my bed and took a quick glance into the living room. Bad idea. Instantly, I slumped back into my bed and put my head under the covers in a panic. Maybe my mind was playing tricks on me, but there was what looked to be a young female watching television. I stayed silent for a few seconds, trying to catch my breath as my nerves were frozen. Once my nerves warmed up a bit, I thought about what I saw and figured it was my tiresome mind seeing things. I slowly pulled my head up from the covers, sat up, and took another peek. The couch was empty this time, but still, a growing feeling of terror lingered within me.

I laid down, staring at the reflections of light off the ceiling for a few minutes. My mind was drawing blanks, and I knew the prospect of sleep was far away. Unexpectedly, a light from the kitchen flickered on. My attention turned away from the reflections as my eyes were focused on the passing light in the hall from the kitchen. Straightaway, a silhouette of a shadow cast on the light from the hallway. As I heard the footsteps coming my way, I wondered what my grandmother was doing up so late in the evening. That was not the case at all.

At the beginning of the hallway (right beside my bed), there stood the same young female whom I saw from the living room. My body became paralyzed from fright as she stood there, glaring at me in a curious manner. I could not scream, move, or even blink my eyes if I tried. Deep inside, I kept telling myself that this was nothing but a nightmare, and none of it was real. My brain did not want to hear it as I felt chained up to an old brick wall in my unconscious state. This lady chilled me to my bones.

Suddenly, the volume from the television started to rise uncontrollably as the female turned her eyes toward the sound. Once the volume reached its peak, it swiftly turned silent—only the reflections of light were active. After the silence, her eyes turned back to my direction once more. I remained paralyzed as the lady started to slowly walk closer to my bedside. She stared at me for a quick second, tilted her head, smiled, and placed her hand on my forearm. Finally, I had woken up from this ghastly nightmare in a panic. Where I was, I did not know. From the drowsiness, all I could see was darkness and bright-red lights on the side of my bed.

21

An Unfamiliar Place

D r. Janaski, please report to room 418 for observation." What sounded like an intercom loudspeaker could be heard in the faint distance. I was in a hospital, but no recollection was registered of how or why I got here. My head was pounding, and my mouth was dry as cotton. Besides my headache, I could not feel much pain at all—hence bandages wrapped around my head. From the clock on the wall, the time was 12:26 a.m. I was trying my hardest to remember anything from today, with not much luck. The only thing I could remember was Nancy. *Did I talk to her today?* I was groggy, lethargic, and completely out of it. Along with those symptoms, feelings of loneliness and a sense of being lost were present until a nurse opened my door.

"Hi, Gretan," the nurse greeted me as she placed her hand on my bed rail. "Welcome back to the world. How are you feeling?"

I slowly rubbed my eyes. "What happened? How did I get here? I just—"

"Well, for starters, I am the nurse assigned to you tonight. Alfreda is my name. I got here shortly after you arrived, so it made sense to assign me to you because I'll be here until 10:00 a.m." She willingly checked my vitals and ensured my IV line was still connected. "On a scale of one to ten, ten being the worst, what is your pain level?"

I was still confused. "I… I'm not sure. Maybe an eight? Wh-what is going on? How did I get here?"

"You suffered a severe concussion last night. Right now, you probably have no memory of what happened or anything else from yesterday. I'm going to give you some more morphine to help with the pain, so you'll be able to sleep through the night. It would be best for you to ease up, talk less, and just sleep."

Exasperation was setting in. "No, wh-when, how did I get here?"

Alfreda nonchalantly rolled her eyes. "I was told an older male and female dropped you off. Maybe your parents, or family?"

I subtly shook my head. "What? No, my parents are dead. I have no other family. Are they still here?"

"As far as I know, they left after they dropped you off." Alfreda sat down and put her hands on her knees. "Okay, here's the deal. I don't know the full details, but as I said before, you suffered a concussion. I don't know what you were doing, where you were, or how it happened, but it looks like someone slugged you pretty hard on your coconut. I don't know the details—not my department. I am here to treat you in any possible way I can until you leave or my shift ends. You will have to stay overnight for monitoring, and the earliest you may be discharged is approximately twelve hours after you arrive. Of course, that's only if the doctor signs off on your release. One more thing: The colony sheriff will want to speak with you about your incident before you leave. I hope your memory comes back so maybe they can find the perpetrators or perpetrator who did this. Do you have any more questions? Concerns?"

"Yes, lots. Why—"

"Please, get some rest. I gave you 10 mg of morphine, so it will help you sleep. You're going to need the rest if you want to leave as early as possible. Rest well, Gretan."

Once Alfreda left the room, I laid back and shut my eyes for a moment, hoping to remember anything I could. Nothing. It was a dark, empty void within my memories of yesterday. Nancy was still ringing a bell, but I could not remember how or when. For some odd reason, the first and only person I thought about was my father. It's strange because I never once thought about him in all the years he's been gone. I guess my consciousness triggered a deep thought about him. I thought that maybe he would still be alive if he never left. Keeping this in mind, I was not even sure he was still alive to this day. I guess it would be nice to have family look after me, considering what transpired earlier. Wishful thinking, I suppose.

****

A few hours passed, and I awoke from a morphine-induced sleep. It was now 6:50 a.m. on Friday morning. My confusion was still prevalent as my memory was starting to come back. I heard stories of memory loss, and quite frankly, I never easily believed any of them. I always believed it was a made-up thing that people embellished for attention. I never bought it, no matter how troubled someone's mind was. Naturally, I stand corrected on my prior belief in that notion.

About six hours ago, all I could remember was Nancy, and I was not even sure how she came up with that equation. I was not sure if it was the morphine or sleep, but something must have triggered a chemical or reset switch in my brain to allow the memories of yesterday to flood my mind. With my memory fully restored, unknown factors were still present. I still had no idea who or why someone clobbered me over the head, but I knew I had to find out.

A nurse knocked and opened my door. "Gretan?"

"Yes?"

"My name is Eliza. I will be your nurse for the remainder of your time here."

"What happened to… Alfreda, I think?"

"She had to leave early for personal reasons, so I took over for her."

"Oh. I guess that's a good thing. She wasn't the most pleasant nurse from what I took in my concussed state."

"Yeah. She tends to rub people the wrong way at times. She's a good nurse. A little rough, but she's one of the best. Anyway, how are you feeling, and what would you say your pain level is?"

"A lot better. I would say it's a three, maybe four. But I'm fine."

"That's good news. I'm not sure if Alfreda told you, but the colony sheriff is here and wants to speak with you. If you are

151

unable to talk and need more time, we can afford that. You let me know whenever you're ready."

"Oh, okay. You can send the sheriff in; I'm ready."

"Okay, I'll be back with him in a couple of minutes."
I knew I had to think quickly about what I was going to say to the sheriff. Telling him the truth was out of the question, for he would probably label me as a psychotic or something worse. I felt like this was not going to go my way as I observed a tall, burly sheriff enter my room with a solemn look upon his face.

"Hello, son. My name is Sheriff Johns, and I am the colony sheriff in these parts. If you're ready, I'm going to ask you some questions about the events that occurred last night. I understand you may not remember all the details, and that is fine. However, the more details you provide, the quicker and easier it becomes for the both of us. Deal?"

"Yes, sir."

"Well, all right, son. This should only take about ten, maybe fifteen minutes."

"I'm ready whenever you are sir."

"Okay, first question. Where were you last night?"
Be smart about this. "I was at Hugo Lake."

"What time around was that?"

"It was right before 8:00 p.m."

"Okay. Now, son, be honest here. I need you to tell me the truth. Exactly what were you doing there, and what were your intentions?"

Here we go. I guess I was totally oblivious to the fact that I would be asked this question; hence, I did not have a clever answer. Obviously, I could not tell him the truth because it was not believable to an ordinary person. Quickly, I had to think of something fast and believable. "Well, this is kind of embarrassing. A girl… I was to meet a girl for the first time whom I met on a dating application. I know, it's a stupid thing to do."

Sheriff Johns flashed a quick smile. "Fair enough. Okay, what happened from there?"

"I saw a car two spots over from mine when I pulled in. I figured it was her. When I got out of my car and approached the vehicle, it seemed like no one was in the car. I then walked back to my car, and… that's all I remember."

"You never saw this female you were supposed to meet?"

"No, only pictures from the computer. I doubt it was even her now that I think about it."

"Does this female have a name?"

Here we go again. "A name?"

"Yes, son. A name."

Think quick. "Rachelle. Her name was Rachelle."

"Okay, do you have any other information on this… Rachelle girl? For example, an address or phone number?"

"No, we never exchanged that information. We agreed to meet there."

"Now you wouldn't be withholding any other pertinent information from me, would you?"

"No. Absolutely not."

"I'm tracking. You look like a bright young man, and your record with the sheriff's office is completely blank. If you don't mind, I'm going to give you some advice that may save your life down the dusty road. Next time, meet someone you've never met in a lively place. It's a lot safer. Hanging around that lake at night is not the safest first date. Going back the past five years, we've seen an uptick of drugs, robberies, sexual assaults, and even deaths around that lake. If you ask me, that lake is no good. I feel like it's *cursed* or something. I'm not one to believe in that stuff, or, what do you call it, superstition? Yes, that's it."

"Deaths? As in, murders?"

"A couple. Even suicides. It's a sad place. Some folks around here believe that it has something to do with the water. But that's an old myth."

Instantly, I thought of Dani. I wondered if he was aware of her death by drowning. I did not want to ponder that thought too much or ask if he knew. I let well enough alone.

"I never knew." I quickly readjusted myself to a more comfortable position. "I suppose I won't go there after dark again."

"Good choice, son." Sheriff Johns took a deep sigh and started up again. "Here's the thing about this case: I'm baffled… I guess I can say. Your keys and wallet were still with you when you came here. So, the intent was not robbery. It's like… they clubbed you for whatever reason, like it was a game of some sort."

"I don't know, sir. I wish I had more to share with you."

"You have no enemies or anyone that would want to do harm to you, do you?"

"No, sir. I always mind my own business the best I can."

Sheriff Johns shook his head. "I thought so. We'll figure it all out, hopefully. One last thing. We had to tow your car to our impound lot. Since you were a victim of this case, we are not charging you any fees. You'll need to find a ride to our office one way or another. The receptionist here has your wallet and keys. The lot closes at 6:00 p.m. today, so if not today, tomorrow, I suppose. Good luck, son. We'll keep you updated if we find anything. I must admit, cases like these are rarely solved. Behind the randomness of it, I'm not too optimistic. No offense, son."

"No, none taking at all. Thank you, sir. I appreciate your time."

Sheriff Johns had exited the room as Eliza returned to check up on me. "Still feeling a lot better?"

"Much better. I'm ready to get out of here. Is that going to be possible?"

"Very much so. You suffered a minor to moderate concussion to the back of the head. It appears that the assailant struck you with a brick or rock of some sort, thus needing a few staples to the scalp. The doctor wants you to take it easy for at least a week. That means no physical activities, no work, and no alcohol due to the prescriptions you will have to take. Easy enough?"

"I can manage that."

"Good. Unfortunately, the earliest we can release you is 8:30 a.m. So, sit tight, relax, and rest up before that time. It'll only be another hour or so. Hang tight, young man. You'll be out of here in no time."

22

The Bishop takes Command

It was now 8:30 a.m., and I was ready for my discharge. According to Sheriff Johns, I was to somehow acquire a ride to the impound lot to pick up my car. Calling for a taxicab was realistically my only option due to my phone being left in my car. Well, at least I think it is, considering I could not remember any of the five phone numbers in my contacts. As I got up to stretch, the room door opened, and Eliza popped in.

"Ready to go home, Mr. Hutchen?"

I scoffed in joy. "You better believe it."

"Good," Eliza walked toward the sink to rinse her hands and smiled, "because we need the bed. No, I'm joking. All you need to do is go see the receptionist. She has your prescription and any other belongings you may have left. Good luck to you, Gretan. I hope they find whoever did this to you."

"Thank you… for everything."

"My pleasure. You know, I like your first name. It reminds me of one of the most courageous friends I've ever had. Her name was Grenlynn."

"Oh, that's nice. She sounds like a very special person."

"Yes, she was. She passed away five years ago, at the age of thirty. Leukemia had taken her. She was diagnosed when she was eighteen years old. Many times, she fought the good fight and seemed to have a grasp on it. Then one day, it came back full circle. No one saw it coming, and when it did, it was fast and ruthless. I guess it was just her time."

"I'm really sorry to hear that."

"She was always happy, full of life, and had that never-quit attitude to live another day. It's not fair, I guess. We were all with her when she passed by her bedside. We, as in family and friends. I tell ya, it's a sad thing to witness something like that."

"I know what it's like to lose somebody. That has been the story of my life. My birth mother left me in a park bathroom right after I was born. I legally died, and I was brought back to life. I was supposed to have many disabilities, but I overcame them all. My adoptive mother was murdered when I was ten years old; they never found the killer. Then, my adoptive father abandoned me about two weeks later—I have never heard from him since. Now, my grandmother passed away six months ago—she was all I had left.

"Life isn't fair, but we need to keep moving and fight that good fight, as you mentioned. You know, my grandmother always used to say, '*Be thankful for all the bad days you have, because you'll never appreciate the good ones.*' Keep your chin up; the rest will take care of itself."

"Wait a second, your adoptive mother. I think I remember that case in the news." She quickly snapped her fingers. "I knew your last name sounded awfully familiar. I was about fifteen years old and remember that case ringing through the news stations like wildfire. For the life of me, I can't remember her first name."

"Florence. Florence Hutchen."

"Yes, that is it. Now I remember. I'm so sorry that happened. I bet it was a horrible ordeal, I imagine. It's a shame they never found the killer. I remember my mother thinking that it was your father. He abandoned you shortly after?"

"My father was a suspect at first but was quickly eliminated. I remember it all like it was yesterday. And yes, he left for good shortly after. He's thought to be somewhere around Peninsula. Who knows."

"Unbelievable, just unbelievable. Well, I wish nothing but the best for you. Good luck again and take care of yourself."

"The same goes for you. Thanks again for the treatment; I can't thank you enough."

"My pleasure, sir, my pleasure."

Eliza was that type of person who people wanted to know, identically similar to Nancy. I felt I could easily relate to her in many ways. I would have loved to continue our conversation and share stories, but I desperately wanted to get home, relax, and brainstorm what possibly could have happened last night. Besides being a little groggy and weak, I wanted to take a nap in my own bed. Plus, I needed to get my car back as soon as possible.

An elderly woman who appeared to be in her late seventies greeted me as I approached the reception desk. If I had to guess, I would say that she has probably worked in this hospital for over forty years. She simply portrayed that warm, nurturing personality that you would want to see in humble people.

"Good morning, sir. How may I help you today?"

"Good morning, ma'am. My name is Gretan Hutchen. I'm checking out. I believe you have a few items for me."

"Oh, yes. Gretan Hutchen. By chance, were you related to Florence Hutchen at all?"

It seems like everyone here knows. After all, she was a nurse here. "Yes, ma'am. She was my mother."

"Oh, dear. I am so sorry. I knew Florence very well. We used to work together here over twenty years ago. You know… I was at her wake and funeral. I think I remember you there." The lady paused for a moment as she was seemingly lost in thought. "Of course, you were a lot smaller and younger, but I remember you. She was such a fantastic lady."

"Thank you, she certainly was. Small world, huh?"

"You're telling me." The lady then went to the counter behind her and grabbed a bag. "Here is your stuff that you asked for. Your keys, wallet, and prescription are all inside. Do you have a ride to go wherever you need to go?"

"No, not yet. I was wondering if you would be able to call a taxicab company for me. I don't have my phone on me, so I'm completely helpless right now."

From the corner of my eye, I could see Sheriff Johns talking to a hospital worker, as it was evident that he noticed me. While the kind lady was sifting through a binder of telephone numbers, he strolled over and decided to strike up a conversation with me.

"Hey, son. Did you get your discharge?"

"Yes, sir. I just need to get a cab, and I'll be on my way to the impound lot."

"Well, I'm about to head that way toward the station. I can give you a ride in my cruiser if you would like."

What a nice man. "Really?"

"Yeah, sure. Anything to help."

"That is a kind gesture, sir. I will take you up on that offer. I need to let the receptionist know that I found a ride, and I'll be ready to go."

"Sure thing, son. No rush at all."

I pointed over to the lady at the counter. "Pardon me, ma'am? I don't need that cab ride after all. The sheriff is going to give me a lift to where I need to go. I appreciate the help, though."

"No worries, young man. Have a great day!" As I started to walk away, the lady stopped me in my tracks. "Sir, wait a second. I forgot to give you this. It was left behind by the people who brought you in, and they wanted you to have this."

I reached over and grabbed the envelope. "Thank you. Did they happen to leave a name?"

"No, sir, not that I'm aware of."

I nodded my head and went about my business. It was a blue envelope with my first name only on the cover. I was not sure what was inside, but I was certain it was a note of some sort. Considering I had fabricated the whole story for Sheriff Johns, I had no need to show him this envelope or let him know about it. I was not ready for a hundred more questions, and this letter could unweave my story like no tomorrow.

As the sheriff and I walked out to his cruiser, nothing was said until we both were fully inside. "Any big plans for the day?"

"No, not really. I'm just going to rest and take it easy. That's all I can pretty much do."

"It would be wise to do so," Sheriff Johns paused for a minute, rubbed his chin ever so slightly. "You know something? I didn't want to say this earlier, but I actually met you a long time ago."

Here we go again, I thought. "No kidding?"

Sheriff Johns smiled as his eyes remained steadfast on the roadway. "Oh, yeah. Rookie year. I was the lowest deputy on the totem pole when your mother's case happened." I could tell he loved his career, while the glow in his eyes hit a peak when he mentioned *'rookie year'*. "I remember that case like it happened yesterday. Those were the days. It's funny how time goes by so fast, and you remember certain things."

I nodded my head in agreement—polite reasons. "Time does go by fast." Three times in the span of twenty minutes, my mother was brought up. Maybe it was a coincidence; maybe this world was smaller than I could ever imagine. I did not want to talk about my mother again, but this man was doing me a huge favor. If I were to be rude and smug, prudence would not be on my side.

"You know," Sheriff Johns chipped out while adjusting his window, most likely for fresh air. "You know, I was recently thinking about taking a look at the case once more."

Taking another look at the case—it would not be unnecessary, maybe a waste of time. "Really? Let me ask you— do you think it's solvable? I mean, all this time, nothing. Don't get me wrong; there is no one more eager to see this all come to an end. I feel after all these years, you'll have a better shot at hitting the lottery."

Sheriff Johns stood still for a brief second, calmly collecting his thoughts. "You know... I think it is solvable. Over twenty years ago, we didn't have the advancements that we have now—DNA reliability, fingerprint recognition, et cetera. Maybe the detectives assigned to the case missed something the first time around. It's possible. I know both detectives are deceased now, one from a heart attack and the other from natural causes. The case has been in our cold files for probably eighteen years. I have a few good detectives who may be able to see the details in a *different* way. Hell, you never know, son."

His idea was intriguing, but I knew better to get my hopes up. "I mean... I'm all for it. I hope it does become solved one day. I won't get my hopes up." I paused for a moment and stared out the window. "I'm tired of false hope. My grandmother used to say, *'Hope for the best, expect the worst, and accept the outcome.'* I guess that's all we can do these days. Accept the outcome."

"I understand where you're coming from, son. I surely do." Sheriff Johns wiped his nose and once again readjusted his window, seemingly trying to get a grasp on a tolerable temperature. "There is someone I would like to talk to—I think he may hold some information that may be vital to this case. Actually…" He hesitated for a moment, as it was evident that he was unsure of his next words. "There is another one I would like to talk to. I talked to him before—around the time it happened, but nothing came about."

I shook my head in disbelief. New testimonies could lead to something breaking. "Okay, who are they? Do I know them?"

Sheriff Johns sighed deeply, finally deciding to close the window. "I would rather not say—you know, protecting the identity and privacy of these two folks is a big part of my job. If something were to come about it—say, information that was undoubtedly verified—then we could make it public. The problem is: we can't find this person, and they may have changed their name, and the other lives in Peninsula."

That was disappointing. "It sounds like you'll have a better chance of hitting a bullseye in the dark from twenty feet away."

He nodded his head in agreement. "I'm a pretty decent shot. But you're probably right on that, son. But it's still a shot." I had to admire the man for being optimistic.

"She didn't deserve to die." I blurted out as I was seemingly confused about what to say next.

"No, she didn't. No one does, considering the way we found her. That—"

"Please… can we change the subject?" I was done talking about this topic.

"My apologies, son. We're almost there—about two more minutes. Yes, sir. Almost there."

My anticipation of opening this envelope was killing me inside. The never-ending conversation about my mother was bittersweet—good points and awful memories were recognized. I figured that once I received my keys and had complete possession of my car, I would open it immediately. Finally, we were here. I could see my car in the front row.

"Well, son, here we are." Sheriff Johns happily spoke out. "Better than a cab ride, huh?"

I guess it was better than a cab ride. "Yes, sir. I can't thank you enough." I reached out to shake his hand. He willfully obliged and shook back.

"My pleasure, son. Before you leave, I wanted to say something quick. Your mother's death was not in vain. I know, I know… it's been twenty years too long for the culprit to still be out there. But I want you to know that I have two options here: give up on the case or do everything I can to fight this thing until the day I die. I choose to keep fighting. I will do everything I can until I take my last breath in this world to find your mother's killer. I swear to you, I will."

It's not that I needed to hear that, but in a way, I did. It made me feel good and restored the dignity that I feel in others. "Thanks, sheriff. That means a lot to me. You're undoubtedly a stand-up man." I reached out to shake his hand again and looked him in the eyes. "Much respect, sir. Thanks again for the ride."

"You got it. Take care, son." He is an easy man to admire. He was a respected member of the colony and appeared to be a rarity these days—a blue-collar, values-first, no-excuse, tough, son of a gun kind of man. It was simple to understand all the veneration toward him—I'm glad I finally had the chance to converse with him.

The impound lot was as *dead as a doornail*. Like counting to three, I was in and out, walking to my car, and ready to see what this envelope was about. Inside my car, there sat my phone—wedged between the center console and the front seat.

Four percent battery life and two missed calls. Gabby called again, and the other number was unknown; both called within three minutes of each other. Gabby at 11:57 p.m., and the unknown directly at midnight. I thought it was a little strange, but I didn't have time to ponder it. My focus was growing fierce for this envelope. I felt like I was riding my bishop piece in chess, about to slaughter my opponent's queen. Unfortunately, there is no time to read it now. The gate guard had a look of annoyance on his face, as he probably felt that I was taking too long to exit, so I exited and went on my way.

A short drive home, my house was exactly as I left it: locked, safe, and secured. It was that time—time to see what the contents within this envelope contained. The handwriting of my name seemingly gave the impression that a female wrote it—not that it meant anything. I can't remember the last time I was so eager to discover something new. It was a strange feeling. I sat down at my kitchen table and began to open it. As I suspected, it was a note. Short and to the point, it read:

Gretan,

> **You are easy to envy, and we are behind you. If you want to learn more, meet at the aluminum park bench next to the green garbage can at Old Falls Park. It's the only bench next to the can. 4:30 p.m., Friday. If not, 4:30 p.m., Saturday. Come alone and keep this to yourself.**

> **DO NOT SHOW ANYONE.**

> **PS – I know who assaulted you. This is not a ruse.**

Well, there you have it. This was huge. Absolutely huge. This game I was invested in suddenly became intriguingly interesting. Without a shadow of a doubt, I had no idea who could've written this letter. As dangerous as it can be, I knew I had to accept this anonymous invitation to Old Falls Park. Declining it would only pace me back two steps and further away from the answers I seek. Moving forward was my only option. Safety was also a matter of grave concern. For all I know, this could be a ruse for my supposed adversary to gain an upper hand. Strange people in a strange land seem to be the norm these days. Stay alert, pay attention to detail, and act fast if necessary. I had it down, and my optimism was brimming with surety.

I had time to burn, for it was only a little past 9:00 a.m. A part of me wanted to check up on Dani, but I had to put myself in perspective. My concussion was taking a toll on my well-being, along with the last dosage of medication I took a few hours ago. I needed a nap—a lengthy nap—so I could shake this headache and be well rested for the evening. I opened my prescription bottle, took two codeine pills out, and placed them on the table. I stared at them for a few seconds, pondering if it was wise to consume them. Pain pills and I have never had a coexistence before—never had a reason to take them. I've only ever heard stories of the effects they may bring: sluggishness, euphoria, restlessness, and vagueness, to name a few. I thought, *What the hell,* and swallowed them without fully thinking of the repercussions.

Thirty minutes later, I now understood how and why it's possible for people to fall victim to addiction. From one standpoint, they made me extremely sluggish, comparable to someone who had not seen sleep for forty-eight hours. From another perspective, I felt like I was on cloud nine. All my feelings and emotions turned numb—a complete absence from all my worries and cares. I was high. There was no way to over or underexaggerate that statement. My conscious was yelling that I needed to sleep, and it felt like some entity was controlling my mind. Sleep—of course, I remember what that was now. Directly after that thought, I must've passed out because that was the last memory I could recollect from that morning.

23

An Identity Revealed

He is me,
And I am him.
He watches me endlessly,
Ever so grim.

He stands in a corner,
Sometimes in obscurity.
Shaking my foundation,
Sharing my purity.

Will he ever leave,
I think nay.
We are both the same,
Till the end of days.

Summers like this were the best. Just the right temperature—not too hot, never too cold. I was casually taking a stroll through a crowded city street in a popular metro area. Where I was exactly, I did not know, nor did it matter. I felt alive. The city was booming. People were all around me, seemingly enjoying the sites and scenes that played into each other. Lovers were holding each other's hands, while kids were playfully running and messing around in their childish games. The aroma from numerous restaurants, coffee shops, and food trucks was prevalent, even with the faintest smell. A sudden gust of wind would convey the flavoring scent of barbecue chicken down a whole block, setting a chain reaction of whispers stating, '*Mmmm, that smells good.*'

Wow, what a magnificent eye piece, I thought as my eyes became glued to this beauty. Toward the end of the block, there was an old colonial-style house that was transformed into an intimate restaurant. This structure was like no other neighboring business regarding the simple notion of contemporary style. I was hypnotically drawn to the extensive mahogany double doors in the front of the entry. My eyes gazed upon the entrance, as each simple thought brought me one step closer to ingress.

I opened the right-side door, entered, and was immediately enamored by the interior's sheer allure. A short, red-haired young woman, who I assumed to be the hostess, immediately greeted me. "Mr. Hutchen, welcome back," the lady eagerly expressed as she quickly fixed her crooked collar on her dress shirt. "Your table is almost ready. Our staff is making the proper preparations for a lovely experience here. I do apologize for any inconvenience we may have caused—"

I mistakenly rudely interrupted. "Table?" I shook my head in confusion and brushed off a bead of sweat from my forehead. "I do apologize, but… table reservation?"

The ever-courtesan hostess gleamed a smile in my direction. "Yes, sir. Don't you remember, Mr. Hutchen? You called about an hour ago and made a reservation for two."

What was going on? Was I in the right place, or the right world, for that matter? This restaurant—I have never been here. A reservation for two, nonetheless. *Who would I invite?* Just act normal and go along with it. "Yes, the reservation." I retorted and humbly accepted.

The hostess grabbed two menus off the podium and smiled again. "Sir, if you would please follow me to your table. How are you on this lovely evening?"

"I am… okay, I guess. A little hot. You know… the weather."

"Of course, sir. I will grab you a couple of waters, and your server, Shelby, will be with you shortly. Would you like me to inform her to wait for your guest to arrive?"

Pretending I knew what was going on was an easy option. Certainly not the easiest to understand, but the easiest to execute. "Yes, please. I wouldn't want to be rude and order before my guest arrives. That wouldn't be prudent."

Again, where in the hell was I? I started to feel lost in some bizarre world that did not exist. The more I thought about it, the more I kept thinking about who was to be my special guest for this reservation that I had unknowingly made. Brian was an easy thought, or even Gabby. Beats me. Whoever it was, I knew I had to act accordingly.

From the distance, I could see the hostess walking back to my table with the waters in her hand. Directly behind her, a tall, peculiar elderly man was following suit. "Mr. Hutchen—your waters." She looked back at the old man and then looked at me. "I see your guest has finally arrived." The old man took his seat across from me. "I'll leave you two be. Shelby will be back to accommodate you two in a few moments."

I nervously kept glancing between the man and the hostess. "Um… I uh… yeah. Thank you."

I was silent at first as the man took off his long, pin-striped coat and placed his old, black flat cap on the corner of the table. Confusion, mixed with a little uncertain fear, is an easy way to describe how I felt. I could not keep my eyes off him. There was something about him—something familiar. Something so intimate yet so strange, it felt like this meeting was reconceived from something that happened many years ago.

"Hello, Gretan." The old man said while he swiped some dust off the top of his flat cap. "And how are we tonight?"

I was beside myself. "I… um. I am… fine, I suppose."

"Of course, you are. Everyone always seems to be fine when their conscious mind is fast asleep and their subconscious is experiencing the unimaginable through the dark maze of their unconscious mind."

I looked downward and thought for a second. "I um… I guess I'm a little confused. Do I know you? You do look oddly familiar."

"Confusion is an expectation for those about to learn. Soon, your confusion will exit all your thoughts, and your grasp for knowledge will fill an empty void within your soul. As for familiarity, we've met before—many, many years ago. You must've been in elementary school at the time—remember?"

Okay, this was oddly starting to creep me out. "My house. You came looking to speak to my father—but why?"

"I don't have the luxury of time to explain. There are other matters that need to be addressed before you wake up from this intuitive dream."

I had to ask. "Who are you?"

"That's more like it." The old man smiled as if he were awaiting that question. "I am the *right* to all your doubts and misgivings. I am the answer to your failures. I am the traveler who travels at night—roaming around your unconscious realm while trying to make connections with your conscious mind. I am the part of you that you'll never see while looking at yourself through a mirror."

"Okay. So, who are you?"

"Gretan, I am you. You created me during a time of tragedy. It was simply a way for you to understand the harsh realities that may travel down your path. I am your subconscious, and I am here now to show you what is to come. You may not like me or grow fond of my timing, but you will learn to accept me."

I did not know how to react or know what to say next. "Okay, you have my undivided attention."

"You see, we are in a dream right now. I get to play your realities, visions, and thoughts when it is necessary to do so."

I shook my head as if I were trying to knock something off my head. "Why does this dream seem so real? I mean, the other ones—I don't realize I'm dreaming until I'm about to wake up. But this… this is real to me."

"This dream only feels real because you demand it to be real. We are almost at the climax of your story—or your '*game*' as you like to call it. You are a major player right now. You may not know it or believe it yet, but you have the possibility to change lives. There is so much to learn, and deep down inside, you know it's true and will have the ambition to learn it and learn it well.

With learning comes failure. You will fail many times. You will also win fewer times. I am here to guide you and share lessons along the way."

"I… I don't really know what to say."

"You don't have to say anything. You just need to understand. Here, I have something to show you." The old man looked past me, then focused his eyes on mine and gave me a signal to look behind him. "You see that family of four sitting behind you?"

I turned my head around in a way that I wouldn't be noticed. I put my hands over my face for a quick second and was in awe of what I saw. It was Claire, her husband, Gabby, and Dani. "How? How is this possible? This can't be. Dani is—"

"Yes, Gret. She is, along with her father. You see, we are powerfully compelling together when we want to see a specific scene. Our mind always knows what is best. You may be asking yourself, 'Why are you showing me this?' Well, it's quite simple. I brought you here today to show you what once was. You can't change what happened in the past. But you, and you alone, can alter a diminished strain on two of the four."

I took a deep sigh and wondered if I would wake up soon. "You mean Claire and Gabby, right?"

The old man lightly hit his palms on the table and smiled. "See, we work well together. I will show you many other things so we can learn, understand, and act when the time is right. It won't be easy, for nothing worth fighting and working for ever is."

I thought deep and hard for what I wanted to ask next. "If you are my subconscious, then why do you show me night terrors?"

"A very good question, that is. Unfortunately, it is time for you to end this deep slumber. You will see me again, and I will answer that question when the time is right. Until then, wake up."

Reality came crashing down within a heartbeat. I awoke on my couch, sweating profusely as an ice cube sitting directly in the sun on a hundred-degree day. My head was pounding painfully hard. It was approximately 3:00 p.m., and I could tell the drugs had worn off during that dream. Besides the headache, I felt refreshed, as lethargy was no longer a thing. This dream I encountered was mesmerizing. My understanding of this whole conflict I was facing became a lot more transparent. I was caught in this '*game*', and I knew I had to endure everything that was coming my way. This meeting was right around the corner, so I knew I had to start getting ready—physically and mentally. It was almost time.

Think big,
Refrain small.
Die little,
Live tall.

Overcast, slight rain, and breezy. It was right above fifty degrees—a tad below the September average. I did not mind the cold weather, only the rain. Except for today. Rain, sleet, snow, or sunshine, it did not matter. Determination was the only thing that mattered today.

I was in *that kind of* mood today, I guess you can say. I assume that phrase can be interpreted in many ways. In my case, I always took it as a way to *get stuff done* with no nonsense in between. The time was now 4:15 p.m., a short way away from arriving at Old Falls Park. What a place to visit, I must say. My fondest memories of this park date back to when my mother used to take me. From the picnics to the simple walks amongst the wilderness area, they all had a special place in my heart. I wondered: *Would this visit be as special?*

I suppose I was quite lucky, for there was not a car in sight. The rain has taken its toll, I figured. The less company there was in the park, the better it was for me. I parked in the first row, deployed my umbrella, and took a quick look around at the benches and pavilions—desolate as can be. Admittedly so, I was a little leery and nervous. The bench by the green garbage can was null of company. According to my watch, I was three minutes early. The idea of this being a ruse started to manifest more than I had hoped for. Regardless, I sat down on it and checked my phone. 4:26 p.m. My watch was a minute faster than my phone. At that moment, it happened.

"Gretan?" An unfamiliar voice called me from three feet behind as I turned around and stared in confusion. "You are Gretan, right?"

My eyes were locked on this middle-aged female. "Who are you?"

The female became quickly irritated that I didn't respond with a one-word answer. "Just answer my question—you are Gretan, correct?"

Instantly, it hit me. In my brief conversation with nurse Alfreda, she mentioned that a lady with another man dropped me off. It was her; it had to be. I just had that feeling. "Yes, I am Gretan." I quickly stood up. "Who are you?"

The lady quickly interrupted. "Look, we have little time. My husband needs to speak with you. I need you to take me to my house, like, right now. I did not drive here."

"Wait, just a minute. I'm not going anywhere until—"

"There is no time for this—any of this! We need to go now. Please, just trust me. If we don't go now, they may see us!"

"Who?"

"I think you know damn well who. Either leave without me now or take me with you. There is no time!"

I could see the fear within her eyes, as I was sure she could see mine once she stressed a quick exit. It was a fear so deep and real that no chances could be taken. I knew I had to act fast, for I wasn't positive about what I was dealing with. I had no choice. "All right, follow me."

I thought, *I must be crazy for doing this.* Keeping pace toward my car, she was seemingly looking in different directions all around her. I dared not ask any more questions before we fled. My mindset was set straight to avoid conflict and abide by her confession to flee fast. Her expression was enough to make me believe that this was no joke. Once I started my car, the conversation started once again.

"Look," she eagerly said as she buckled her seatbelt. "Just take a right once you exit the park. You will drive for about four miles. I'll let you know when the next turn comes. Just listen to me, and this will go smoothly."

"Okay," I responded in a curious tone. "Are you going to tell me who you are and what's going on?"

The lady scoffed like she was annoyed to repeat herself. "I told you that my husband needs to talk to you, and I was sent here to guide you. Please, no more questions. All will be answered when we arrive at our destination."

I shook my head while keeping my eyes on the road. "I get that, but… well, can you tell me anything?"

"For crying out loud, I already did. I told you we needed to leave quickly and that my husband wanted to talk to you. I was specifically instructed not to answer any questions other than that."

"Wait. Does he *need* or *want* to talk to me? You said two different adverbs."

She looked at me in annoyance. "You pay attention to details—that's pretty good. In the meantime, just shut up and drive."

I slightly chuckled and smiled, trying to turn adversity into humor in this peculiar situation. "I feel that I'm getting a raw deal over here. Am I?"

"I told you, no more questions. Just drive. It'll be worth it for all of us."

"All of us?"

She looked at me once again—this time with a blank stare. "Just drive."

To say this car ride is awkward is the understatement of the year. Here I had this pregnant lady, most likely a few years older than me, instructing me to make right and left turns to some unknown destination. Whatever this situation may be, it was making her perturbed to the point in which she was glancing in the side mirror every five seconds. I still wanted answers. As much as I wanted her to talk, I did not want to upset her even more, so I kept quiet.

The ride was quite long, roughly twenty miles, until we pulled into our destination. I did not say anything, but something in the driveway snagged my attention right away: the maroon coupe, plate number GEK-8837. It was evident that this lady and her husband were my mysterious stalkers. The riddle to the car was halfway solved, at least I thought.

"Listen," she said before we exited the car. "Just follow me and take a seat on the couch. Don't look around outside or make it obvious, like you've never been here. He will be with you shortly. Understand?"

"Oh, I understand. Act like a robot—I shall."

She got out of the car and looked my way through the car. "Are you always this difficult?"

I exited the car and glanced right back at her with a smile. "I won't answer any more questions until I speak to your husband." I was anxious beyond all measure. Not nervous, just anxious. This meeting would go one of two ways: great with endless possibilities, or not so great and an utter waste of time. I leaned on the greatness, for I was optimistic.

The lady opened the front door as I followed. "Please take a seat on the couch. Make yourself at home as I go grab my husband."

"Thank you."

Once she left the room, my eyes were wondering all over the place. Living room décor is a good indication of what kind of people take up residence in an unknown place. Clearly, I took them as 'artsy' people by the canvas oil paintings and framed movie posters all over the walls. They were collectors—anyone could tell by the sheer number of expensive pieces they possessed. I liked that a lot. I knew they weren't low-life, petty people who were a drain on society. Anyone with a collection like this values the beauty life has to offer. Then again, maybe I was wrong.

A man walked in carrying a couple of beers and sat down on the loveseat across from me. "Hello, Gretan. I'm glad you were able to make it here. Now, the first thing I… my apologies." The man quickly reached out with a beer in his hand and offered it up. "Beer?"

Why not. "Sure. Thank you."

He took a quick swig and wiped his chin. "So, as I was saying, it was a bold decision to accept my invitation. I respect that. To be frank, I'm not sure I would've accepted it."

"You're saying that this was a mistake on my part?"

The man waved his hand in a convincing manner. "No, no. Well, let me rephrase this. Yes, and no. It is how you decipher it and how far you are willing to partake in what is to come our way."

I took a quick sip. "Our way?"

"Well, yes. In retrospect, the three of us and... your friend."

"Friend? Wait... who are you referring to?"

The man took a long sigh and finished it with another drink. "Your Sleepless friend. What is her name?"

Here we go. "How... how do you know about her?"

"Because Gretan—I am like you."

"You mean to tell me—"

"Yes, I can see them too. It's a rare gift we have. Of course, some may call it a curse—I call it a gift. It runs in the family. Grandfather had it, mother had it, I have it, and I suppose if my wife has a daughter, she will have it also." The man got up from his loveseat and peered out the blinds in the window. "Yeah, funny old life."

I decided to turn the tables a bit. "So, what kind of man seeks another man out, sends him an invite to his house, gives him a beer, and won't even tell him his name?" I wasn't finished. "Oh, and may I mention, the man supposedly took him to the hospital after he was ambushed and knocked out by some mysterious perpetrator. Lest I forget, I've spotted your car not once, not twice, but three times around places I was. So... are you going to tell me who exactly you are?"

The man halted his view from out the window and returned to his seat. He stared at me for a couple of seconds while shaking his head up and down to a slow beat. "You certainly don't know who I am, do you?"

I rolled my eyes in slight confusion. "No, should I?"

"Well, by appearance, I would've guessed that you may have *some* idea."

"No, I have no idea whatsoever."

The man then pressed his hands together and smiled tremendously, as if he were about to give away a grand prize of a million bucks to some lucky winner. You could tell he was waiting and had planned this moment out for some time. "Okay, now bear with me here. I have no reason to lie or make up fairytales. My name is Carey—Carey Kline."

I hesitated for a second, scoffed, and took a short breath. "You mean… I… Kline, as in my—"

"Yes, Gret. I am your grandmother's son and your mother's brother. Or, if you prefer, your Uncle Carey."

Veracity Verified

I was speechless. Flabbergasted, if I'm to be honest. Even if I had something intelligent to say, I wouldn't even know where to start. The credibility gap from what I've known to believe to his astounding confession drew narrow. From no family to family, this admission came to me like a bolt from the blue. Last night, my opponent made their most decisive move. Today, this was my counter.

"Gret," Carey said, looking me in the eyes, his sincerity gleaming like light in a mirror. "Do you understand the solemnity of all this?"

I covered my face for a moment to soak it in. "I mean… I… I do. How do I know you're telling me the truth?"

"Your grandmother's name was Patricia. Your mother's name was Florence, although we used to call her 'Flo' for short. Your father's name was Jarrick—not a *chipper* fellow." Carey tipped his head. "Would you like me to continue?"

"Where have you been the last… thirty years?"

Carey took in a deep breath and flashed a smirk. "It's a long story, Gret. I guess some of it was my fault, but not really. I loved my mother and sister. Unfortunately, your grandmother had crazy ideas, and Jarrick was constantly brainwashing your mother. It was your grandmother who had forsaken me. Before I get into any further details, what do you know about me? The whole family? Have you ever heard anything?"

"Absolutely nothing. I never even had suspicions that the family would go to the grave with a secret like this—until recently. When my grandmother passed, I was with her in her last moments. The hardest few minutes I've ever had to endure. She took my hand, held it close, and, harboring a barely audible voice, whispered something to me I'll never forget. Something about me possessing a rare gift and *'to protect'*… I… I didn't know what she meant. Fast forward a week or two later, and I understood what she meant by a *rare* gift. But the whole *protect* thing threw me off for months—until I found something buried in her possessions. It was her journal. She went to great lengths to keep it hidden, as was evident by keeping it stashed within the confines of another book." I shook my head. "I never figured out why she did that."

Carey interjected. "I know why. Your grandmother knew about the evil that lurks among us. She wrote about it and kept it well hidden because she knew that they always knew our business when they wanted to know so."

"They?"

"You know—and don't pretend you don't. I know for a fact that you've had a few *experiences* with them. They've been scouting you and your house, trying to get a good read on you. Habits, timing, sleep schedule, and so forth. At Claire's… a few times, mind you. I know you've seen Sebastian, Rodick, Lucian, and a female… whom I've never seen before but who seems to be around you the most. She must be a new recruit—hence her many outings… I don't know. As a matter of fact, she's the one who knocked you in the back of the head at Hugo Lake."

I was astounded by this admission. "Are you sure you had nothing to do with it? After all, your car was there. Your plates were the last thing I saw before the blackout."

Carey slowly nodded his head and briefly smiled. "No, not at all. Saffron and I were tracking them that night. We hid out under a pavilion by the lake. They were trying to kidnap your Sleepless friend that night. Fortunately, your presence deterred them, and you paid the price for their failure. After it had happened, they fled too fast for us to even interject. That's when we scooped you up and rushed you to the hospital.

"You may not understand this, but since that day you interfered with their routine to kidnap, they slapped a big bullseye on you. If they find out I'm helping you now, I fear Saffron, and I will receive the same." Carey got up again and peeked out the blinds. "Hell, I wouldn't be surprised if they already knew I was helping."

I had to ask the million-dollar question. "What exactly are they?"

"Beyond a doubt, I hoped you weren't going to ask me that." Carey returned to his seat, pounded a third of his beer, and took a deep breath. "But since you asked, I'll tell you what I know. We call them the Ancients."

"Yes, grandmother referred to that name also in her journal. Who, or what, are they exactly?"

"Of course, as I was saying, they've been around for hundreds and hundreds of years. They were once people like you and me. Living a life only to die and become a Sleepless—kidnapped and turned to what they are now by their leader, Aza Azura. How they originated—only one man truly knows, so he claims he does. I haven't seen that man in over fifteen years. His name is Quintt. He taught me everything I needed to know about our abilities and the Ancients. I was seeing him regularly around that time, helping me grow stronger with every visit. Then, one day, he vanished like a *feather in the wind*. Maybe they got him; I don't know."

I scratched my head as my ears begged for more information. "Okay, what do they want?"

"Well, for starters, they want your Sleepless friend, and possibly you. Many times, when they hunt these Sleepless, they sense an *ability* within them. Some of them have certain abilities, or powers, I guess you can say. From what Quintt told me, there are five abilities: future sight, past sight, vision, sound, and the most gifted of all, mental and physical telepathy. As the years go by, their faction grows. Once they become what they are, death is not a thing to them."

"What do you mean by that last statement?"

"They live an eternal life at the age they convert. They don't sleep, they don't need to eat or drink, and they keep living their lives under the obedience of their master, Aza Azura. Their end game—I suppose it is calamity. I could be wrong, but most likely, I believe I'm right."

"They can't be killed?"

Carey took a long, hard look at the wall, evidently thinking of his next move. "They do have one poison, one weakness."

"Which is …"

"The atomic number of 46, palladium. As mildly scarce as it is these days, that is the one thing that can turn them to ash."

I lightly scoffed and chuckled for a moment. "Palladium metal turns them into ash? What then? Do they fade away in the wind? This now sounds like something from a fantasy tale. I can't—"

Carey was quick to interrupt. "Gret, this is no joke. I wouldn't have you come here if it wasn't. I am serious as a heart attack. You obviously have a caring nature towards this Sleepless at the coffee shop. If you stick by her, they may eventually dwindle off. However, you need something for protection. Hang tight for one second and let me grab something." Carey got up and left the living room in a hurry. I had a lot more questions—too many to count. I wanted to know everything. Their movements, their demeanor, their hostility, and most of all, their abilities. I wondered if Carey was the right person to fill me in. I wanted to believe him, and I truly did. However, this man waited so long to contact me and claims my life is in danger. To me, that seemed kind of odd and suspicious of some possible scheme at play.

Shortly, Carey returned to the room with Saffron and a couple of what looked to be *daggers* in his hand. "Check this out, Gret." He slowly handed me one in a brown sheath. "I want you to keep this one. It needs a good sharpening, but as it is now, it'll still do the job. You'll need to keep this at a close distance from now on."

I reluctantly took the blade out of respect. "I'm… I'm not a killer."

"No, you're not." Carey clapped back as he took the other blade out of its sheath and ran his finger on it. "But you'll need to defend yourself if the time comes. Make no mistake, it's coming."

"You mentioned names earlier for some of these… ugh, people. How do you know so many?"

Carey briefly looked at Saffron as she presented a half-smile towards him. "My wife and I had some—I guess you can say—dealings with them before. I'm only alive right now because of what I did. That was a long time ago, though. It was nothing to be proud of, but I had to do what I had to do to stay alive. Please, let's not delve into that subject too much."

I knew. It didn't take a genius to figure it out. "You're like me—the ability. You traded locations of Sleepless for your lives, didn't you?"

Once more, Carey and Saffron stared at each other for a second with looks of regret. "It was a long time ago," Carey said in remorse. "Whenever Aza needed to add to his *family,* he would reach out to me for locations of Sleepless. In return, he kept us alive."

I had to ask. "You didn't tell them about Dani's location, did you?"

"Dani? I'm guessing that is your Sleepless friend?"

"I'm not friends with her; I never even talked to her. I know that she's—" I instantly stopped myself for what I was about to say. Keeping Gabby and Claire out of this was paramount in a situation that I knew very little about. "I just know she goes to that coffee shop a lot."

"To answer your question, no, I did not share her location with them. If I were to guess, she has a gift—ability. They are hard on her trail, and Aza will never back down until he has what he wants."

I clenched my hand into a fist as I felt a little adrenaline rush. "Well, he's not going to get what he wants this time."

Carey shook his head and smiled. "That's my boy. My *good boy.*"

A bell instantly chimed within my head. "Oh, so you left that note on my car?"

"I sure did. I witnessed you put a monkey wrench into their poor attempt to kidnap her."

I looked down and spoke silently, "They better get used to it."

"I like you boy. I truly do. I always knew we would meet someday. Fortunately, that someday is now under *not-so-pleasant* circumstances. I wish the family was still around—and we all got along with one another."

I almost forgot to ask. "Speaking of family—why did they banish you?"

Carey pressed his hands together and took another quick drink. "As I may have mentioned before, it was your grandmother who banished me. You see, this intuition we have runs deep in our family. I have it; she had it—and did nothing with it, may I add. Her father also had it, and somehow the adopted son of my sister has it, and it's as strong as ever. Some are born with it already enhanced, while others need it enhanced by someone who possesses it. I was born different, with it dialed close to the maximum. Your mother didn't have it or even know it existed. So, your grandmother spun up accusations and stories about me falling into hard times with drugs and alcohol. She sold it well to your parents. Flo and Jarrick were straight as an arrow; they never drank or did any of that *bad* stuff. Well, your father used to, but went sober for a long time. Long story short, they influenced your grandmother to cut loose any affairs involving me. Hell, they even threatened me with harassment charges. Your grandmother then—"

Something was off, so I had to interrupt. "Wait, it doesn't add up. Why would having this ability cause you to be an outcast?"

Carey pointed to me and chuckled a bit. "I was just about to make my point. You see, when you were a little tyke, your grandmother informed me and swore up and down that you had our ability, but it was dormant. I didn't know how she thought about this, and she wouldn't even tell me or explain her reasoning. All I knew around that time was that I wasn't allowed to visit her house anymore." Carey shrugged his shoulders in confusion. "Whatever. A couple days go by, and I decide to stop over at her house to talk to her about it. Instantly, she cursed at me for stopping over and refused to allow me to step inside. We chatted briefly on her porch for about ten minutes, all about you. I wanted to enhance your abilities. Her, not so much. I felt that not enhancing your gift in the present time was exactly what it was—a waste. Her, on the other hand, feared for her and your life if it were enhanced. She felt that the Ancients would catch on and put a quick end to us all. I never thought that would be the case. Of course, she disagreed, which led to our demise. Her, your mother, and Jarrick all got together and offered me a lump sum of money if I were to move away. Financially, I was going through a hard time, so I took it. I regret it this day ever since. But that's life for you. You live and learn."

I saved the most burning question for last. "Did the Ancients kill my mother?"

Carey stared at me long and hard as if he was trying to read my mind. "I'm not sure, kid. I'm not sure at all."

"Fair enough." I wasn't buying his answer. "So, what do we do now?"

"You keep doing what you've been doing. Stay alert, remain cautious, and follow her every moment you can. You're already invested, and there is no backing out now. Your presence alone makes them leery and throws them off a little. They'll never admit it, nor will they see it in their eyes, but they fear you as much as you fear them. Never take them for granted. They are unpredictable."

After a moment of silence, their house phone began to ring. "Carey," Saffron called out his name after viewing the caller's identification on the phone. "It's coming up as an *unknown number.*"

"It's them." Carey said while drifting his attention my way. "They know you're here. Don't answer it, Saffron."

My nerves were starting to get to me, for I did not understand what this meant. "How do they know?"

"They always know, Gret. They always know." Carey set his beer on the end table and stood up. "I think its best that you leave now. Can you meet here tomorrow around the same time?”

“Umm … sure. May I ask, if they know I’m here, is it not safe for us? I mean… I guess I’m trying to think of a logical way to stay safe.”

Carey walked over to me and unexpectedly wrapped his arms around me and gave me a hug. “We’ve already crossed the threshold of safety. They know. Now, we must prepare for our next move.” He shook his head and stared right through my eyes in solemnity. “There is no safety now.”

That message right there was a gut-check. The meeting had now come to an end. We had agreed upon another meeting for tomorrow at the same time. An unexpected rush of adrenaline was flowing through my blood. It’s an odd feeling—something I wasn’t used to. I knew what I had to do. I was ready to turn the page and fight for what is right in this world. I’ve never been one to fight, or confrontational, for that matter. However, this meeting changed it all.

**

7:55 p.m., Friday night, Lake Hugo. My obligation was to do the same thing as last night. This time, maybe I will not end up in a hospital again. I was a little wiser and more cautious this time around. Not to mention, I had the palladium blade that Carey bestowed upon me. If tonight was anything like last night, Dani should be here any minute for her descent into the lake. Luckily, the rain had seized, and there was not a cloud in the sky. It was a perfect night for a not-so-ideal situation I was living in.

I took refuge under the easternmost pavilion, which enabled a clear view of the entrance to the lake. It was an easy site to see, but also an easy site to be recognized. I didn't mind, though. Considering the beautiful night, others were out enjoying the natural splendor of moons and stars reflecting off the massive lake. About 150 yards away, a couple sat on a quilt, holding each other close—most likely stargazing. A man and what appeared to be his son were sitting on a dock near the west side—night fishing in hopes their luck was plentiful. Splendid sites on a gorgeous night were great to witness, but I was about my own business—for I started to feel her warmth inside me.

From a distance, I could now see her in the same exact direction and routine as last night. I maintained a steady state, watching as her footsteps portrayed a vision of her walking on water. The closer she got to the entrance, the closer I moved to the edge of the pavilion, as my eyes were steadily focused. No diversions were noticed—only the small crowd, which took no notice. As last night, she edged up to the entrance, looked up, returned her eyes straight forward, and strolled into the lake once more until she was fully submerged. A sad scene for the faintest at heart, I must say.

For a couple of minutes, I stood there, staring at the spot in the lake where she went under. I felt like I was in a surreal dream, filled with sadness, agony, and regret. If only I had known her before her demise, maybe I could have made her see life differently. Maybe she, Gabby, and I would've all been great friends who could depend on each other when times were tough. Maybe I could have saved her life. Undoubtedly, it was a reach to think that, but I could not help but think of the possibilities of the past. Locked in my emotional daze, I became unaware of my surroundings as a hand violently grabbed me on the shoulder.

"I knew I would find you here," Carey blurted out rather quietly. "You can't stay away, can you?"

"You scared the crap out of me!" I said as I was trying to catch my breath.

"You need to be more careful, kid. You're doing right by keeping tabs, but if I were one of them, I may have had to take you to the hospital again. Or, you may have been a corpse." Carey paused for a moment and was glancing around my hip area. "Where's your blade?"

"Oh… that… my blade. I must've left in the car—by accident, of course."

Carey shook his head. "That's not an accident, kid. I don't think you've grasped the seriousness and relentless malevolence they strive for. I don't want to see you dead." He put his hand on my shoulder and tapped it a couple of times. "Take it everywhere you go now."

I agreeingly shook my head. "Yes, sir. I will. It won't happen again."

"It better not. The living, the Sleepless, and the Ancients aren't done with you yet. I see something in you—something I haven't seen in a long time."

"And what is that?"

"Change. I feel that whatever the outcome is, you will endure, and the change you will present to others will go a long way."

"Those are kind words. Thank you. I must say, I didn't expect you to be here tonight."

"I figured you may need some backup, you know. Come on." He tapped my shoulder once again. "Let's get out of here."

Minding my surroundings was never my strong suit. I suppose it was a wake-up call for me—stay vigilant and be on my toes at all times. Carey's surprise visit and words resonated with me in such a way that reality was undoubtedly real. I could've died tonight, or maybe become a hostage, or another trip to the hospital. The *change* comment hit me the hardest. If his words rang true, what change could I possibly make if I wasn't always ready and adapted to my surroundings?

Speaking of surroundings, our two cars were the only ones left in the parking lot, as I could see them from a distance. The young couple and the father/son fishermen duo had left for the night. Lake Hugo was as quiet as could be—only to hear our footsteps inching closer to our cars. That all changed, and Carey halted his brakes and reached his hand out for me to stop as well.

"Shh," he whispered quietly. "Do you feel that?"

I did not understand him. "What am I supposed to feel?"

"Fear, anger, malice, agony. They're here."

"How do you know?"

Carey bent down to pretend he had to tie his shoe. "Don't look right now. 150 yards to your three o'clock position. The entrance to the pines—that's them."

As I said before, keeping tabs on my surroundings wasn't my thing. However, viewing a scene indirectly without being noticed seemed to be my forte. With my head down, I scratched the back of my neck and slightly to my right. "I don't see anything—or anyone, for that matter."

"They're there, trust me. Just keep moving towards the parking lot, and we should have no issues. They are like a pride of lions. They will sense your fear if we were to run. Hell, they probably already sensed your fear tonight."

"I'm not afraid."

"Yes, you are. Even if it's a little, and rightfully so. I can see it in your eyes." Carey paused for a moment and scoffed. "They scare me."

I shook my head in subtle disagreement. "Let's get out of here."

"Right, kid."

Carey wasn't wrong, but he wasn't necessarily right either. I was a little afraid, but in a primal way. My fear pumps my adrenaline, and my adrenaline drives me to carry my confidence in any endeavor. This was new territory—a territory in which I needed to adapt quickly. I thought about that notion until I was halfway home; then, my phone rang.

I picked up my phone to see it was Gabby. "Hey, Gabby. What's up?"

"Hey, Gret!" She replied in a jubilant manner. "What are you doing right now?"

I had to think of something quick. "I was, uh… heading home from the store. You?"

"Fun. I'm not sure if you heard, but I'm home now for good. It's a long story—well, it's not that long. Anyhow, I'm at the Meeting House right now. Would you like to join?"

"I was in the hospital last night and was just going to rest. But, uh, yeah. I can use a little company."

"How… why? No, we can do this another night."

"No, I insist. I'll be all right. Trust me."

"Why were you in the hospital?"

"It's a long story. I'll tell you about it when I get there. Hang tight, and I'll be there in a few minutes."

"Great! I'll be waiting!"

I feel my kindness has always been a great weakness for me. Staying at home and getting some good shuteye sounded better than spending time with Gabby. It was nothing against her as a person; I was emotionally and physically drained from everything that transpired today. She was my friend, and I knew she needed a friend tonight.

8:43 p.m., Friday night. From the outside, the Meeting house appeared to be the place to be tonight. Rightfully so, it was a mildly cool night set on the moons being full. Full moons have always intrigued me. I've heard stories about how they insinuate superstition and carnage among the worst people. Nevertheless, I was never one to be superstitious—maybe just cautious and modest in my beliefs.

Inside, the Meeting House was as advertised by the full parking lot—packed to the brim. Gabby was easy to spot, considering she was flying solo. At the bar, she was lonely, with an empty chair next to her. She was like the last time I saw her—holding her Malbec like it was a crux. From a short distance, I could see Kristina taking an order for some patrons. She was so tall that I couldn't help but smile and shake my head. Jokingly, I walked right up to Gabby's side and planted myself right next to her, pretending not to notice her.

"Hey!" She joyously shouted out and threw a one-armed hug my way. "Man, I missed you!"

I threw my arm around her and patted her on the back. "I missed you too. So, how's it been going?"

"I'm done at Hoborg... for the time being. It was too much for me. I, you know, needed a break." She took a sip of her wine and continued. "This hospital story—I want to know all about it."

Think. Think quick. "It's actually the strangest thing. My garbage disposal was leaking water, which was pretty bad. So, long story short, I slipped from the water and hit my head on the counter. I barely remember anything from it. It's the damnedest thing. The doctor put me on some strong pain meds, which means I can't drink any alcohol unfortunately." I thought about that last statement for a second. "Well, maybe one drink."

"Wow, what a story." Gabby signaled to the bartender as she made her way towards us. "May you please get this man a rum and soda." She looked back at me. "That's what you want, right?"

"That's fine. Thank you." I turned my attention back to Gabby. "So, what else is new? I'm sorry about you leaving Hoborg."

Gabby took in a deep sigh. "Yeah, me too. Now I get to wallow in my self-pity with alcohol. It is what it is, I guess."

It was quite evident that a problem had manifested within Gabby. Glossy eyes, slightly slurred speech, exuberant hand movement, clearly drunk. Gabby was depressed and using alcohol as a disguise once again. "What time did you start drinking?"

Gabby refrained from looking at me and stared at the bar top. "Umm, I think like… five. Maybe six. But I swear, I didn't drink much."

I had to diffuse her away from this activity. She needed to stop. I hated to suggest it, but it had to be done. "Hey, Gabby. I have an idea. How about we finish these drinks and get out of here? I was thinking—maybe my house. You know, maybe catch up a little bit someplace where alcohol is not served."

"You don't have any alcohol at your house?"

"No, but I have plenty of water." *Man, I sounded like an old man.*

"Well, I have to work in the morning anyway—why not?"

Willingly, that went a little easier than I thought it would. As much as I did not want to entertain a drunk Gabby at my house, it was the right thing to do for a friend. She desperately needed someone, and I was here for her.

Before we were to leave, Gabby had to use the restroom, so I thought it would be a noble idea to pay for her bill. Five glasses of wine, one rum and cola, and thirty-eight dollars. It was the least I could do to ease her sadness.

Gabby started to walk back from the restroom and took her seat next to mine. "Let me pay my bill, and we can get out of here."

"No need to—I already paid it."

Her eyes grew wide, as it looked like she was about to cry. "Gret, you didn't have to."

"I know, but I wanted to. Let's go."

She lunged toward me and presented me with a giant hug. "Thank you. You're seriously the best, for real."

I shrugged off her generous comment. "Eh, I'm… okay."

We were on our way. During the ride, not much was said other than a miniscule conversation. The alcohol was starting to subside, leaking sadness into her bloodstream. She was sinking into her bad habits, but for her, it's what took the pain away.

We arrived at my house in under five minutes. Once inside, she took a seat on my couch as I went to fetch her a large glass of water. She needed it, and lots of it, if she was going to work tomorrow. To my surprise, she made herself feel at home while she was browsing the pictures on the wall.

"I love your home," she confessed, and I turned my way with a smile. "It's very accommodating."

"Well, thank you. I try my best to maintain it." I handed her the glass. "Here is your water—you're going to need it."

She graciously accepted. "Thank you. You know, I must say, you do a great job at maintaining it." She returned to the couch and smiled immensely at me. "Don't take offense, but you are quite the… as they would say, *lady* decorator. I would've guessed a female was living here based on the interior decor and tidiness. Not a typical *man* house."

I smiled right back at her. "I get that a lot, actually. No offense taken whatsoever."

"Keep it up. It's a great quality for a man to possess."

Deep inside, I was dying to know more about her move from Hoborg. "So… what about your recent move? Tell me all about it. That's if… you want to tell me."

Gabby rubbed her right eye and sighed. "Yes, I will tell you. I know I can trust you. I won't sugarcoat it or make excuses." She paused for a few seconds and kept a stoic stare at the floor. "I tried to do something to myself while I was away.

Well, kind of… I don't even know anymore. I hate even saying the word… makes me sick." She took another deep sigh as a tear rolled down her eye. "I took a bunch of pills, but it was never my intention. I knew the consequences, but I didn't care. I wanted to be pain-free.

"An hour had passed—at least it felt like it. My roommate found me on the floor and quickly called emergency services. The odd thing is that I heard everything that she was saying, but I could not comprehend why I was on the ground. My eyes couldn't even move. They were fixated on a spot on the wall. It felt like I was *dead,* but not.

"So, they overnighted me at the hospital—the whole thing was a blur. The next thing I knew, my mother was at my bedside in the morning and told me she was taking me home. I remember that car ride home—ridiculed for what I've done to myself and what a waste of money it was for me to enroll this semester. Her condescending words were all I heard. She never comforted me, consoled me, or even tell me that *'Everything will be all right.'* She didn't care. She never does. I don't know anymore."

In the middle of her confession, I knew what I wanted to say. It was unconventional, but it needed to be said. "Listen, I can give you advice that 99 out of 100 people would give you. I'm not going to do that with you. I think you need a quick reality check."

"Okay, I'm all ears. Go ahead."

"If you're thinking of harming yourself, then do it. If you're thinking of living, then do it. If you do choose to end it all, remember this: Once it's done, it's done. You can't take it back. Think about your life, and then think about the lives of all the unfortunate people who continue to live in poverty-stricken conditions from the wars of the past. Some of these people wish they were dead, but they keep living. Why? Because sometimes it's the only way.

"So, here you are—healthy, some school under your belt, food on your plate, beautiful on the inside and out, and maintaining a job. Even though your mother shuns you, she still loves you immensely. I know she does because she told me the day you left for school. Your mother is different, and she is hardheaded. Hell, most parents are, and rightfully so, to keep their kids on the path to success.

"Hands down, Gabby, you are loved by many. You will always have people there to lend you a shoulder and have your back. I know we've known each other for only a short time, but I'll always be there for you."

Gabby hung her head low and slowly nodded. "You know, you're right. I've never had someone tell me to kill myself, though, but I see where you are coming from. You have a flattering way with words and a unique perspective. I appreciate that."

"You'll get through this; I know you will."

"Yeah, I believe I will. I need to work on myself when it comes to raw emotions and impulsive tendencies. I hope the relationship between my mother and I will veer off the broken path. Wishful thinking, I guess."

"Just give it time. Time and patience heal all wounds."

Both of our heads perked up as my house phone began to ring. "Do you want me to answer that, considering the phone is right next to me?" Gabby asked.

"What does the identification say on it?"

Gabby stood up and looked. "Unknown number. Maybe it's—"

I hastily interrupted. "No, don't answer it. Just let it ring."

"Are you sure? Let's have some fun. Let's say—"

"No, don't."

"All right," Gabby smirked, "too bad!" She answered the phone. "Hello?" She paused for a moment as a look of confusion overtook her. "Hello? Who is this?" She then hung up the phone.

"Damn it, Gabby," I lashed out in anger. "I told you not to answer!"

"Geez, I'm sorry. I wanted to have a little fun."

"Well, did they say anything?" I knew who it was.

"No. All I heard was heavy breathing, muffled by strange noises."

Not good. Not good at all. It was them, and now they knew she was with me. Whether or not this meant imminent danger for her, I had no clue. I should have never met with her—I knew it would be a mistake. I had to get her out of here as soon as possible, and time was wasting. "Say, I hate to do this, but I'm not feeling too well now—you know, the concussion and all. I'm going to have to take you home if you don't mind."

Gabby shrugged her shoulders in despondency. "Well, that's fine. I was hoping to stay a little longer, but I suppose I need to go home. Thanks for having me over. I love your pad. We'll have to do it again sometime."

"For sure. Hang tight for a second; I need to grab something from the bathroom." Of course, that bathroom trip was intended to take two pain pills, with the intention that they would kick in by the time I came home. I needed sleep—good, restful, uninterrupted sleep.

The drive to Gabby's house and back was exactly what it was—an uneventful drive home. I think my advice resonated with her in a way that she would consider life's options before doing something rash again. Once I sat back on my couch, those pills were starting to deliver a knockout punch to me. I knew I was on the brink of comatose—hardly recollecting the events from the day. I sat there, staring at the picture of my grandmother and I on the wall. That was the last thing I remembered from that night.

Such a sterling mind,
One made for the ages.
Never once to doubt,
One whom can turn pages.

Denial shall be ignorance,
And Ignorance is always bliss.
Reality will become certain,
By the bitter touch of her kiss.

She is always watching,
Sometimes she will wait.
Steadfast as can be,
The bearer of unwavering fate.

There she was, again. "We meet again, young man." The pale lady said as she brushed back on her hood. "'Twas to be expected, as well as our next meeting. What do you think this meeting is about?"

"I… I don't really know. Where are we? Wh—who are you again?"

"As I mentioned before, prior to this dream, our meetings will revolve around transparency. You are now in the second stage—translucency. Do you understand yet?"

"This old house next to us—it looks familiar. What does this have to do with translucency?"

"An excellent question always propels the mind forthwith. You see, think of your translucency as a frosted window in your bathroom. Light will pass through, but you are still unable to see the pureness that shines on the outside. Imagine someone holding up a scripture to the outside of that window. You can see the placement and movement of it, but you are unable to decipher the letters and words in an astute fashion. You can see the truth, but your understanding of it is not fully developed yet. It will come in time. In time, my blessed child."

"But ... I ... I don't understand the meaning of all of this."

The pale lady put her hand on my shoulder and smiled. "You must enter the house. It is my duty for you to understand what is to come. You see the end, but your grasp on it tends to slip. Like others, your life is inevitable. You shall see." The lady looked to the sky as if she had to voice something from up above. "When the waters rage and the stars are shining brightly in a clear, black sky, we shall have our final meeting."

I joined her by looking up toward the sky for a moment, turned my attention back to her, and she was gone. Here I was, standing alone outside an unknown house that looked oddly familiar in an unexplainable way. The entrance door was red— a *turn-of-the-century-style* door with three micro-viewing windows spaced evenly at six feet high. A magnificent hand-carved design of a lion man, a sheep man, and a hybrid rooster man were perfectly centered right below the second window. Directly in the center of all three, a shield with what looked like a family crest was perfectly placed on a platform. All three presented one hand on the edge of the shield as they were joined in unity. The more I stared at it, the more it left me wondering what it meant. As old and peculiar as this door was, it shone a warm and inviting energy toward me as I grasped the brass handle to open it.

Once inside, I was certainly in unfamiliar territory. Directly to my right, stairs led down to a large basement. A robust smell of mildew lingered in the air, undoubtedly originating from the basement. The lights in the basement were off, but I could easily see the old sage-green carpet that seemingly had no end.

Straight ahead, six weathered linoleum steps presented the entryway to the main level. It looked as if no one had entered this house for some time; hence, the steps were strewed with dust balls and black dog hair from severe neglect. Up the stairs, an empty dining area cluttered with dilapidated furniture was directly to my left—seemingly uninviting. To the right, a short hallway was a gateway to other rooms. A two-level staircase lay directly to the right, most likely leading to bedrooms. I elected to pass the staircase and started to hear voices to the room up ahead on my left. In the hopes that the people inside wouldn't notice me, I stood firmly outside and peered inside. To my shocking surprise, scattered within the family room were my grandmother, mother, father, Jacob, Jaret, Carey, and a few others whom I did not recognize.

I stood by the entrance with hopes that eyes would be set on me with a warm welcome to take a seat and enjoy the moment. Nothing. No eye contact, no greetings, or no mentions to each other about my arrival. It appeared as though I was a ghost that was invisible to the naked eye. I walked in, and just like I was standing by the entrance, no one took direct notice of me or acknowledged me. My mother was seemingly quietly arguing with my father about something, most likely about work or money. Jacob and Jaret were both locked in a conversation with Carey, as deep focus portrayed all three men. My grandmother was sitting next to my mother—expressionless, staring off into blank space.

I planted myself in an empty chair, about two-arms' length away from Carey. I sat and observed everyone around me, still unnoticed. A thought began to trigger within my head if I was in a bazaar time warp and this may not be my family—at least not yet. The whole scene was strangely ambiguous, with no one knowing what might happen next. Just as I thought, things were about to become even more odd.

From across the room, my grandmother started to shake her head and close her eyes every few seconds. It looked as though she was trying to get a word out as her lips were starting to move up and down. An epileptic seizure, I thought. I got up from my chair and gave quick aid to her. "Grandma, are you okay?"

She responded in gibberish.

I put my hands gently on her shoulders. "Grandma, please answer. Are you okay?"

Gibberish once more.

I lightly shook her. "Grandma, you're scaring me."

Her slight convulsions seized, and she looked up at me with a menacing face. "Lies… lies."

Confusion overtook my senses. "Lies? What are you talking about?"

Her voice started to accelerate in volume. "Lies… lies… lies."

I took a quick step back. "Grandma, what do you mean?"

She took a quick glance around the room and returned her stare towards me. "Lies... lies!" She yelled, sat up, and began to walk toward me. "Lies! Lies! LIES! He tells LIES!"

Frightened and inching back, I suddenly bumped into a guest. I turned around to apologize and instantly recognized the guest. There he stood, that eerie old man donning his pin-striped suit and flat cap—my subconscious, as he claimed. For a split second, he stared at me and gave me a peculiar smile. Instantly, I woke up in another intense sweat.

29

By Any Means Necessary

6:30 a.m., Saturday morning. I was well rested and, surprisingly, in minimal pain. After waking up around 2:00 a.m. from my mysterious dream, I managed another four plus hours of sleep, which was surprising. Maybe it was the medication, or maybe it was my deep sleep; however, I did not know where I was for a couple of seconds when I woke. I could not explain it, as many of my dreams fell into obscurity and confusion.

I got out of bed and was ready for the day. I had a couple things on my agenda: breakfast at Claire's and another meeting with Carey. I had to keep a close eye on Dani, and my meeting with Carey was essential in hoping he figured out a plan for these Ancients.

It was right before 7:30 a.m. when I arrived at Claire's. My bank still had an hour and a half until the doors were open, so killing time with a big breakfast was easy to do. I thought about using my keys and leaving the papers on my supervisor's desk, but I had time on my hands to stop in and say hello.

Nancy caught my attention the moment I entered. "Hey, Nance. Good morning to you."

Nancy smiled back in a joyous manner. "Hey, Gret! It's good to see you again. Up early today, aren't ya?"

"Yeah, I'm normally an early riser. Say, I ran into Gabby last night at the Meeting House. Is she in yet?"

"Not yet. She'll be in around nine, I believe. Just in time for the brunch crowd. Claire is here—in the back doing payroll."

Terrific. I was a little nervous to interact with her considering the last time she practically chased me out, pleading for me to tell her about what I saw. After my conversation with Carey, I knew it was vital to keep a *hush status* regarding what was and is going on to avoid danger. Unfortunately for Gabby, it may have been too late for her to answer my phone. Only time will tell.

Considering the early breakfast crowd was moderate, it was easy to get a good seat and fresh coffee expediently. I knew Dani wasn't here yet, but I needed a piece of mind to confirm my suspicion. After Nancy came over and took my order, I got up and started to make my way towards the restroom. I was right; she was not in her usual seat. I stepped into the restroom, did my thing, and made my way back to find a surprise waiting for me at my table. Claire.

"Hello," she said with a half-smile. "How are you today?"

I smiled and scratched my head. "I'm fine, I guess. Been under the weather as of late."

"So, I've heard. Gabby mentioned something about a concussion?"

"Yeah, you know. I slipped on some water from a leaky sink and hit my head on the countertop. I was in the hospital overnight, but I'm fine now. I guess I need to take it easy."

A look of concern overcame her face. "What night was that?"

"Um… Thursday night. Yes, Thursday."

"And I take it you hit the back of your head?"

"Yes, right square in the back."

Claire shook her head in an arrogant manner. "That's interesting. Did you see the sheriff blotter in the morning newspaper about a young man who was attacked at Hugo Lake by an unknown assailant and sent to the hospital?

She was good, too good. "Um, no. I did not read that." *Quick, think of something.* "You know, I think I do recall hearing something about it on the local news early Friday morning. It never phased me, I guess."

"Ah, the local news. You watch the news a lot, don't you?"

"I try to." I had to stop this after expressing an obvious sigh. "Look, I'm not sure what you're trying to get at. Between me hitting my head, the attack at Lake Hugo, concussions… I simply hit my head in my kitchen. I don't know what else to tell you."

Claire chuckled for a moment and slapped her knee. "You're too funny. I'm not trying to make comparisons between two totally different stories. I'm not trying to put you in a corner. I find it a strange coincidence. That is all."

I knew she was full of it, but I pretended to believe her. "I apologize if you took my words wrong. I just—"

She quickly interrupted. "Please say no more. I actually need to apologize to you. Look, I'm going to be honest with you. There is something about you, and I can't put my finger on it. To be honest, I'm not sure how I seemingly feel about you. And don't get me wrong, it's not a thing between dislike and like; I think there is something about you that makes me wonder.

"My daughter has taken a liking to you, which makes me want to know you a little better. I must understand that you are a customer, and I must treat all my customers with respect and dignity. With that being said, I am sorry for that little outburst from the other day. It wasn't my place, and it won't happen again."

"You have no need to apologize. No hard feelings at all."

Of course, Claire had too much pride to walk away without saying what she needed to say. "Glad to hear that. I am sorry, but I still think you saw something in here."

I scoffed and let out a little chuckle. "Claire, I don't know what you want me to tell you, but I didn't see anything in here. I don't even believe in that stuff anyway. Maybe, if I saw something, I would tell you."

"Would you?"

It was at that moment, sitting across from me and asking that question, that it happened. I felt the warmth; it was becoming stronger by the second. Much to no surprise, Dani made her way through the door. This time, she did not bypass the main dining area to get to her usual seat. She took two steps in, looked around for a second, and walked right over to the table next to Claire and me. She stood over the seat from across my view, took a hard look at her mother, and sat down, staring straight ahead.

Mesmerized, shocked, confused, and excited—all these emotions hit from every direction. It felt like I was in a trance, with the air being sucked right out of me, preventing me from answering her question. For a moment, it felt like I didn't even know where I was or who I was. I couldn't even remember what Claire had asked me.

Claire got a little louder as she took notice of my obvious state of mind. "Gret? Gret! Are you going to answer my question?"

I quickly shook my head back and forth and snapped out of it. "I'm… I… wait—what did you ask me?"

Claire looked at me like I was a fool. "Really? Do you have dementia or something?"

Suddenly, it all came back to me. "Oh, your question. You were asking me if I would tell you if I ever saw something in here."

Her eyes became distinctively wide. "That would be the one."

I made it obvious so Dani would hear loud and clear. "Yes, Claire. If I ever saw anything out of the ordinary in here, I would have no qualms about telling you the truth."

Claire slapped both hands on the table. "Okay, I'll leave you be. Sorry for bothering you. Enjoy your breakfast."

From the corner of my eye, I could see a smile on Dani's face when Claire started to lose her patience. That smile alone put me at ease. I felt bad for lying to Claire, but in a way, I did not. This is a place of business, and a customer should not feel pressured or hounded about questions that they do not want to answer. She had to let it go, and it probably would not be easy for her.

I could see Claire go back to the back room of her office. Once that happened, Dani stood up, pushed her seat in, and planted herself in the same seat that Claire sat in. If I had learned anything from my thirty-two years, it would be that nothing surprises me these days. Except this. This was on a level of surprise and belief for me to initially comprehend. I was nervous and knew I couldn't make it obvious that she was sitting across from me. My composure was maintained for the time being.

Dani looked me square in the eyes. **Why are you following me?** Her voice echoed inside my head. **If you're wondering, I can communicate with you inside your head, and you can also. So, why have you been following me?**

I was beside myself. "It's not that—"

It's not... what? Don't make it obvious you're talking to me. Try inside your head.

I was lost in a dark closet without a flashlight. To say I was nervous felt like an understatement. I was beyond nervous, as I could feel a bead of sweat run down my right temple. I tried to do as she said, but not a word or a thought felt like it was going through. I had to cover my mouth to speak. "I'm trying to, but I don't know how."

Here, lay out your hand on the table, and let me help.

I took a quick look around and nonchalantly followed her advice. She reached out and placed her hand on top of mine. At first, her hand felt like a block of ice. A couple of seconds had passed, and that ice instantly turned into a comforting and warm feeling. It was a feeling I've never felt in my whole life.

She took her hand off mine and smiled. **Okay. Try now. Just think of what you want to say and then say it in your mind. You'll hear yourself in your own mind. It's tricky at first, but you have the strength to do it. I sense it.**

I closed my eyes for a moment and remained calm. *Can you hear me now?*

Dani instantly smiled. **You got it. See, it wasn't that hard, was it?**

No, not at all. I must say, this is pretty amazing and surreal.

Yes, it is. This is a first for me—you know, talking to a real person since... well, you get it. Say, how can you see me?

I couldn't stop smiling inside. *Well, I have a gift. To be honest, I'm not sure if it's a gift or a curse. I see people who have passed who remain in this world. There are very few in between, but occasionally I can sense and see them. You're the first I've communicated with.*

Do you know who I am?

Yes, I do. Your name is Daniella—Dani for short. Your mother is in the back room, I think, and your sister Gabby works here also.

A look of surprise overcame her face. **How did you know that?**

Well, for starters, you probably know that I've been here a lot during the last week. And... I've hung out with Gabby a couple times already. She showed me a picture of you two together. So, I put two and two together, and... there you have it.

Wait, you're dating my sister?

I scoffed out loud and took quick notice that I should've done that in my mind. Luckily, no one noticed it—at least, I thought. *No, Gabby and I are just friends.*

She probably likes you. It's always been easy for her to fall for handsome guys like yourself who give her more than two minutes of their time.

I felt my heart pounding faster and faster. *Thank you for that compliment. I must say, you are... beautiful.*

You are very sweet. She paused for a moment. **So, you've never interacted with one before as you are with me?**

Once. I tried to interact with a young boy but ended up scaring him away. I believe he was terrified at the fact that I noticed him.

Yeah, I would probably be scared also. Why do you think I ran into the woods while you were following me in your car?

I apologize for that. It was the only way. I... never mind; it's nothing.

No, please tell me.

I can't right now. It's not that I couldn't; I didn't know how to tell her.

You can. One way or another, you will.

What does that mean?

Dani reached out her hand, directing me to do so also. **Here, let me see your hand again.**

I eagerly obliged as she set your hand on top of mine. This time, it was different from the first instance. There was no warmth to be felt, only an ice-cold hand. As transfixing as all this was, I was not ready for what was to come next. At first, I felt it in my chair. A low, yet subtle, shake came from underneath as if it were a quake. Next, a split-second tremor violently shook the foundation of the whole building as everyone took serious notice. Dani quickly removed her hand and remained silent. In the background, voices were heard about their concern about the tremor, as quakes around our colony were not a normal reality. I looked around, pretending I was in disbelief to sway any fault that could have been blamed on myself.

Claire was standing by the register with a bemused look on her face. "Gret, did you feel that?"

I knew I had to play along, like I was startled. In retrospect, I was. "I did. It must've been a quake. I can't say I've ever felt one before." Dani sat there with a smile on her face.

Claire looked away from me and quickly looked back. "Yeah, me neither." She paused for a moment, and her eyes grew narrow. "Strange, isn't it?"

I shook my head. "I guess so." I quickly shifted back to my mental focus with Dani. *What was that?*

I guess you can say, like you, I have a gift. I can see the past within others. I tried to go back a few days within your past to answer my question that you couldn't tell me. Although it didn't work with you. You have, like, some kind of block. I never knew that was possible.

Wait a minute, you've tried this before? I guess I'm confused on how you would know this because, from what I gathered in a short time, you've had no interaction with the living before me.

No, I've tried it before. I did it to my sister once while she was taking a nap at home. She never knew, and the room didn't violently shake like it did. Once I was in, I was in her memories. That shaking you felt was me exerting everything I had to try to pry into your memories.

Wow, that was intense. You know, your mother is on to me—or us. I meant 'us' as in that she doesn't know it's you.

Yeah, I've gathered that already. My mother is an enigma. Borderline crazy and insane, if you ask me. I laugh it off now, knowing what I've become.

Understandable. I believe she has it in for me.

Nah, she likes you. If she didn't like you, she wouldn't even talk to you. Trust me, I know. She never liked any of my boyfriends or even boys who were just friends. Not to change the subject, but can you tell me what you were starting to say about following me in your car?

I knew I had to, and after what occurred, it made it that much easier. *Okay. This isn't easy to say, but I'm not the only one following you.*

A subtle look of bewilderment and terror came over her face. **I was afraid that's what you were going to say. I've noticed a woman and a couple of larger men seem to know who I am. Am I right about that?**

Sadness, but mostly concern overcame my thoughts. *I wish I could say you're wrong, but I can't.*

Who are they and what do they want with me?

I took a deep breath and let it all out. *I'm not sure exactly who they are or what they are. I know that they aren't human like I am. Maybe they were before; I don't know. I know all this because of the couple of resources I have. They are known by people who long ago came before us as the Ancients. From what I understand, they are trying to kidnap you to convert you to one of them. I know it sounds crazy, but I have no reason to lie.*

Okay, I guess I'm a little skeptical, but I never thought I would be what I am. Are they some kind of, like, cult?

I'm not really sure. I wish I knew. I have to meet with my uncle later about this. He knows more than I do about all this, and his help is what we need right now.

We?

Well, it's not in my nature to sit on the sidelines and let this happen—especially to you.

Dani smiled immensely. **Okay, what do we do now?**

I never thought of an answer to this question, but I knew I had to use some quick thinking. *Right now, I believe you aren't safe here. If it's fine with you, I need you to come back to my house with me. It's the safest place I can think of.*

How much danger am I in?

I wish I had a straight answer. It may be a little, none, or a lot. But we should leave here as soon as we can.

May I ask a question?

Of course.

Why would you possibly sacrifice a lot and do this for a stranger you've just met?

A sudden jolt of adrenaline ran through my spine, triggering a warm sensation. *Because Dani, this is now my duty, and I'm here to protect you by any means necessary.*

30

The Truth Within Her

Huge. This was a huge step. Having direct contact with Dani was my most decisive move in this game. It was bold, but I knew I had to do whatever it took to protect her. My confidence and optimism were brimming, but whatever Carey's plan was, it had to make sense. Introducing her to Carey was a little nerve-racking, but it was my only choice. Considering her vulnerability, it may work against us or may not. She was now by my side, until life decided otherwise. This game was now in full motion, and it was moving rapidly. It was their turn to make a move, but not if we counteracted first.

It was around 8:30 a.m. The bill was paid, and Claire had left to pick up Gabby for work. Of course, Claire could not resist the temptation of favoring me with a non-verbal smirk before she left. She was obviously upset, and I could not blame her. I know what it is like to look for answers that come to no avail. I felt for her, but it's the way it had to be.

Dani opened the car door and made herself comfortable in the front seat. "How long of a drive is it to your house?"

She was now speaking to me directly, which made me a little confused. "Very short, maybe ten minutes or so." I knew I had to ask. "Say, I'm a curious man, so to speak. I guess what I'm trying to say is that I didn't know our communication was a two-way street. Can others hear you speak out loud, or do they have to be like me? Can others not like me see you open imminent objects such as doors?"

"No, they can't for both. Even though we are face-to-face, I am in a different realm. You see and hear both of them—others can't.

"Interesting. I guess it's true what they say: You learn something new every day."

"I guess so." She turned and looked at me while I was driving. "How old are you?"

I kept my eyes on the road. "Thirty-two years old."

"Your name is Gret, right?"

"I take it you've been listening well at your mother's place."

"It's the only thing I can do. To live vicariously through others is all I have. Do you live with your mother and father?"

"No, my mother is dead and my father… my father is… gone. My mother died while I was young, and my grandmother raised me. She's passed too. It's just me these days."

"Interesting."

"Interesting? How so?"

"No reason."

It felt like a chilling response. There was no sympathy, no empathy, and no emotion whatsoever. Her *interesting* comment somewhat flabbergasted my mind—not setting right with me. I don't know; maybe she knew something I didn't know. Maybe she was a little *rough on the edges. Or* maybe it came with the territory of who she was now. Regardless, I thought it might be best if the conversation ceased until we arrived at my house.

Fortunately, my house was the way I left it. I pulled in my drive, and before I killed the engine, I decided to do a 360-degree look out my windows to check if danger was lurking. Nothing—a good sign thus far. Dani sat there, looking straight forward in some sort of trance. With her eyes wide open, it looked as though she was sleeping awake.

"Dani?" I asked as she maintained her position. "We are here."

Her stare did not move an inch. "It wasn't supposed to be like this."

"What wasn't?"

Suddenly, her head slightly shook as she awoke from her state. "I'm sorry, I must've spaced out."

"It's all right. Would you like to come in?"

No response. She seemed strangely reluctant to exit my car. At first, she placed her hand on the door handle and froze. Maybe she was sensing fear, as her trust in me was not fully there. I got out, rounded the car from the rear, and opened her car door.

She turned to me and smiled. "You passed the test."

"What test?"

"The gentleman test. I forgot what it felt like to have a gentleman open a door for a lady."

I smiled and offered my hand. "I wouldn't have it any other way."

That comment alone lifted a huge weight off my shoulder. I felt more inclined and relaxed, knowing that her comfort level was rising. Nonetheless, it was a great feeling.

I opened the front door; she stepped inside and seemed taken back. "Your home… it's… it's beautiful."

"Thanks. It was my parents' home, and my grandmother practically raised me here."

"They did a good job." She walked over to my couch and took a seat. A sudden look of sadness overcame her. "It wasn't supposed to be like this."

I walked over to her and sat next to her. "You said that in the car. What does that mean?"

She looked down and turned my way. "What does what mean?"

"What you said—you know, 'It wasn't supposed to be like this.'"

A look of confusion sprouted on her face. "Did I say that?"

"Yes… twice already."

"Here," she said, reaching out her hand with an intention to gain mine. "Let me show you."

I hesitated at first. "I thought it doesn't work on me."

"On you, yes. But I can show you my memories." I reached out my hand as she took hold of it. "Take a deep breath and relax."

All of a sudden, my mind was placed in a deep, lucid dream state. Like Claire's, my furniture was shaking as I could hear a glass fall off my coffee table. My body was sitting on the couch, but my mind was at Hugo Lake. I could see and feel everything—the warm breeze, the smell of fresh-cut grass, and the birds chirping relentlessly. I casually walked over to the lake and stopped short at the shore. Emotional pain was weighing heavy on me, and the depression within was uncontainable. I suddenly felt the urge to take off my shoes and walk in to soothe my pain. I got to about neck deep, and something overcame me. It was a feeling of relief, as the pain was starting to subside. I stretched out my arms, took in a deep sigh, and tears were starting to roll down my eyes. I was born again, baptized with a new look on life from the pureness of the lake. Joyous laughter had overcome me as I felt that special feeling. That feeling of *"Maybe life isn't that bad after all."* I was alive, and it felt good, until something happened that I wasn't anticipating. Suddenly, my body started to convulse, and my mind was absent as control over my movement was gone. I was having a grand mal seizure. Slowly, I started to go under—I knew I was about to drown. Once I was fully submerged, Dani took her hand off mine, and I snapped out of it.

She looked at me with utter concern. "Did you see it?"

Breathing heavily and trying to catch my breath, I was in a state of shock. "You… I… what was that?" She nodded her head and didn't say a word. "You… suicide. Gabby was right. You didn't—"

"No, I didn't. But that's what they all think."

"How long was I in that memory?"

"A minute, at most."

"It felt like ten minutes. I really don't know what to say. Wow."

"They always do. This… what we have here right now is very real. The spirit realm is real." She paused for a moment. "Now that you know, would you like to hear what happened that day?"

"Um… I mean, sure. If you would like to tell me, that is. If not, I understand."

"I've never had a chance to tell anyone, so I will now." Dani closed her eyes for a moment and took a deep breath. "When I passed, I did not know that I was deceased. One minute, I was standing near the deep end of the lake, and the next, I was in a dark room with a subtle, ambient light bulb hanging from the ceiling. I thought maybe I blacked out cold and was taken hostage somewhere. The room was tiny, almost the size of a small shipping container. It was shaped in a rectangular shape, with a locked door at each end. I sat there, completely helpless and lost. I remember that the only thing that was on my mind was my sister. I missed her and wondered if I were ever to see her again.

"Anyway, twelve hours must've passed, maybe more. Then, one of the doors opened, like a snap of a finger. I walked through, and somehow I was back at the lake. I was confused— even more confused when I turned around to see the room; it was gone. All I could see was the lake and the scenery around it. I thought that maybe I was in a dream, but now I am awake. I felt different, though. I felt like I had a new lease on life. I rushed home as soon as I could, eager to share my experience with Gabby. When I walked in the house, Gabby was standing by the sink, washing dishes from earlier. I sat down at the kitchen table, grabbed the morning newspaper, and called out her name. She didn't respond. I kept calling her name, thinking she was trying to be cute or clever, but she did not answer back. Still, no response. I got up from the table and went to give her a playful shove, but something stopped me. From the inside of my body, something froze my motor functions, prohibiting me from making contact. At that point, the realization of my livelihood was shattered. It hit me and hit me hard. I was no longer among the living—I was dead.

"I walked back to the lake and sat in a secluded area for some time. Tears were overflowing on my lap as I wept for hours on end. Then, an unexplainable force overcame my body as I started to walk towards the lake. I started to walk in, confused and unable to control myself. I was scared, but for some odd reason, I wasn't fighting it. I slowly started to submerge, and once I was completely under, everything went blank. The next thing I knew, it was morning, and I found myself by the entrance to the shore. I was confused at first—I didn't know what to do. The only thing that came to mind was going to my mother's coffee shop. So, I went and sat in the back, listening to the sweet sounds of life that I was no longer entitled to. The day passed, and when dusk had fallen, I found myself going back to the lake once more.

"So, this was my new life. Wake, my mother's place, lake, repeat. It's a sad routine, but it's all I had. I was never one to believe in any of this. And by any of this, I am talking about the spiritual realm. As I said before, it's very real—and I'm proof it exists."

I felt melancholy within, but I knew I had to show her that I was strong. "I'm… I'm taken back by your story. I just wish—"

Dani put her hand on top of mine and looked me right in the eyes. "Shh, say no more. Everything that has happened was for a reason."

"I get that, but sometimes the reasons make no sense."

"They always will make sense in the end. One day, you will see."

"I hope so—for Gabby's and your mother's sake."

"They aren't doing so well, are they?"

I thought about lying or not overindulging their situation, but I couldn't hold back. "No, they need help. Gabby is a wreck. She dropped out of college and is back here for the time being. Apparently, she took a bunch of pills without thinking of the repercussions. Her roommate found her passed out, and they rushed her to the emergency room. Luckily, the doctors got her stable, and she was going to live. She swears to me that she never took the pills with the intention of suicide, but I don't know what to believe. Now, she is drinking heavily and even told me it's the only thing to ease her pain.

"On the other hand, your mother, well, is your mother. She's one-dimensional when it comes to Gabby and how she should act and be. There is no empathy, sorrow, or forgiveness towards her daughter. Gabby told me how much your mother chastised her for dropping out of school and taking those pills. I'm not sure what your family's life was like before tragedy struck, but it seems to me that your passing and your father's shortly after changed her drastically."

"My mother has always been difficult. Accepting it became harder the older we became." Dani looked down and paused for a moment. "They will find peace. It will take time, but they will."

"How do you know?"

"Because—everything happens for a reason."

Compared to Gabby, Dani was a 180-degree difference. She was tougher, with a lot more durability in her skin. Understandably, though, as she portrayed how an older sister would act and should be. Dani was unique—different, as I could not recall ever meeting a lady like her. It felt like we could talk for hours without a dull moment in between. The serious conversations and small talk made me forget why I even brought her here in the first place.

"May I ask you a question?" Dani readjusted herself for comfortability. "These people who are following me—do you know anything else about them?"

"I don't, really. Other than that, they are trying to kidnap you and… wait. I think I know why they specifically want you."

"Why?"

"My uncle, Carey, mentioned something about them wanting Sleepless with specific gifts. In your case, it is your gift to see the past. They want to turn you into one of them."

"Sleepless?"

"According to my grandmother's journal, that's what they labeled you as."

"I would like to see this journal. That's if it is okay with you?"

I had no reason to object her request. "Sure," I pointed to it on the end table, "it's right over there."

Dani walked over to the end table, grabbed the journal, and sat back down on the couch. I curiously watched her with great interest as she nonchalantly flipped one page over another. At about the five-minute mark, she stopped and set the journal down. "I have two questions."

"Okay, what are they?"

"This war, as your great-grandfather told your grandmother about it—do you think it's real?"

"It could be. I don't have a definite answer to that. I wouldn't be surprised if it were, considering the truth that you've shown me. I guess what I'm trying to say is that everything going on in my life never surprises me. If someone were to tell me months ago that this would all be real, I wouldn't have believed it."

"Did you read this whole journal?"

"No, just a few parts."

"Your grandmother was quite a lady. Did you know that the last entry she wrote was right after your mother passed?"

"No, I did not get that far."

"Did you read about the auto accident?"

"Auto accident? What auto accident? Wait, how do you know this information? You breezed through the whole thing like it was nothing."

Dani looked deep into my eyes and smiled. "I didn't need to turn the pages to know. Once I set my hands on it, I saw your grandmother's past and her entries. She was a remarkable lady and a fierce protector, I must say."

Her statement was itching a scratch. "Wait a second. I was under the assumption of my uncle, and from what I read, she decided not to act against the Ancients."

"I have a feeling you will see the truth soon." Dani reached her hand out and placed it on my shoulder. "Let us not speak on this matter anymore."

I was a little confused by her objection. "Okay, I guess. I was curious, that is all."

"I understand, I truly do. But you need to understand that everything that has and will happen to you is for a great reason. It is now your duty to seek out and understand the meaning of everything that comes your way. Do you understand?"

I shook my head. "Yes, I do."

"Okay, great. Now, what would you have me do considering the people after me?"

"For now, stick with me. Until I know what the next course of action is, I will do anything I can to keep you safe." I hesitated for a moment. "May I ask you a question?"

"Sure, anything."

I took a deep breath. "Why do you return to the lake every night?"

A look of anguish overcame her face. "I… I don't know. It's like a part of me. Something inside me triggers a return every night. It feels like a life force to a certain extent. Before I return, I feel so tired—beat down. When I awake, it's like my spirit has been re-charged. Does that make any sense?"

It looked like that question took something out of her. "Yes, it does. Look, I'm sorry I asked. I meant no harm by it."

"You don't need to be sorry." Dani leaned back on the couch and made herself comfortable. "So, what are we to do for the rest of the day if I am to remain by your side?"

"Well, I need to meet my uncle at 4:30 p.m. He's like I am—in terms of being able to see you. He will have a plan for us and is exceptionally knowledgeable on this subject. I would like to take you to meet him. That's if… you would want to go?"

"I would love to see something new. What about before?"

"We can stay here if you would like?"

"I would like that. May I ask you a favor?"

"Of course, anything."

"Can we watch the television?"

I chuckled and cracked a huge smile. "Most definitely."

"Do you think that you would… oh, never mind."

"No, please finish."

"I wanted to know if you would be able to hold me while we watch."

I couldn't see my face, but I'm certain I probably blushed. "I would love that."

She was scared and nervous—and rightfully so. By that request alone, I knew the fear trembled inside her. This poor girl was caught up in the crosshairs of unbeknownst evil. Evil that is so pure and vile, it shook the foundation of everything good in this world. I had to be the difference-maker, the one to prove that good would always triumph over evil. I had to protect her, for it was my duty.

31

Am I Safe Here?

Life's possibilities,
Harboring infinite peace.
Clutching eternal hostilities,
Dreams manifest a release.
I fear they will never cease.

I awoke from a nap on my grandmother's couch. The television was blaring, and the blinds were set three-fourths down, shimmering with a glimpse of light from outside. I was puzzled. I figured my grandmother would be sitting in her favorite chair, enjoying her favorite pastime of knitting, but she was peculiarly absent.

Taking an interest, I rose and walked toward the kitchen. Empty. The kitchen table was proper, the stove was empty, and the pantry was shut. Everything was in its right place. Neglected and soiled, not so much. The kitchen looked as if it were prepared for an extended period of inactivity.

Attached to the kitchen was my grandmother's bedroom. The door was shut, as it was 95 percent of the time. Beyond the door, a soft voice was lingering in the bedroom. At first, I thought my grandmother must be on the phone. Curiously, I placed my ear on the door, listened in, and determined the voice to be unrecognizable. I placed my hand on the door handle, attempting to open it slowly. To my luck, it was locked.

My consternation started to grow as the peculiar voice was carried within my mind. I knew I had to gain entrance somehow, and then it hit me. Every door in her house had a safety lock mechanism from the outside. All it would take was a little flathead screwdriver or a butter knife to open it.

I crept to the silverware drawer to obtain the easier mechanism, the butter knife. Long forks, short forks, spoons, soup spoons—not one butter knife. *Odd.* As a second resort, my grandmother kept a simple junk drawer filled with batteries, tools, and random knickknacks. *Easy enough,* I thought. However, there was not one battery, tool, or any other random objects that could be found in it on any day. Today, it was filled with what must've been over fifty butter knives. Strange, indeed, but pondering it would take my attention off the task at hand—gaining access to my grandmother's room.

I inserted the butter knife through the middle of the handle and applied a little pressure. Instantly, the door lock popped open, and I now had access. I stepped inside and shut the door behind me. To say the least, I was a little disappointed to find out that the voice I heard was nothing but a talk radio show playing from the nightstand radio. However, something still felt off. After taking a quick glance, I noticed that my grandmother's tall dresser was not where it normally was—flush against her accent wall. The dresser was primed up against the back corner so that an empty space was created behind it. Instinctively, I knew there was something behind it. I walked up to the dresser, put my hands on the top edges, and gave it a firm jolt. Instantly, whatever was behind it moved in a manner to readjust in what was seemingly a hiding place. With one hand on the back side of the dresser, I pulled the right side out from the wall with ease. Under a black and white quilt was the shape of what looked to be an extra-wide tire. Without thinking, I pulled off the blanket, took a step back, and quickly gathered my thoughts.

There, laying down in a fetal position, was a young lady with her arms over her red hair. After she realized that she had been found, she slowly turned her head towards me while maintaining the same position. "Am I safe?" She said, trembling in fear. "Am I safe here?"

Pow! Pow! Pow! Something, or someone, started to violently bang on the other side of the door. I looked back down toward the mysterious female, and she was gone. Immediately, I woke up to a cold feeling on my couch. *Who was that red-haired girl?*

3:30 p.m., Saturday afternoon. I didn't even remember falling asleep on my couch with Dani by my side. Yet again, I awoke from yet another vague dream. Dani wasn't wrapped in my arms when I awoke. She was sitting at the other end of the couch, watching television, and seemingly interested in it.

I sat up, and she turned my way. "Are you okay?"

I rubbed the crust out from my eyes. "Yeah, I guess I dozed off."

"You sure did. I had to get up from where I was lying next to you because you began to shake violently. Did you have a bad dream?"

"Something of that nature, I guess."

"I used to dream a lot. I always thought of them as truths that hadn't been told yet. You know, signals from your subconscious are trying to trigger your conscious mind while in an unconscious world. I always wanted to focus my life on oneirology—the study of dreams." She paused for a moment as she thought about what she was about to say next. "Can I tell you something that you may find hard to believe?"

"Please, regale me."

"Okay. This is going to sound crazy, but... I really shouldn't."

I smiled and chuckled. "Well, you kind of have to, now that you started. If not, I don't know what I'm going to do for the rest of the day. Quite frankly, the rest of my life."

Dani playfully smirked. "Oh, come on. I can tell you're a jokester. Anyways, I dreamt of you some years ago."

Okay, now she had my attention. "Of me? You can't be serious, are you?"

"Yes, I'm serious. One night, I dreamt I was alone and walking through a vast wooded area. I remember all the details, from the snapping of the twigs under my feet to the smell of the pine needles collecting on the ground. I thought I was in a warm place, I guess you can say. But the further I kept walking, the

223

darker the forest became. I started to become concerned and turned around. I then realized that the area behind me was nothing I could remember. Panic started to set in. I started to turn in every direction, and everything I saw seconds ago had changed drastically. The forest was now dead. I remember that it was hard to catch my breath as I felt a panic attack setting in. Then, out of the blue, someone tapped me on the shoulder from behind. Low and behold, I turned around, and it was you. That's when I woke up.

"Of course, at that time, I didn't know who you were. But once I saw you at my mother's shop, I knew you were the man who rescued me from my nightmare. I knew it." Dani wiped back a tear from her right eye. "So, here we are now. You are still full of life, and I'm... well, you know."

Her admission of having a dream about it signaled a warm feeling in my blood. "I... I literally don't know what to say; other than it's a shame we hadn't met around that time, but I'm glad we finally got to meet."

"Yeah, you're right. Like I said, everything happens for a reason."

I knew it may be in my best interest to change the subject to veer away from the sadness. Considering our situation, I had no idea how long we would be side by side, within each other's company. I didn't want all our conversations to be centered on pity and sad stories. Besides, it was about time to go visit Carey.

I turned my attention toward Dani and clapped my hands together. "So, did you still want to visit my uncle with me? We'll need to leave in a few minutes if you want to go."

"Would you like me to go?"

I sat up and took in a quick stretch of my upper half body. "I would prefer it, but I can't make you go. I want you to be safe until... you know, nighttime."

Dani got up from the couch, walked right up in front of me, placed her hands on top of mine, and stared into my eyes. "You know, you don't have to do this for me. You literally just met me." She closed her eyes for a moment. "I guess what I'm trying to say is that you're risking your life for me. As much as I want to say no to you in regard to your sake, I... I can't. Yes. Yes, I'll go with you."

I bolted up and clapped my hands together. "Alright. Well, let's get going then. Hopefully, this won't take long."

"Are you sure this will be, okay?"

I placed my hand on her shoulder, knowing that I had to lie. "Of course. Everything will be fine."

She looked down at the floor and smiled. "Okay, I'm ready."

Certainly, I was a little leery about taking her to Carey's. It had never been my place to bring an uninvited guest to someone's house, let alone someone who was new to me. I had no choice, for I knew it was risky to dismiss her for the rest of the day. She was now my investment, and I had to keep her safe.

The ride to Carey's house was nothing more than it was— a ride. We talked little—nothing more than hobbies of sorts. One-word answers followed by an occasional five-to-ten-word answer were normal. Her anxiety was evident. To be frank, I'm sure my anxiety was even more evident.

Once I parked in Carey's driveway, I froze for a moment and thought about what I was to say. "Okay, look. When we walk up to the door, stay to the right of me so you're out of sight. Let me explain it all to him first. Easy enough?"

Dani nodded her head slightly. "Okay."

With Dani about three feet to my right, I knocked on Carey's door, and he answered. "Gret, you made it. Please, come on inside."

"Before I enter, there is something I have to tell you." I glanced over to Dani. "Well, more like something I have to show you."

Carey peaked his head out the door, glanced at her, and then turned his worrisome face towards me. "You brought her?! Do you know what this means now?"

I tried to downplay the situation. "Carey, look— "

He quickly interrupted and shook his head in frustration. "This is not good. Now they know, and you probably infuriated them even more with this stunt. We're as good as dead now because we probably lost the element of surprise. Good grief, this is not good."

Dani quickly spoke inside my mind. **Gret, can we please leave now?**

I looked toward her to calm her down. *Just wait a minute, please. Let me try to reason with him first. We need him.*

Carey's frustration and hostility quickly turned into curiosity. "Wait a minute. Do I think what just happened just happen?"

I knew he knew. "If you're referring to mental telepathy, then yes. Look—we desperately need your help. Without you, we are lost. Please, Carey. Please help us."

Carey scoffed and took a deep breath. "Okay, come inside. I don't like it, but it's probably already too late. I suppose we are all fully invested now." He pointed over to the couch. "Go take a seat, please."

I took a seat, and Dani took one right next to me. "Thanks again—you know, for having us over. Is your wife here?"

Carey took a quick sip of his beer. "No, she's working right now. You know, you're a lot stronger than you think. Definitely stronger than I am. You must be a level three."

"Level three? What's that?"

"The man I told you about, Quintt, explained it all to me. Level one is when you can only see them. Level two is seeing them and communicating with them." Carey pointed sharply at me. "Level three is seeing, verbally communicating, and mental telepathy. Last but not least, there is a level three-plus. That's all three levels, with the ability to create a portal to send them to the next world, whatever that may be."

Dani adjusted her posture. "You know, Gret didn't know he could mentally communicate with me until I helped him. Maybe you have it too. It's like a campfire. You need wood and fire. Maybe you only have wood."

Carey smirked and scoffed. "No, honey, I don't have it."

I decided to butt in. "You never know. Let her try to help."

It was easy to tell Carey was becoming a little agitated. "Trust me, I don't have it. I know because… here, I'll tell you what." He turned his attention toward Dani. "Try to speak to me through telepathy, and let's see if I can hear you.

Dani eagerly agreed. "Okay." Her stare toward Carey was as stiff as one could manage. "Did you get it?"

"Nothing. I told you."

Dani extended her hand toward Carey. "Take my hand; I can help."

Carey looked down and shook his head. "I don't think so."

"Just try it," I said. "What do you have to lose?"

Carey looked all around the room like he was expecting an answer on the wall. "Well, okay. I know it won't work, but I guess you never know."

Carey's reluctance was as clear as day. Maybe he did not want to risk the chance of being proven wrong, or maybe he knew something that we didn't. I was not certain about how much knowledge he possessed on this topic, so it was important for me to keep an open mind.

About eight hours ago, Dani placed her hand on mine for a few seconds and enhanced my ability. Five seconds, maybe six, was all it took. However, this was not the case with Carey. After a couple of seconds of their hands joining together, the expectations took a rather odd turn. With her eyes closed, her whole body started to shake ever so slightly. The lamp on the corner end table started to flicker, while it felt like the temperature of the room dropped 10 degrees at the snap of a finger. Carey was confused as he looked around the room in a frantic panic. A few seconds later, Dani's eyes opened, and a troubled look of disappointment overshadowed her willingness to help Carey.

Carey quickly snapped his hand back from Dani's. "See, I told you. Nothing. I don't have it."

"I tried," Dani said, "I'm sorry."

Carey shrugged his shoulders. "It's… whatever. I don't really care, I guess." Carey grabbed his beer, took a long drink, and lightly slammed the empty can on the end table. "Now, let's get down to business."

Before he started to talk about business, Carey began to ramble on a quick story about his wife and how they met. I wasn't paying attention because Dani started to speak within my mind. **Gret, I need to do something. I need to leave. Please, don't worry about me. I'll be okay, I promise.**

No, you can't. They may be around, for all we know. Please, just stay.

No, darling, you cannot go where I need to go. Please, just trust me. I need to take care of something. Considering everything that has come to light, this may be my last night, or maybe not. I need to do something before it's too late. I can meet you back at your house by 7:00 p.m.

How are you going to get there?

I can walk. I'll run if I have to.

Listen. If they approach you, you run as fast as you can away from them. You run like hell, no matter what it takes.

I promise, I will. One more thing. Thank you for everything.

You don't have to thank me, and you never will. I'll tell Carey you have to leave.

What she had to do and where she was going were beyond me. Certainly, I was nervous and hesitant to let her out of my sight, but something in her eyes affirmed my senses that she was going to be all right. Meanwhile, Carey was still rambling on about his wife, seemingly lost in his own words. I signaled my hand to gain Carey's attention. "Carey, um… sorry to interrupt, but she has to leave right now. If you don't mind, I will stay here for as long as you need."

"Yeah, that's fine," he replied. "Do what you have to do."

"I'm going to step outside with her for a moment. I'll be right back."

Neither Carey nor Dani said goodbye to each other. I sensed there was a little hostility toward each other, for whatever reason. It didn't matter, though. We were all on the same side. This was not a time to play mediator or pick sides; we all had to be in this together.

Once outside, I put my hand on Dani's shoulder. "Look, please be safe. You do what you need to do. I'll be thinking about you until your return."

Dani flashed her biggest smile I have seen thus far. "I promise I'll be back. But… I need to tell you one more thing." Dani quickly pointed to her head, insinuating telepathic communication. **From the start, I knew your uncle didn't have the ability to talk like we do.**

How did you know?

I just… did. I can't explain it.

Okay, but if you knew, why would you even try?

I didn't try. I looked into his past.

My eyes became large. Sneaky. *What did you see?*

I… I would prefer to tell you later. She grabbed my hand and gazed into my eyes. **Please be careful with him. I'm sorry, Gret, but I don't trust him. Trust yourself before you trust him.**

What would you have me do?

I don't know. Everything he says, every story he tells you—take it all with a grain of salt. Look, I'll tell you later tonight.

Okay. I gave her a hug, and we said our goodbyes. *Please be safe.* She nodded her head, and she was on her way. I stood outside for a few moments until she disappeared beyond the trees. Her words about not trusting him were troublesome for me. Keeping an open mind and remaining cautious were all I could do. He was family, and I simply needed more answers.

I re-entered the house to find Carey in the same spot, where there seemed to be a fresh drink in his hand. His fixed gaze on me and amusing smile suggested that he was finding something humorous to be amusing.

"Her," he said while chuckling a bit. "What is her name again?"

"Dani, short for Daniella."

"You're quite taken by her, aren't you?"

I shook my head and smiled. "Man… I want to help her, nothing more."

Carey opened a huge smile. "You want to help her." A short outburst of laughter sprung from his mouth. "You had to think about that answer, huh?"

"Alright, alright. Can we get on with the business at hand here?"

Carey took a quick sip. "Sure." He paused for a moment. "You do know I was serious about the Ancients knowing about all this, right?"

My blood was starting to simmer. "Yes, I know—you already told us. Look, there was nothing I could do. It's not like I sought her out and purposely brought her here. She sat next to me at Claire's because she knew I was following her."

"Still, should've never brought—"

I quickly interrupted, as my patience on this topic was wearing thin. "Look, I'll leave if you want, and you'll never see or hear from me again. If you seriously have a problem with this, then let it all out now."

"I do have a problem with it. My wife is pregnant, and now I fear we will all be dead in a day or two because of what you did." He took another drink and shook his head like he was shaking water from his hair. "But you didn't know better—so I can't be mad. We have to work on a plan to overcome them."

I felt a little relieved. "For what it's worth, I'm sorry. Heck, maybe they'll never know… you know… that I brought her here."

"They know, Gret. They *always* know."

"Okay, so they know—big deal. Do you have any ideas on a plan?"

Carey leaned back and extended his arms to stretch. "I … I don't know. Kind of, I guess. I think the only way to counter them is to lure them out with your friend. The lake would be perfect for that."

"You don't think some kind of sneak attack would work?"

"No. Aza has a couple followers who have the gift of sight and sound. They would know you're coming a mile away. It's pointless."

"Well, maybe it's not. Dani said—" An alarm was set off in my head. I thought it was best to keep Dani's gift a secret.

Carey's attention was starting to pique. "She said what?"

"It's… I… I was going to say," I had to make something up fast. "I was going to say that Dani said that she had seen them separately before. You know, maybe the followers with sight and sound won't be there."

"No, we have to lure them out. It's the only way. They normally travel in pairs. Very often, you will not see more than two together. However, I did see three that one day at Claire's while you were there. Lucian, Rodick, and whoever that new woman is. I haven't seen Aza yet, but that's typical of him to not be seen."

"I have a random question. I can't remember if I asked you this before, but how do you know their names and their movements?"

Carey took in a long sigh. "Well, as I mentioned yesterday, my wife and I have experience with them. I was once a prisoner to them. I don't want to dig into this topic, but I've done things that I'm not proud of. Promises that were broken. So, they took me in and held me for a few days. They demanded payment—I paid them."

"How much was it?"

"No… no money. Locations."

"Yeah, I guessed that yesterday."

"Yes, you sure did. I helped Aza find Rodick and Lucian. This was a long time ago. Much long ago. I'm sure Rodick and Lucian have hated me ever since. I had to do what I had to do in order to survive. That meant traveling with them and getting to know them pretty well. I know I'm probably a *coward* for it, but it was my life on the line." Carey took another quick drink. "That's how I know them pretty well."

I started to become slightly worrisome. "Considering we have the same gift, do you think they would do that to me also?"

"It's hard to say. I believe they only consider you a threat now because of your insertion into your Sleepless friend's routine. Not to mention, I'm sure they have set their radar on me also."

"For what it's worth, I'm ready to do whatever needs to be done. I do not fear them."

Carey scoffed. "I admire your courage, kid. I respectfully do. Just don't go out and get ahead of yourself. They will always expect the obvious, for they are always watching. You never want to look for the fight. Let it come to you."

"Okay, that all sounds like roses to me, but how do we do this?"

"Give me some time at least until tomorrow morning or afternoon. I'll devise a plan. Just trust me on this; we'll see to it that it's done."

Trust him, he said. That magical word came up again at the crossroads of my own decisions. According to Dani, I had to trust myself before I trusted him. I had no choice but to trust him at an arm's length, for going into this alone was not an option.

I got up and started to walk towards the door. "So, you will get ahold of me tomorrow?"

"Yes. I'll figure something out."

Before I made my exit, I walked towards Carey, looked him in the eye, and offered a handshake. "Thanks for everything. Once this is all over, I certainly hope we can keep in contact and, you know, catch up."

Carey obliged with the shake, nodded his head, but couldn't look me in the eye. "Yeah, I hope so too."

I've seen and met all different people throughout my life. I've always favored a firm handshake and a look from eye to eye as a signal of honesty. Undoubtedly, I am not foolish enough to know that it doesn't always work out that way. Many have presented a limp shake while looking past me—some of those were honest. Meanwhile, some could have reciprocated—some of those lied. For Carey, something was amiss. His gesture of goodbye was seemingly hiding something. I've been wrong before; hopefully, this time is one of them.

The meeting was over, and I was on my way back home. Overall, I would say the meeting was productive and interesting. It was reassurance that we all stood a chance, no matter how deep the threat was. Eyes on the road, I started to wonder if Dani was safe and if she had accomplished what she needed to do. I also wondered: Would she be honest and tell me what she saw within Carey? Whatever she saw, I imagine it was not pretty, judging by the way she left. Carey gave his word; for now, that was good enough considering our dilemma. After all, what good is a man's word if we have nothing left to stand by?

6:30 p.m. I arrived back home with thirty minutes to spare before Dani said she would return. From the outside of my residence, everything looked in its place. I unlocked my door, took my shoes off, and walked to the kitchen for a glass of water. To my surprise, she was already waiting for me at my kitchen table. "Jeez! You scared the hell out of me!" I took a deep breath, as it was obvious that I was shook up. "When and how did you get in here?"

Dani smiled as she seemingly enjoyed her little scare tactic. "About ten minutes ago." She lunged out of the chair and attacked me with a hug. "I know this sounds a little… barmy, but I categorically missed you."

I wrapped my arms around her and swayed her left to right. "I missed you too. I'm glad to see you are okay." The hug was released, and we both took a seat at the table. "So, how did you get in here?"

"You forgot. Your realm is different than mine. You see a locked door, and I see an unlocked door."

"Fair enough. Did you do what you needed to do?"

"Yes. Yes, I did."

"And?"

"All in good time, you'll see."

I didn't want to press the issue. "All in good time is right, I guess."

"How did the rest of the time with your uncle go?"

I shrugged my shoulders. "Good, I suppose. He's devising a plan for us all. Hopefully, it'll all end soon."

Dani frowned and looked at the floor. "I need to talk to you about him. I know he's your uncle and all, but you should know something about him before you agree to this plan."

It was the moment of truth. "What is it? What did you see?"

She took a deep breath. "I saw two distinct things. Do you want the worst of it first or last?"

"It doesn't matter. Just tell me whatever way you think is better."

"Okay. First, everything he said about your family and him, he lied. I guess you can say that he was a *menace to society.* He's an alcoholic and addict, and he has seen the inside walls of a jail cell many times. While he said that he wanted to convince your grandmother about your ability, that was all a lie. He did it to sweet-talk you. You know, for you to trust him and find him credible. Your mother and grandmother never told him to disappear; they gave up on him. In turn, he gave up on the family for his sad life."

I buried my eyes with my hands and thought for a moment. "Hm, that's interesting. I don't know what to think. Maybe he's trying to make amends—I don't know. I suppose I must take him for what he's worth." I paused for about ten seconds and looked at the clock—it was now 6:39. "Was that the worst of what you saw?"

"I'm afraid not. Well, maybe for you. Not for me."

"What does that mean?"

"The Ancients only knew about my whereabouts because of him. He conspired with them as part of a deal they made a long time ago. The deal was that he would seek us out and inform them of our whereabouts and habits. By doing so, he had a quota he had to meet every so often. I was the last one on the supposed contract. If he failed them, the deal was off."

"What would've happened if he had failed them or not?"

"From what I gathered, it was a little hazy, but he wants to be one of them. It was more of a *tryout* for him. I saw their leader, Aza, in his memories. I saw both sitting down and discussing the matter. Something tells me that Aza doesn't want him but finds your uncle's attempts somewhat amusing, like it's a sport. If he did fail, I can only imagine it would be horrible for him. I didn't delve down that street; it didn't exactly captivate me."

I shook my head in disbelief. "I would be a liar if I told you that I wasn't surprised by everything you told me. I know he's a shady guy. It's not hard to see it written all over his face. That is why we will take his trust in stride. We have to act like we trust him, but in reality, we know we are smarter than him." I had to ask. "Is that all you saw?"

Dani lowered her head in shame. "No. I didn't want to tell you everything. I wanted to spare you the last thing I saw. I'm sorry; I know I was wrong to do so. I shouldn't have lied to you. You have the right to know what else he did."

A powerful mixture of curiosity, anger, and disappointment in the form of acid felt like it was piercing through my veins. I wasn't mad at her, but I was mad at what else my *so-called* uncle could have done. "Well, what is it?"

"The night your mother passed. He called her at work and begged for forgiveness. More than less, he needed money. Your mother refused all pleas and told him that it would be best if she didn't have a brother anymore. Then... he did it. He was infuriated with anger and told your mother about his, your grandmother's, and your *possible* ability to see us. I could not see beyond that phone call he made, but I think you know the rest of the story. I fear he may have been the cause of what happened to your mother."

"And you saw all this, the whole story—the whole everything—inside his memories? Do you think he killed my mother?"

"Yes, Gret. I wouldn't lie. As for your mother, I don't know. I would guess not, and it wouldn't be right for me to speculate."

It had felt like a heavy gust of wind had entered my body, wreaking havoc and sucking everything out of my insides. Being a believer in circumstance over fate, I believed that his phone call may have triggered a chain reaction of all the unfortunate events in my life. The audacity that man had—it was hard to stomach.

His selfishness was above all else that night. I was distraught and angry about this confession, but I knew I couldn't let these feelings subjugate the game we were involved in. As much *red* as I could see, a part of me had to believe that he was here to help and make amends for all his mistakes. I could not let my anguish conquer me. Deep down, I was all in. I had to take this chance.

Dani got up from her chair and put her hand on my shoulder. "Gret, I'm sorry. I wish I had something better to tell you. I want to be honest with you."

I placed my left hand on top of hers and looked up at her. "Okay. Look, here's the thing. Am I mad? Upset? Sad? You better believe it. A part of me wants to make him suffer in ways I could never imagine. But, without him right now, I don't think we stand a chance. If we don't go along with him, they will eventually find you and turn you into something that we don't know much about. Let's listen to what he has to say. If we don't like it, we bail and come up with something, I guess. I promise, I will keep you safe."

Dani released her hand from my shoulder and sat back down. "I've asked you this many times, but why are you risking your life for me?" A tear rolled from her eye. "You don't owe me anything. For me, it's hard to fathom that someone I just met would risk everything to keep me safe."

I handed her a tissue. "I feel that everything in my life, from battling sickness to losing loved ones, now to this very day, has come to this moment." I took a deep breath and slightly nodded my head. "One day, I will die. It is inevitable. But before my last moment, do I want to ask myself, *Could I have done more?*"

"Oh, Gret. I don't know what to say. You are simply an amazing person. I will never forget you."

In that instant, an unexpected moment had occurred. Dani leaned over from her chair, embraced my body, and planted a kiss on my lips. A warm, tingling sensation instantly ran through my body. I know well enough that this feeling wasn't excitement or gratification; it was simply love.

"Wow," I said in amazement. "I wasn't expecting that."

She started to become nervous. "I'm so sorry, Gret. I didn't mean to. I just… couldn't stop myself."

"No, it's fine." I leaned back over and kissed her again. "I'm glad you did."

"Really?"

I smiled and reached for her hand. "Of course."

She instantly blushed. "As much as I would love to kiss you more, I have to cut this short. It's about that time."

"You can't stay… maybe a little longer?"

"As much as I would love to, I can't. You know what I have to do. It's a part of me now."

I nodded in subtle agreement. "I understand. May I at least drive you there and watch you to ensure your safety?"

Dani graciously smiled. "I would love that."

It was now a little past 7:30 p.m. We were now on our way to Hugo Lake. I was glum, but I was also grinning from ear to ear from the inside because I knew I would see her tomorrow. The whole ride, she sat there in a happy daze while looking out the window. It was the happiest I have seen her since I first laid eyes on her. Not only was she happy, but I was happy too. Happy as can be, but a little sad once we pulled into the parking lot to the lake. Damn, I wish this moment could last forever.

I parked and left the car on for a few seconds. "Well, we are here."

She looked over at me and smiled. "Are you going to be a gentleman again and walk with me? And maybe… a kiss goodnight?"

I quickly opened my car door, got out, and turned to her. "Hold that thought for a second." I ran around the back end of my car, only to open her door for her. I reached out for her hand, which she gladly accepted. "I wouldn't have it any other way."

The night was calm, with a little breeze pushing from the west. For safety measures, I equipped my palladium blade on my side as a precaution. Hand in hand, we made our way over to the closest park bench. It was surreal, like I was walking on cloud nine. Right before we reached the bench, she froze, turned to me, and kissed me once more.

"Well, I guess I'll see you tomorrow?" she asked.

I planted a little kiss on her forehead. "Not if I see you first. Where do you want to meet?"

"I can meet you at your place if that's okay?"

"Perfect. Wake me up if I'm still sleeping." I winked at her. "I'll leave the door unlocked for you."

She giggled like a little girl in love. "You are cute. See you tomorrow."

One last time, we both leaned in simultaneously and kissed for a few seconds. Mindful of our surroundings, I watched once again as she walked into the lake and disappeared underneath the water. This night was simply perfect. I took it as, *the calm before the storm.*

Where I stand,
In this peculiar land.
Truth shadowed in darkness,
Uneasy to understand.

My emotions are gray,
Thoughts in disarray.
Never doubting reality,
My conscious led astray.

I have seen far too much,
Innocence to bear, no such.
Awaiting her gentle touch,
Awaiting her gentle touch.

The waves ripped the ocean apart as the wind swirled from the south. Torrential downpours mixed with thunder and lightning strikes were all but a couple miles away, signifying the worst has yet to come. The notion of a capsize entered my mind, silver-lined with doubt of rescue. Unbeknownst to me, why I was aboard this grand ship was beyond any logical explanation. Confused, troubled, and alone—at least I thought. There she was again, the pale lady. She held her position well at the ledge with her hands on the rusted rails, keeping a mesmerizing stare at the dark sky. "Here. Come here, my child."

I walked up to her in a reluctant, but yet curious manner. "You, again. I take it that this is our last meeting."

She kept her gaze glued to the sky, exhibiting zero expression. "Yes. Yes, it is. I want you to look at the sky and tell me what you see."

I placed my hands on the ship's rails and obliged. "I see… nothing. Just a dark sky filled with a few stars that are scattered behind the clouds." I looked toward the forward of the ship. "I also see we are heading directly into a storm."

"Yes. The dark sky holds many truths and much superstition. Many believe that their fate will come true during the darkest night. They also say that stars that shine brightly resemble life's most precious commodity—hope. I'm not one for superstition; I only know truth. The darkness is unforgiven." She desisted for a moment and turned her head toward the forward of the ship. "Often, light will oppose the darkness, prolonging the inevitable."

My nerves started to become uneasy. "Why… why are you telling me this?"

The pale lady ceased her gaze and dispensed a cold stare upon me. Her eyes were dark, her posture stiff, and her skin paled. "This is simply clarity—the last stage of your transparency. You now see it all clearly—the way things are, the way things should be, and the way things will be. Your truth shall reveal itself when you know it's time to look upon the dark sky." She then flared a smile toward me. "You will see me no more in this realm. Our time is now up."

I shook my head in confusion. "What does all that mean?"

Refraining from my question, she raised her arm and pointed at the door to the ship hold. I turned my head and looked. "You must enter now. We shall meet again in this lifetime."

Those last words—chilling. Within my mind, I did not think about it much. I figured that maybe she thought that one more meeting was necessary. Like the other two meetings, she vanished at the snap of a finger. I had no choice but to enter through the door she signified.

Alone, I found myself at the helm of the ship, enclosed in a little ten by fifteen room that must have been the captain's headquarters. According to the compass on the dash, the wheel was locked to head south. Somehow, traveling south into the storm did not resonate with me. I knew I needed to travel north, away from the storm. I placed my hands on the helm and, with all my might, attempted to turn the ship around, but to no avail. The helm would simply not budge. Improvising for a better grip, I snagged a little thin rubber mat in front of the wheel to strengthen my grip. Before I could even re-attempt to turn the helm, I discovered a little trap door that was hidden underneath the mat. Attached to the latch, a key was perfectly placed right next to it. Something told me that this key wasn't placed there by mistake but an intentional act—begging me to enter.

My inquisitiveness surpassed any indecision. I unlocked the hatch, shone my flashlight down beneath, and counted twelve steps on the ladder below. The descent was surprisingly easy, considering the only light I could utilize was from up above. I reached the bottom and pointed my flashlight towards the end of the long, narrow room. Disbelief.

I believe that there are times in one's life when they are meant to find what they are particularly looking for. On the other side, there are moments when one finds something or someone that maybe they were not supposed to find. This was one of those times. Down below, this long and narrow room was filled with coffins, lined up as far as the eye could see. The more I started to move forward, the more coffins were seen. There must have been over one hundred—everyone standing upward at the foot of their foundation. For every third coffin I passed, a dainty, old-style light bulb turned on as if it were a motion sensor.

I continued straight ahead the dreary path. Keeping a slow pace and making subtle observations in all directions. Nothing but sealed, tight coffins on each side begged the question within my head. *What was this ship meant for?* Simple thoughts were beginning to fester and suddenly ceased as I reached the end of the tunnel. Certainly, something was amiss. Every coffin was sealed, apart from the last one on the left. Oddly, this coffin was also the only one painted red. Without much thought, I placed my hand on the door and attempted to shut it. It simply would not lock into place, as I had no other option but to leave it open. At that moment, I knew I was not supposed to be down here.

At the front of the entrance, a sound rattled throughout the tunnel as it was like someone, or something, dropped a heavy object down the ladder. Instantly, I braced myself against the back wall in a panic, as the trap door had now slammed shut. One by one, all the lights started to slowly burn out in sequence, beginning from the entrance to where I was standing. I was now in complete darkness. Numbness overcame my position as my panic-stricken mind had lost all sense of direction. The darkness only got worse from that point on. In the distance, I could see four red lights approaching me from straight ahead. The left two lights were at least six to eight inches below the right pair. The closer they became, the more petrified my fear became. I was in peril— frozen like a deer in headlights, unknowing what to do. Then, out of the blue, they disappeared from twenty-five feet away. Directly after, all lights flickered back on as visibility was yet again established. This was my time for a grand escape, as hesitation was no such thing.

My mad dash came to a screeching halt as it happened again. This time, all the bulbs shut off simultaneously. Once more, I was surrounded in utter darkness. I stood by for a second, did a couple of circles of scrutiny, and contemplated my next move. Suddenly, without warning, what felt like a hand grabbed me by the shoulder and swung me around. I was now face-to-face with the four mysterious red lights.

Another night, another nightmare. This time, I jerked up on the bed and let out a harrowing scream. Words could not simply describe the terror I felt. *Will they ever go away?*

35

Purpose

Sunday, 9:00 a.m. I slept longer than I was anticipating. I also figured by now that Dani would have already woken me up. Not the case. I wasn't all too worried, for I would've bet she was downstairs watching the television. Unfortunately, that was also not the case.

After I scoped out the living room, my next guess would be the kitchen. Once more, no Dani. It was quiet as a mouse as I started to become a little worrisome, for I feared the worst. Frantically, I ran around the whole house and then checked the outside—no Dani.

My heart was heavy. It was that feeling of it sinking straight down to the toes. Maybe she was late, although I highly doubt it. Getting lost was a possibility—an unlikely possibility, but still worth pondering. Deep down, I knew I should have met her at the lake first thing. Failure was starting to enter my mind, but I had to be optimistic about her safety.

For the next ten minutes, I sat at my kitchen table, hoping to hear a door open or any sign that she was entering. Wishful thinking, I suppose. The only conclusion I could come up with was that she either was kidnapped or got lost and made her way back to the coffeeshop. Time was becoming the essence. Without caring about my appearance, I quickly threw on some clothes and sped off to Claire's.

It was now about 9:25 a.m. At this time and on a Sunday, Claire's was packed to the brim, as I barely found an open parking spot. It didn't matter, though; I was only there for one reason. Just my luck, I was greeted by none other than Claire the moment I walked in. "Well, well. Good morning, Mr. Gret. What brings you here today?"

"Good morning to you also." I briefly looked around to see who was working. "Is Gabby or Nancy here?"

"No. Unfortunately, Nancy called off sick, and Gabby is off today. As you can see, we are unexpectedly a little busy. Did you need something from them?"

Before I could spout off an answer, I took notice of the bright yellow rope barely showing towards the back dining area. "Say, what's with the rope in back?"

"We have an overhead water pipe leaking over the tables, so we can't seat anyone there today. On any normal day, we don't even have to use that area. But of course, the day we would need it, this crap happens." Claire quickly turned around for a quick view of the tables. "As you can see, it's going to be a wait if you want a table. Maybe fifteen or twenty minutes."

I had to think of something fast. "I think I'll come back when it dwindles down. I'm just going to use the bathroom quickly. You know… coffee at home… didn't have to go ten minutes ago."

Claire stared at me with a callously suspicious demeanor. "Okay, you don't need to share details with me."

I nodded my head at Claire and casually walked towards the back. *That was a little too easy,* I thought. Halfway to the bathroom, I started to feel her warmth inside me as instant relief struck. Before I was to make contact, I turned my head around to see if Claire was watching. Luckily, she was out of my sight. Once I turned the corner, Dani's eyes lit up as she stood up with a huge smile. **Gret! I'm so glad you came back to find me! I had a lapse of memory and got lost for a little bit.**

It's okay. You're safe, and that's all that matters. We should get out of here, considering your mother is here and it's quite busy.

Okay, I'm ready. Dani quickly dug in her pocket and pulled out what looked to be a photograph. **I almost forgot. Take this.** She handed me the photograph. **When I left your uncle's house yesterday, I went to my mother's and retrieved this photograph of Gabby, my mother, and me. This picture was taken at our cousin's wedding a few years ago. We all went shopping together for the dresses we wore. This picture**

was always my mother's favorite of the three of us. She used to keep it attached to her bedroom vanity mirror, but it was taken down after I was… well, you know.

Okay, do you want me to keep it?

No, I want you to leave it here on this table. She'll find it. You'll see.

Her answer was vague, but I think she knew what she wanted out of it. *Okay, done. Now, let's get out of here.*

I wish I could say that our exit would be *uneventful,* but it was anything but that. Right before we were to turn the corner, Claire stopped me in my tracks. "I thought you had to use the restroom?"

I was at a loss for words. "Oh, well, I did use it. Quickly, of course."

"Then what in the hell were you doing in my roped-off back dining area?"

"I… I was… looking for the source of the leak."

Claire then stood on her tiptoes and looked behind me. "What is that on my table?"

Oh, shoot. Here we go. I looked back at the table. "What is what?"

"It looks like a piece of paper or something," she replied with a curious tone.

I knew we had to exit stage right quickly. "Look, I have to run. It was nice chatting with you again. See you soon."

I was so perturbed, I never even looked back to see if Dani was following me, as I was about seven paces away from Claire. Once I did, I witnessed something I wasn't expecting at all. As Claire stood there and stared at what she discovered from her distance from the table, Dani's hand was placed on Claire's shoulder, as both were seemingly frozen. It had felt like time stood still, and I was dumbfounded about what to do. Luckily, I didn't have to do anything. It only took Dani a few seconds to do whatever she needed to do with her contact. After that, I did not know if Claire went to grab the photo or even looked back at us. My eyes were straight forward the whole time after leaving the establishment in a hurry.

While in the car, the burning question was boiling up inside me. "What did you do to your mother?" I asked.

Dani kept her eyes straightforward and smiled. "I just gave her a reminder. You'll see soon enough."

I kept her answer at that, for I didn't want to think more about it. Now that I found Dani, my mind was focused on one thing and one thing only: The endgame of this all. After a short ride home, Dani discovered a folded-up note tucked below the door mat for an easy find. The note read:

Gret,

Meet me at Hugo Lake tonight at 7:00 p.m. sharp. I have devised a plan, and I'm sure it'll work out for us and her. She needs to be there too. As a matter of fact, she must be with us in order for this to work. Do not talk about this plan in words with her or me, for they may hear you speak of it, and it will ruin us all. Just be there by 7:00. I promise, it'll all work out for us. Don't forget your protection. See you soon.

Sincerely,
Carey

I handed her the note to read so she would heed the warnings Carey informed us about. She began to shake her head. "I have a bad feeling about this."

"Yeah. I understand and get it. We have no choice."

"We always have a choice."

"Do we have one in this case? I mean, sure, we can delay this and have them keep coming. But one slip, and they'll have you. We must hit this head on."

She reached out for my hand and gazed into my eyes. "I trust you."

I nodded my head slightly. "I promise, I won't let anything happen to you. Let's go inside before someone sees us out here."

Dani smiled. "They won't see me. Remember?"

I chuckled. "I sometimes forget about that."

We had plenty of time to kill before we had to meet Carey. Rest, television, and simple conversations are what I had in mind. Deeply, I knew there was a good chance that this plan might go south. I couldn't let her see through me—I had to keep ensuring her safety and the defeat of our enemy. I had to savor these hours spent together, for they may be our last together.

She took a seat next to me and placed her hand on my thigh. "Gret, I need to share something with you."

"Okay, what's on your mind?"

"Something," she shook her head for a quick moment. "Something happened to me last night that has never happened before. I was amazed, so to speak."

"What happened?"

"You know how I explained to you that at night, my memory and mind go blank once my night is over? Well, after last night, that statement was no longer true. I had a dream last night."

My eyes grew large. "Really? What was it about?"

"I dreamt I was in an eerie place. A dark place. It seemed like an old, abandoned hospital, but I'm not certain. I was running nonstop from a man—at least I think it was a man. I never precisely saw him. He was dark and was almost like… faceless. No matter how fast or far I ran, he was always a short distance from me. Finally, I came across a rustic, old door that was obviously *out of place*. I could tell that this door—this door—was not meant to be here. It was red with an unusual design on it. The paint was riddled with claw-mark scratches all over it, like people were desperate to get in.

"Suddenly, as I attempted to open it, the door swung open like it was meant for me. I didn't hesitate to step inside, for the fear of that man chasing me was still real. I never looked back to see if he was behind me. It didn't faze me because, deep down, I knew I was going to be safe.

"I was right. Once I stepped inside, I was somewhere new. I was in a beautiful green field filled with wildflowers, as far as the eye could see. The funny thing is that my father used to call me his *'little wildflower'* when I was younger. Then I turned around, and the door was gone. Right then, I knew I was somewhere safe. I was happy again. I could swear that this was the afterlife. Next thing I remember, I woke up by the lake. Gret, what do you think this means?"

I took a deep breath and shook my head in amazement. "I think it was a premonition of what may come. How our dreams become implanted into our subconscious mind into our unconscious state of slumber, I believe that they don't just happen for no reason. There was a reason you had that dream. It wasn't a coincidence or sheer luck. That dream will come true. That's what I believe."

"It felt so real and so right. I want that feeling again."

Her sadness floored me hard. She never admitted it, nor have I asked, but I could see she was tired of this life. This life—if you could even call it that. It had now been over a half-year since I discovered that the Sleepless existed. I had seen many—more than I could have ever imagined. I only wished there was something I could do for all of them. Especially Dani.

I put my arm around her to console her. "I know you're sad, as I am sad for you. As long as my body breathes its last breath, I will always help you and be there for you anyway I can. You may not see it or feel it like I do, but you have changed my life in so many ways that I can't describe. There will be light at the end of the tunnel, but until then, I will shine my light as often as I can to ease your sadness."

"She placed her head on my shoulder. "I don't know what I would do without you. I wish things were different. But they can't be. One day. Yes, maybe one day."

"One day is right. Little wildflower—I like that."

"Me too. I miss those days."

For the rest of the day, we both rested on the couch as I continued to hold her tight. We talked, listened, and were enjoying each other's company immensely. I was genuinely falling for her. I know that statement sounds strange considering, but I couldn't help myself as I was falling deeper into these feelings. Indeed, life is a funny thing.

Before we knew it, it was around that time. "You ready for this?" I asked while I was slowly preparing myself.

"As ready as I can be, I guess."

"Remember, if it looks shady once we arrive, we bail. Trust ourselves and each other. Take his words and trust with a grain of salt. I promise, I won't let anything happen to you."

Dani smiled and nodded her head. "I know you won't."

We were on our way. My palladium blade was tucked between my hip and pants. I was ready. This game was possibly going to reach its climax. While driving, I could see her nerves were riding high—as were mine. High nerves cause higher silence. Not one word was heard until we pulled into the parking lot.

Carey was already waiting by his car. "You made it. Did you bring your blade?"

I pointed to my hip. "I'm ready."

"Good boy. Okay, here is the plan." He pointed to Dani. "You are going to be positioned by the entrance of the lake. You will practically be our *bait,* if that makes sense. Gret and I will be hidden behind those trees over there, observing. If my senses are right, they will approach you from the east side. Once they pass us, we will charge them and strike first. I don't know who will show up today, but if we can at least take two out, that's a start. I imagine they may back off if they see how serious we are."

Instinctively, I had a bad feeling about this. "Are you sure this will work?"

Carey shook his head. "Yes. The element of surprise will be on our side."

"I need to speak with her before we do this… privately."

Carey rolled his eyes in frustration. "Do you not believe me?"

"No, it's not that. It's personal. If not, we walk away."

Carey scoffed. "Okay, but hurry. We need to get in position right after."

Obviously, I was not in favor of this plan. Dani's expression held a solemn truth of doubt, too. It had to be done, though—we had to take this chance. I had to convince her that everything would be all right.

We veered about forty feet away from Carey. I held both her hands. "Look, if anything goes south, you run. Run as fast and far as you can. Run into the lake if you can."

"I can't. It's not that time yet; it's too soon."

"Then you run. Everything will be okay."

Dani simply nodded her head and spoke no other words as we returned to Carey's side. "Okay," Carey said as he pointed to the lake. "Dani, go stand right in front of the lake. Gret, come with me. We'll be behind those trees."

We took our positions and were ready for whatever was to come. I felt the adrenaline flow through my veins. I had a strange sense of urgency that I'd never felt before. The urgency is to strike hard and fast. Sure enough, I didn't have to wait much longer.

Carey took a few steps forward and started to squint his eyes as he looked in the distance. "Gret, check this out. Am I seeing things, or are they approaching from the west end?"

I stepped forward and looked. "I don't see anyone."

"Here, take a few steps closer and look very hard."

I took a few more steps. "No, I don't—"

BLACKOUT

36

The Climax

Gret. **Gret, wake up.** Her voice inside my head was only dialed to two—ten being the maximum. **Gret... are you all right? Wake up, please.** Slowly, her voice was gaining traction, and I was starting to fall into coherence.

I didn't move a muscle. *Dani... I... what... what happened?*

Carey. He hit you in the back of the head with some kind of pipe. We are hostages now.

That word *hostage* sent a jolt within my conscious. He did it—I should have known. I have now come to terms with the fact that Carey has betrayed us, but for what? My arms were bound together behind a tree, and Dani was lying in a fetal position with her arms and legs bound. I blinked my eyes a few times, ridding myself of the blur I suffered from the attack. I could barely make out Carey as he stood ten feet away, watching me like a hawk. A pompous smile lit up his face once he realized I was now awake.

Carey marched towards me and kneeled right next to me. "You know... It never had to be this way."

I slowly lifted my head and gave him my undivided attention. "Why? Why did you do this?"

"You would never understand. I did it because I had to. This last-minute deal was an incentive for my wife and me. It was the only way out."

I looked over at Dani and glared back his way. "You're a coward. You did it because you're a coward."

Carey shook his head ever so slightly. "No... no." He let out a fast chuckle. "You fail to see that we would've lost against them, even if we tried. Don't get me wrong; I was on your side from the start of all this. You let your emotions come

into play. You made us weaker by bringing her to my house.
They knew—they always knew. I... ”

Dani quickly interrupted. “I told you he couldn’t be trusted.”

Carey looked over at Dani in disgust. “Will you shut your mouth already? This is all your fault. All yours! Now, you will be responsible for his death. Isn’t it funny how this works? He tried to save you, and now you will get to witness his death—most likely.”

“You know,” I stared daggers right through his eyes. “What would your mother think of all this?”

Carey scoffed loudly and arrogantly. “Do you stupidly think I care what she would think? Or, better yet, what about your mother? The sister who allowed my dismissal from the family—all orchestrated by my mother. So, yeah... I don’t give a damn about what they may think.”

“They outcasted you because of your negative proclivities.” Dani said before she turned her attention to me. “I’m sorry, Gret; I should’ve told you all the details.” She then turned her attention back to Carey. “Your drug use, alcoholism, constant debt collectors, and time spent at the colony jail. Instead of being reliable to your family, you were nothing but a sad, pathetic liability.”

Carey burst out in deep laughter as a maniacal smile overcame his face. “So—that’s why Aza is after you. The cat is out of the bag! You never tried to help me communicate; you saw my past.” Carey walked over to Dani, knelt next to her, and started to caress her hair. “You’re a pretty one, aren’t you?” He then made a motion to whisper in her ear. “You know... Aza is going to love you. So pretty, and such a rare gift. Yeah... you will make a great addition to his family. Don’t you worry, he’ll be here soon.”

“Carey,” I called out his name in desperation. “You don’t have to do this. There is a way out of all of this. We can help you. Why are you doing this?”

"That's easy, Gret. You see—as I said a minute ago, the moment you brought her in the equation, we were doomed. It made them angrier and more aggressive. So, I made a deal with them. The deal was that I give them the both of you, and they leave myself and Saffron out of this. I had to do it—my wife is pregnant." Carey walked over to me and patted me on the shoulder. "Know this—it's nothing personal."

I shook my head. "You told me you made these deals before." I looked over to Dani. "You even traded her location in hopes of gaining favor with them. I guess old habits die hard, huh?"

Carey callously smiled and laughed. "You are correct on that. You know it all, don't you? To be honest, I can care less." Carey turned away from the both of us and was looking toward the opening. "Well, here they come." He took a closer look. "It appears to be… Aza and… Ziah. You've seen her a couple times."

"I thought you said you didn't know who she was?" I blurted out.

He threw his hands up. "Oops, I guess I lied again.

"Frickin' coward." I muttered under my breath. Bound to the tree, I watched in astonishment as Aza and Ziah took their place next to Carey. Aza simply looked like a monster. He is easily 6'5" tall, 280 pounds, and had a harrowing look that undoubtedly demanded respect. His dark trench coat covered up what looked to be some kind of black dress attire. He was a man of power. On the other hand, the female was easily recognizable. After running into her twice at Claire's and that unforgettable stare the second time, she looked the same— tattered, black clothes, and neglected hygiene. Still, she couldn't keep her eyes off me from the moment she arrived.

Aza pulled his hood back, took a glance at Dani, and focused his vision on me. "Gretan, make your acquaintance; pleased I am. I am Aza Azura." He pointed towards Ziah. "This… is Ziah. Focused one, she is. Flaws are many, she is asset." He paused and took a couple steps towards me. "Stories many of them of you, I've heard. Boy with valuable gift, death defying short in a lifetime. Special… are you." He then turned to Dani. "You… you gift possess past recollections all of. Much need, we need. Important gift, vital very to my family." He then looked at Carey. "Carey… happy and pleased, I am. Perfect … plan."

Aza's speech was nothing like I've ever heard before. It was quite evident that he had a speech impediment. The way he talked and sounded, I could only imagine how long he has roamed this world for.

Carey started pacing his hips back and forth. "Sir, Aza. I believe we had a deal. Am I free to walk now?"

Aza smirked. "Ah, yes. Deal struck, it was. Two for two, much fair." Aza slightly nodded at Ziah. "First, witness you shall on objective, ours. Very serious."

Carey shrugged his shoulders. "Understood. Do what you must do, and I'll be on my way."

"Your fidelity, promising it has been. Word of man, man of my word—I am." Aza looked over to Ziah, presenting her with a subtle nod.

Steadfast as a loyal subject, Ziah beelined towards Carey and stabbed him once in the chest and once below the ribcage. Dani let out a bellowing scream as I sat there, frozen in shock. Carey had met his demise. Once he hit the ground, he was gasping and choking as blood started to spew from his mouth. Disturbing, it was. Aza walked over to him, bent down, and put his hand underneath his chin so he could look into his eyes one last time. "You know," Aza said as he smiled at Carey. "Deal kept, I, did so. Promise your life, never. Your wife and unborn child, I did. Nothing personal."

Aza then let his hand loose from underneath Carey's chin as his head hit the ground while lying motionless. Carey had passed. It was a sickening scene for a sick man—one I will never forget. Aza turned his head towards Ziah and nodded again, and his attention quickly shifted towards us. "Apologies, must I confess, for this mess. Both, you, will come with us.

First, weary I grow, Ziah few words she speak must. Leave before we go."

Ziah took a few steps towards me like a predator stalking its prey. It was easy to tell that she was about to reveal some kind of hidden agenda. "I was never a dreamer," she said with her eyes fixated on mine. "I always thought that those who tried to live out their dreams always faced uncertainty and certain failure. A pessimist is what I was. But I knew... I knew... I knew the first day I saw you in that coffeeshop; I knew who you were. I thought, *wow... I'm I dreaming?* For so long, I was never a dreamer—until that day."

I was confused, to say the least. "Okay... what are you trying to say?"

"You... you don't know who I am, do you?"

I shook my head, briefly looked over to Dani, and returned my attention to Ziah. "I'm afraid I don't. Should I?"

Ziah smiled and nodded her head. "You should, and you will." She then circled around me and placed her hands on my binds to ensure there was no certainty of escape. At that moment, I knew this was serious and braced for the worst. She then returned in front of me and got on her knees, so we were face-to-face. "Gretan, I... I..." She quickly turned her head to Aza for approval. Of course, Aza nodded his head. "I am your mother."

"My mother is dead."

"Yes... yes, she is. Both are dead and long gone. I gave birth to you in 2160."

Everything around me suddenly got blurry and hazy. A sudden emotional rush ran through my veins as I could feel my heart pounding hard. My whole world was now failing. "Wait... what?"

"I was seventeen years old. Pregnant, homeless, and strung out on drugs. I gave birth to you prematurely in an alley. No one was there to help me, but I managed. I was young, ignorant, and stupid. My mind and body weren't right. You were so small, so sickly… I… I only thought you had a few minutes to live.

"Then, shortly after, I was carrying you in a blanket while I was on my way to meet up with some people in the park. When I arrived, they weren't there—nor did they show up. I looked down at you, and… and I… I thought you were dead. I went into the bathroom there and splashed some warm water on you in hopes you would wake up, but you never did. I failed. I failed so badly. I then snuggled your lifeless body in the blanket and placed you on the sink. By gosh, you looked like an angel. Then I ran out of the bathroom and decided never to return to that park.

"Three days later, I was so distraught and fell into a deep depression. I ended up passing away from a drug overdose. I then became a Sleepless." She quickly pointed at Dani. "In death, I realized what a bad place my mind and soul were in while I was among the living. I regret it to this day. Realizing the error of my way, I tried to seek you out while you were an infant, trying to right my wrongs so I could gain closure. Not only closure, but I wanted to be there for you.

"Nonetheless, Aza found me first and showed me a better life. A life in which I was on top. I had the sweet taste of freedom. Nothing could stop me. I felt… I felt alive again. The promise of immortal life and bliss is what I needed. Now, if you willfully join us, I can show you this life that is worth having. I can be your mother again."

"I had a mother," I said with no remorse. "Her name was Florence Hutchen. You're a nobody."

Ziah deeply sighed as a look of disappointment overcame her face. "So be it. I guess I tried." She started to walk back towards Aza and paused for a moment. She quickly turned around towards me, smiled, and approached me with the intention of whispering in my ear. "One more thing that I think you should know, my sweet child. I took your mother's life, and I enjoyed it. Don't worry, she didn't suffer—well, maybe a little." She glanced at Carey's lifeless body and returned to her whispering position. "Your uncle helped me—he told me when and where she was. Life sucks, doesn't it?"

Rage was starting to boil within my blood. The *red* is dangerous. "Your claims… lies… they mean nothing. Our lives are all inevitable. I see the utter *clarity* of all of this. You may win the battle tonight, but you will never win this war." I had an arrogant smile. "You're pathetic."

"My son, I envy your enthusiasm. You will be a great asset to Aza and the rest of us. I will let my forgiving nature shine bright tonight. I will give you one last chance to willfully join us. Your friend will join us also, so we'll all live happily ever after. I promise, my son."

I heard her voice within my head. **Gret. Do what you think is right. Not what you want, but what you think is right.**

Not a second, minute, hour, or day could change my mind. "No, I will never join you."

"Bring him to me," Aza declared in a towering voice. "Weary, I quite am growing."

Ziah grinned in utter disregard. "You made your choice. Know that your fate will be in our hands for an eternity."

"There's no fate, only choice."

Ziah's displeasure with my statement could be seen as clear as day. She walked over to me, gave me one last stare, and walked behind the tree to unbind my hands. Before she could start, I had one last statement to make. "You will never be my mother. Trash."

She stopped what she was doing and returned face-to-face with me. "What did you say?"

"You heard me. It's not fate that you will never be my mother; it's a choice. My choice!"

Her face quickly winced as she shook her head, subtle like. "Well, that's a shame. How's this for a choice?"

I knew it would eventually come, and it did. A moment after staring me squarely in the eyes, Ziah thrust a dagger into my left rib cage. No doubt, she clipped my lung as I felt the sudden taste of aluminum within my airway. Dani let out another harrowing cry as my head sank in hopelessness. I was slowly dying, and I couldn't do anything about it. Everything started to turn green as a sickly feeling started to harvest within. Then, two things happened that I will never forget for as long as I live. As my near-lifeless body remained tied to the tree, I could feel my binds moving and becoming loose to a point of escape. I couldn't explain it or ponder it. Then, something triggered my mind in such a sharp fashion. Carey never disarmed me of my palladium blade.

I felt new life within me. I knew it was probably temporary, but it was a sudden rush of adrenaline that was screaming for retribution. Without hesitation, I yanked both hands free from the binds, jumped to my feet, and lunged toward Ziah with my blade in hand. The whole scene was hazy—it felt like a surreal dream. Stabbing her in the back and falling back to the ground was one of my last memories of that scene. It was until then that I heard her voice one last time within my head after I hit the ground, slowly dying. **Gret. Look up at the sky. The stars are out. I love you.**

37

A Choice To Make

Memory loss. I was sitting on a foldout chair in a room that was maybe 10 by 15 square feet. How I got there or where I was exactly hadn't yet registered within me. Another chair was empty, facing me—five feet from my toes at least. Suddenly, a beautiful blonde-haired, barefooted hair woman wearing a white church dress took a seat across from me. I knew; I just knew that I'd seen her somewhere.

"Hello, Gretan," she said, taking her seat as one could tell she was all about business. "Here sits the boy, now a man, who continues to defy an inexorable demise. We know about her visits—she wasn't wrong for that. She taught you transparency, and now that must become a reality. For your good fight, you now have a choice."

I was confused as ever. "What choice? Wh-where am I?"

"You are somewhere you will never forget, and many will not have the chance to recollect. You saved her. She is safe, I promise. She loved you deeply, and your love for her will not go unnoticed. You are gravely hurt right now, which leads you to one important decision. You will— "

"Wait… what is this? Who are you?"

The lady smiled in the most elegant way. "We are simply the light.   The stars that shine above are watching your journey. We are inviting you now to join us in a life of bliss, happiness, and the absence of hate."

I knew—right then and there. "You are the woman from my dreams. Singing to the cattle."

"That I am. We simply presented you with a little taste of our world. Is that all you remember of me?

"Yes, it was a dream."

"Oh, my sweet boy. It was more than a dream. That dream was a continuation of many years. I was the one who found your lifeless body in that bathroom. I brought you back because we all knew your life would matter when it counted most. As of right now, it does. You have a choice to make. Stay in this world and continue to fight the good fight, or join us and live in eternal bliss with her."

"Her?"

"Daniella. She is here with us. Your family is here as well. They continue to watch you. You never fail to amaze them with wonder."

"If I stay, what will happen to me?"

"You will suffer greatly. Loneliness will become all too familiar in your soul. You will have many burdens. Life will be horrible at times, but also rewarding. You will help many others during tribulations. Through you, many will come to terms that the spiritual realm is real. Now, what is your choice?

I knew there was only one choice to make. "I… I choose to stay."

Immediately, a shock overcame my body, and it felt like my soul was traveling a million miles back to my body. I could see the stars all around me, shaped like blurred and stretched-out faces. It was an amazing feeling, as pain and suffering could not be felt. In a blink of an eye, it was over, and I found myself on the ground at Hugo Lake. My pain had departed, almost like my stab wound had healed instantly. I quickly lifted my shirt to see that the wound was nothing but normal skin. The only evidence from my wound was blood spurts around my side and a hole in the side of my shirt.

It was as quiet as could be—only crickets chirping their nightly melodies could be heard. Aza was gone, as his whereabouts were a mystery. Dani's ties were strewn across the grass, confirming that she was set free. Ziah's body was also missing, presumably deceased. Only her clothes were left behind in a heaping pile. Oddly, another pile of discarded clothes was also piled about three feet away. Since the events that had occurred were still perplexing me, I did not give it much thought. As for Carey, he lay in his own grave, which he created for himself. Yes, he was deceased. Right next to his lifeless body, I dropped down to my knees, closed his eyes with my right hand, and checked to see if his blade was still equipped. Strangely, it was missing.

In the end, I figured an anonymous phone call to the sheriff about his body was the right thing to do. The battle was over, at least for now. I could only wonder if Aza and his pack would ever return. That single thought was chilling, and I feared it might ring true someday. But not today, tomorrow, or anytime soon. I was tired—I desperately needed a break from all this. This funny old life, I thought. I needed to go home, and home I went.

38

The Calm After the Storm

1 0:30 a.m., Monday morning. It felt like any other morning from the past. I felt well rested and ready to return to my daily routine. Astonishingly, I did not think about or ponder the events from last night. To me, it was over and finished, just a memory. The pain, betrayal, and sacrifice were too much to bear. I know it would take time to heal my emotions, for there were many.

I was hungry and in need of some company. A basic interaction with a stranger at a restaurant would do. Unambiguously, anyone from anywhere would suffice—except Claire's. I knew it was too soon. Maybe in a week or two, I will feel comfortable returning. Claire was my only wildcard there. Making amends with her was on my agenda, but time needed to pass first.

Frankly, I decided to skip lunch and do something that I had never done before. Drive for miles on end with nowhere particular to go. I needed to clear my head from all of it. Driving in the wide-open country scenery was an easy decision.

****

Two hours had passed as I kept driving south down the old country roads and highways. The weather was pleasant, and the air was as clear as could be. I did not know how far I wanted to keep going, nor did I think about it. I kept driving, enjoying the beautiful scenery that was bestowed upon me.

At one point, I came across a neglected park and decided to stop. The park had no name, as it was obvious it had been closed for some time. The grass grew as high as two picnic tables, which were beaten and degraded over time. An old swing set was still present, with one seat fully intact while the other was hanging by one chain. Thinking about old times, I decided to take a seat and gently sway back and forth. The way I felt—

this wasn't me. I was letting myself fall into depression, and I needed to put a fork into that thought. I needed someone to talk to—someone to tell me that life was going to be okay. I could only think of one person—Gabby. I pulled out my phone and decided to call her.

She answered her phone on the first ring. "Hello, Gret! How are you?"

"I'm a… I'm fine. How are you doing?"

"You may find this shocking, but things are great! I can't talk that long; my mother and I are out shopping right now. We haven't gone shopping in, like… forever. What are you up to?"

"I'm out and about, running some errands here and there. Shopping, huh?"

"Yeah, shopping is one of my favorite past times. My mother also surprised me with a little getaway this upcoming weekend for the both of us. She won't tell me where, but she swears up and down that I'll love it. It's strange; she's being super nice to me all the sudden. She was also encouraging me to go back to school next semester if I feel like it."

"That's great! I'm so happy for you that everything is going well. Maybe we can get together soon."

"Of course! But hey, my mother just got out of the restroom. I'm going to have to let you go. Can I call you later?"

"Yeah, I would like that. Just call me anytime."

"Oh, and hey, my mother says hello."

"Tell her I said hello. Talk with you soon, buh-bye."

"Bye, Gret."

Sometimes, life works in mysterious ways. Those mysterious ways had a special place in Dani's heart. I now knew what her intentions for leaving behind that picture were. She alone couldn't do it; she needed me to. A simple reminder that life is short and precious. Love your family, love your friends, and be kind when tragedy shakes the mold of what once was. Be thankful for what you have, and never let it go. Cherish them. Never take them for granted. Claire needed that reminder, and

she received it. I could not be happier for both, especially
Gabby. As I sat on the swing, I could not stop smiling. I felt
that from everything that had culminated in this whole ordeal,
this was the bow on the wrapped present. Metaphorically
speaking, as perfect as this bow was, there was still a slight tear
in the paper. I had one more task to help seal the closure I was
desperately seeking. I had to make the most important phone
call I was ever going to make. I had to call Sheriff Johns.

I was a little nervous as the phone started to ring.
"Sheriff Johns is speaking. How may I assist you?"

"Hello, Sheriff Johns. It's Gretan Hutchen. Do you
have a minute to speak?"

"Hello, son. For you, I have more than a minute. What
may I do for you?"

I took a deep breath as my nerves were starting to draw.
"I've been thinking. I would like you to close out the case
involving my mother."

"Close the case? Why?"

"I feel that it's important for myself to finally gain
closure. I have faith that whoever committed this heinous crime
will receive justice on one level or another. Please, this is
important to me."

I could hear his sigh through the phone. "Well, young
man, you are the only surviving kin. It's your call. You will
need to come by my office to sign a document or two."

"Thank you, sir. I think this is for the best."

"You are the only one with the right to that opinion. Just
stop by my office anytime in the morning. If I'm not in, my
secretary will call me back to the office. We'll take care of you,
son."

"Thanks again, sir. Thank you for serving us and
keeping us safe."

"My pleasure, son."

Closure was now in the palm of my hand. It had felt like
a huge weight was lifted off my chest. I sensed new life within
me—a clean slate that presented new beginnings. My mother

and grandmother made me who I am today, and I had to live every day to the best of my ability. No more sulking in this little road trip. It was time to head home.

About an hour away from my house, I decided to take the more scenic route. I was in no rush to get home and favored the view of nature's beauty. My map came across this old country road that presented an endless horizon of beautiful green fields, as far as the naked eye can see. I felt a sudden urge to pull over and catch the scent of the warm breeze. I stepped out of my car, took a few steps forward, and froze. I closed my eyes, took a deep breath, and let it all soak in. It felt like I was in my own heaven. I opened my eyes, looked around, and observed something that didn't quite register within my mind at first glance. In the grass alongside the road was a single wildflower sprouting to potential. Within two seconds in my gaze, I knew right away what it meant as a single tear rolled down from my eye. It was a sign from Dani. A sign signifying that she was safe and watching down on me from the next life. I dropped to my knees, put my hand on the side of the stem, and felt the warmth of her flow inside my body for one last time. I missed her, but I knew this was her telling me to move on and live my life. Help others the way you would want them to help you. Continue to find good in people, even when evil within the shadows takes hold. Defend those who are weak, and save as many as I can. This—this is my life now. My one and only life.

I tasted a sweet spice,
Ascended the highest peak.
Lost in near memories,
Anchored in a muddy creek.

I miss her ever so,
She replays in my mind.
A voice of sweet elegance,
Always set to rewind.

I must move forward,
The past is unforgiving.
Patience is a virtue,
A life worth living.

A cold, brisk night. The chilling air from the north cut like a knife through butter. Unlike the darkness a night ago, the sudden dip in temperature was a sign of things to come. A sign, unfavorable by many, but accepted in time. Seasons will always change; they come and go at times without warning. Many would say it would not be bold or selfish to admit that a relentless, frigid winter was on the horizon. Out of the shadows, two sounding rustles in proximity to each other were inching closer to the scene that had unfolded.

Out from the tree line, two mysterious figures made their presence known, examining the atrocities of sheer violence. To their left lay a middle-aged man, seemingly deceased by knife wounds to the chest and left torso side. To their right lay another man—seemingly younger than the lifeless man. This man, unlike the deceased, was unconscious and barely clinging to his life by a single thread. Both of his hands were positioned to his side, trying to contain what looked to be a knife wound by the side of his torso. Directly in front of him, a pile of clothes lay strewn—for whatever reason. After quick observation, both figures drew closer to the unconscious man, watching down on him and waiting for one to speak.

Finally, the male figure took the first crack. "Is this what you expected?" He spoke in a nervous tone.

The female figure shook her head with certainty. "No," she said, and then took a couple steps back from the man. "Not at all."

For a reason that could not be explained, the woman thrust a dagger directly into her counterpart's back. The man instantly dropped to his knees, his body disintegrating into the cool, dark air. There was no regret exhibited or any redemption to be had. A cold, ruthless act during an even colder night.

After the woman did her due, she calmly walked over to the unconscious man and stared at his body for a few moments.

Her thoughts were unclear, but it was quite evident that hostile feelings were not present. The woman's observations weren't finished yet, as she made her way over to the deceased man and kneeled beside him. Very subtle, she scoffed to herself, shook her head, and paid close attention to the man's palladium blade. Neatly sheathed, she unbuttoned the clip, and she claimed the blade for herself. She then stood up and casually walked away from the scene. "No more," she said to herself as she walked back into the shadows of the dark forest.